MW01444673

*[signature]*

# ARTLESS

7/25/14

Artless
Copyright © 2014 by Mark Bernard Steck

This is a work of fiction. Any resemblance to actual place names or characters is purely accidental.

All rights reserved. No part of this publication may be reproduced, distributed, or transmitted in any form or by any means, including photocopying, recording, or other electronic or mechanical methods, without the prior written permission of the publisher, except in the case of brief quotations embodied in critical reviews and certain other noncommercial uses permitted by copyright law. For permission requests, write to the publisher at the address below.

Artless Gallery
413 Alexander Ave.
Columbia, M0 65203
www.artlessgallery.com

Ordering information:
For details, contact the publisher at the address above.

Printed in the United States of America

ISBN 978-0-9903214-0-8

First Edition

Work

Front cover:
*Artless* by Joey Wagner
Acrylic on canvas
48" x 72"

Back cover:
*Book Monster* by Joey Wagner
Acrylic on canvas
48" x 72"
2012

Inside illustrations:
Mark Bernard Steck

Cover design:
www.DesignsDoneNow.com

Proofreading:
Sarah Zurhellen
szurhellen@gmail.com

# Dedication

*For my folks*

# ARTLESS

Mark Bernard Steck

*The best works of art are an expression of man's struggle to free himself from this condition, but the effect of our art is merely to make this low state comfortable and that higher state to be forgotten.*
—Henry David Thoreau

# PART 1

# Nordic Waif

He was standing shirtless on the street corner, staring wide-eyed down the block, his long, blond hair rippling like a flag, faraway eyes watering in the wind, like some kind of lost Viking, a savage puncture in the civilized world.

I was sitting inside Coffee Zone, trying to finish an article for the *Jefferson City Telegraph*, but I kept staring out the window, distracted by his strange barbarian presence. He towered stoically above a few quiet pedestrians who kept a comfortable distance. They were mostly state workers, wearing suits and ties, pencil skirts and pumps, going to and from normal, everyday jobs. Standing alongside this lanky, bare-chested figure, they kept their gaze straight ahead or looked down at their watches while waiting for the signal to cross.

The light turned green, and everyone crossed the street except him. He stood alone, purposeless, ruddy nippled, eyes blank as vacant lots. He waited out a couple more lights, then turned in my direction and ambled down the sidewalk, passing by the window of the coffee shop, then out of sight. I got up from the table and walked outside, just as he turned into one of the buildings down the block.

I followed after him. I had to know who he was, where he was going.

I stood on the outside of the building I thought he must have gone into, face pressed against the cold storefront glass of 124 High Street, hands cupped tightly over my temples to block the afternoon glare. The window was nearly opaque with black acrylic paint, a continuous stream of words painted over words painted over words, an accumulated strata made impossible to read. I peered through a counter in one of the vowels, but it was too dark inside to see anything.

I took a step back from the window and lit a cigarette. I had passed by the block before but never noticed this window. It was easy to overlook. The building was narrow, the entrance set back a little from the other businesses. And it was the only one that had no sign.

When I tossed my cigarette onto the sidewalk, I noticed there was a slight crack in the door. A chunk of red brick was wedged in the threshold, just enough to keep it from latching. I looked up and down the block. People filed by, but no one paid attention to this building. I pulled the door open and slipped inside, trying to keep quiet, but the hydraulics were broken on the door closer and it clanged shut behind me in a crash of weighted metal. The sound reverberated for an uncomfortable moment, followed by a long silence.

"Hello?" I called out. "Anyone here?"

No answer.

The building was a shotgun, exposed brick down the right side, an unfinished wall down the left, high ceilings, floor covered in wreckage. It looked like it had been abandoned for years. There was a thick layer of plaster peeling off the bricks, slabs of it laying in piles on the floor. Stamped tin panels on the ceiling were coated in flaking paint, one of every few bent or missing. Empty wine bottles and cans of Stag lined the base of the walls. Saws, hammers, random construction tools scattered around. Piles of broken lumber and material waste everywhere.

"Hello?" I said it louder but still no answer.

The air was chalky with dust and ash. A faint smell of sweat and bread yeast. The light from the front window grew dimmer as I walked farther into the building. On the left was a set of stairs with no railing. I put a foot on the first step, tested if it would hold weight, then went up to see if the second floor was as chaotic as the first.

Upstairs was ripped down to a skeleton of stud walls dividing the rooms, electric wiring and water lines weaving through the wood. In the center of the main room was a large desk, the surface covered in wine-stained rings. I pulled open a drawer and found a collection of crushed cigarette packs. Several musical instruments lined the walls. An old parlor guitar with finger indentations worn into the fretboard, a couple missing bridge pins replaced by 16-penny nails. A six-string banjo with only four strings. A brass trumpet with two pistons permanently engaged. A quarter-inch reel-to-reel recording deck.

The room next to this was partitioned, the stud walls draped in heavy-mil plastic with a vertical slit cut down the doorway. I pulled the plastic back and went in. On one side of the room were gallon cans of acrylic, some of the tops left off, the brightly colored paint drying inside. The opposite wall had canvases stacked against it, some primed with gesso and some finished. In the center of the room there was a canvas lying flat, a gallon can under each corner to suspend it above the floor, the surface covered in a violent flurry of paint, poly, and what looked like beads of caulk. I put my finger to one of the glassy areas of the canvas. I was surprised to find it wet, a pool of polyurethane still hardening. When I pulled my finger back, some of the viscous material clung, then broke off, leaving a bubble on the surface of the painting. I started to worry, afraid I had fucked it up. I waited, and eventually it sagged back into the two-dimensional, finding level again.

I left the room and went downstairs, saw again what a vast, open space this was. There was something happening here. I wondered what it was, who was using the space. I was about to leave, questions unanswered, when I heard a moan coming from the back of the building. There was an old diner booth seat, upholstered in black vinyl, barely visible in the darkness. A pair of boots were hanging off the end and someone was in them, a dark mass of hair buried in the crevasse of the bench, one arm crossed over his eyes.

This is how I found the gallery and the person in charge of it, passed out in the afternoon, between all the wreck and rubble, in a dull fug of sweat, tobacco soot, and cheap, stale booze.

# Underlayer

A week earlier, I was gazing out a vinyl-cased window in an enormous shell of an unfinished house, as the sun heaved up over the monochromatic reels of identical rooftops rolled out through the suburbs. I should have been working, doing drywall. Instead, I was watching birds circle outside the window, wings splayed against the sky. Somewhere above those anemic houses, past the bulge in the distant horizon, a different city waited. Some place where artistic people were making the scene, going against the grain, taking whatever success or failure they inherited, and investing it all in the idea that *living* was not a thing to be earned.

A low, labored moan seeped through the opening of one of the walk-in closets. The doors hadn't been installed yet. The closet alone was nearly as big as my studio apartment.

"You okay in there?" I asked.

"I'll be fine," Travis replied. "Go ahead, start without me."

"No, thanks," I said. "I'm in no hurry." I picked up a flat construction pencil and utility knife, sharpened the gnarled end back into a point, and scribbled out a random quote across the grains of an exposed wood stud.

*The pen is as valuable as the plow—Rimbaud*

I'd been writing different quotes all over the house as it was built. Finding blank spots in the walls, the floors, the seams. I knew it would all get covered over in the finish, but I liked the idea of it still existing there, beneath the surface layers of Formica, linoleum, Masonite, laminates, all the artificial veneers made to replicate the natural world.

I heard the teeth of a zipper close, then Travis appeared in the doorway carrying a bucket of drywall mud. He wore a crisp button-down shirt under an Argyle sweater vest and a tweed fedora with a narrow brim turned slightly up in the front. Drywall was one of the filthiest jobs in the lineup, but he refused to dress in normal work clothes, and his fashion was always in step with his latest subscription magazines.

"Now we can start," he said, dropping the bucket in the center of the room.

Inside was the thick white joint compound we used to fill the cracks and tape the walls. And on top of that was a fresh, menacing turd. The toilets hadn't been installed yet either. Travis stood there grinning, playing the clown, waiting for me to react.

"Pretty funny," I admitted, unsurprised. "But also disgusting. I have to use that too, you know."

"Blowback," he shrugged. "You'll be okay. Just think of the greater good. Some schmuck will come along and buy this house, and I want them to have a little part of me with it." He picked up the drill and shoved the long mixing paddle down through his feces and into the bottom of the bucket. He flicked on the drill and spun the paddle, watching as the turd slowly sank and disappeared into the vortex, swirling brown streaks before it finally diluted into the mixture.

"I'm not using that," I said. "You're on your own until it's gone." I went back to what I was doing, finding a blank spot on the subfloor.

*A work of art is the unique result of a unique temperament—Oscar Wilde*

Travis rolled his cuffs neatly back, filled a drywall pan full of the contaminated mud, and started spotting the screws in the drywall. Spreading it over a line of holes, then wiping it flat, spreading it on, wiping it flat, working his way around the room with deft wrist movements, never allowing a single drop on his dapper clothes.

"Drywall's kinda fucked up," I said, looking for another good place to write. "The whole idea isn't to make something stand out. It's to make it as unnoticeable as possible. To cover every one of these cracks and imperfections with this flat, colorless mud."

"This one will have a little tint to it, at least."

"Think about it," I said. "Our job is to make it look like we were never here. Like we never even existed. No one who comes in to buy one of these houses is gonna give a shit how the drywall looks. It doesn't mean anything."

"We find ourselves in a thankless occupation." Travis shrugged. "Whattaya gonna do?"

I knelt down to write along the bottom of the wall, behind where the MDF base trim would be.

"Then again," I said. "I guess it's like some of the Modern painters, the ones trying to make the canvas as flat as possible, hiding all the brushstrokes, then taking out all the color, trying to erase the fact that someone actually painted it. They may as well have been doing drywall."

*Art washes away from the soul the dust of everyday life—Picasso*

"Yeah, right. I can just imagine going into a museum and seeing people standing around a cutout of this hanging on the wall. Or people bidding millions at an auction for a sheet of drywall with a little mud on it, just because some asshole signed the corner. Then they'd get it home and hang it on a wall made of the same shit, which they paid monkeys like us time and materials to install."

I held out the pencil to him. "You should sign one of these walls," I offered. "You can make it a work of art right now."

"That's okay." He held up the pan. "I already did." He carefully spread another line of parts-per-million on the wall, then wiped it flat.

"Someday your talents will be discovered." I was trying to ignore the foul smell permeating the room.

"Don't say that. I'd hate to think I actually had any talent. You never wanna be too good at anything, especially this. Spend too much time perfecting the art of spreading white mud on a wall, you'll wake up one day to find you can't do anything else."

"Well, I won't be here much longer. I'm getting the fuck out."

"Yeah, right," he said.

"Seriously."

"Sure you are."

In the middle of the drywall, across one of the seams, I wrote another line.

*Do I contradict myself? Very well then,*
*I contradict myself—Walt Whitman*

Eventually, I picked up a pan and knife and reluctantly filled it with the tainted mud. I walked over to the quote on the seam and spread a layer across it, then wiped it down flat, covering it over.

# Landscape

The winter bled out all the chlorophyll, leaving the suburbs an umber pall below the duct-taped sky. To get the engine to turn over on the old Ford work truck, I had to lean in close to the wheel. Push the gas without pumping it. Wait for the right moment. Feel the engine catch fire. Then let off the pedal. I sat outside the job site and waited for the cab to heat up, warming one hand with the other.

    One job down, one to go. My other job was back in town, and navigating the way out of the suburbs required reverse engineering. The houses were identical. Brick front facing the street, vinyl siding around the other three sides. Bricked mailbox at the end of driveway. Their identity was found only in the master plan.

    I knew I would outlive all of these houses, leaving no history in this neighborhood. They were a minor infection, a row of boils. Once they began to show signs of wear there would be no reason to save them. A great hydraulic finger would come along and pop them like pustules, scraping them off the face of the earth in a cold, antiseptic swab.

I made my way through the maze and to the overpass, merging onto the highway that led back into town, out of the expanding adipose of suburbia, the empty calories of municipal fat. It faded in the rear view mirror as I crossed over the ecotone between urban and suburban, past and present, vertical and horizontal.

The small skyline took shape as I crossed the bridge over the Missouri River. This was Middle America, girded in rust belts and Bible belts. Here was the Mule Capital of the World. The Paris of the Plains. The Show-Me State. But a cultural centrifuge still pulled artists out to the rim of the American wheel. Heading out into the cities that never sleep, cities of notions, cities of angels, cities of broad shoulders, golden cities, emerald cities, rose cities. If I was ever going to do anything, I knew I needed to go elsewhere.

I took the exit into downtown. Jefferson City was more small town than city. It was the government seat of the state, and at the end of High Street, the dome of the capitol building rose like a monolithic fist over the river, a tribute to Thomas Jefferson. A bronze effigy of him stood proudly before the Corinthian structure, lording over the town like an American Zeus, despite the fact that he had never actually set foot there in his lifetime.

The rest of downtown had been slowly deteriorating. Most businesses relocated to wider boulevards, long stretches of strip malls, plazas. Fractals of grand national commerce. The old buildings left behind were converted to offices or left vacant. After-hours, when the state workers had all gone home, lights flicked on in the smoky pubs and pool halls that remained, dives I normally dropped into at the end of the workday.

I turned the truck off High Street and pulled into the drive-through lane at Central Bank. This was the commercial home of Samuel Cole, a member of the ruling class. The One Percent whose names were etched into fountains, university buildings, the cornerstones in the national foundation. I'd never seen him in person, but I knew he happened to have one of the largest private art collections in the country. Inside the great, glass-plated edifice were priceless works, decorating the administrative offices and conference rooms. A strange anomaly, having some of the best artworks in the country, but I didn't know of a single working artist.

I flipped my paycheck over and signed the back on the steering wheel, depositing it through the automated teller, then pulled away.

I made my way to the west side and pulled into the parking lot of the country club. I sat a while, smoking a cigarette and looking out the window of the truck. There were things about the town I would miss. Maybe I appreciated it more because I knew I was leaving. I lit another cigarette, not quite ready to go in. The cab now warmed by the engine, radio playing a forgotten song through a curtain of static. A light snow began to fall, but nothing stuck.

# Grayscale

You can't get a job unless you have experience. You can't get experience unless you've had a job. This was true of a lot of things, but writing seemed to me one of the most difficult. You had to take what you could get. This is why I was sitting around a table in the library of an old country club, surrounded by walnut shelves full of dusty classics with unbroken spines, with a group of geriatrics celebrating the 30th anniversary of their bridge club. I was writing an article for the *Telegraph*, the hyperlocal weekly newspaper. They paid three cents a word, and their editorial turnover was higher a restaurant wait staff. The sort of place where it was possible to get a start as a writer.

The elderly bridge players sat four to a table, grumbling and shifting, creaking like antique chairs. I sat down at a table that had a couple of open seats and explained that I was there to do an article. At the head of the table was a woman anxiously shuffling and reshuffling a deck of cards, looking at her watch. Across from her was a man with a permanent scowl, gray roots under his dyed hair, hands folded in front of him.

"Now, I can't help but wonder how the newspaper knows we're having our 30th anniversary?" he asked, looking across the table. The woman had put the cards down and pulled a tube of coral lipstick out of her purse, spreading it around her furrowed lips, a nice color contrast with her galvanized hair. "Any ideas, Mrs. Thompson?"

Mrs. Thompson's face blushed to a shade darker than her lipstick. "Mr. Bradford, you know how word gets around," she replied.

"Uh huh." He turned to me. "Tell me son, you a member here?"

"Me? No," I replied.

"Didn't think so," he said, glancing at my Carhartts. "You ever golf?"

"Not at all."

"Me neither. Can't stand the game."

I pulled out a pen and notebook. "You're member of a country club, but you don't play golf?"

"Pisses me off, tryin' to smack that little ball around. No, I just come here for the ambiance," he said sarcastically. "Now don't be writin' that down. That's off the record."

Another old man walked in, plopped down at the table, coughing into his fist.

"Well, well. Glad you decided to show up Fergus," said Mr. Bradford. "How's life treatin you?"

"Bout as good as I'm treatin' it," he replied. "Where's Mary?"

"Fergus Thompson here is an investor," Mr. Bradford said to me. "You ever want to join the country club, you should talk to him. You gotta start now, while you're young. What you need to do is focus on your *investment strategy*. You want some advice, you talk to Fergus."

"Uh, well…I'm focusing on cash right now," I said.

"Good, that's good. Cash is king, right Fergus?"

"Need a drink," Fergus snarled. "Where's our girl, anyway? MARY!"

"Please don't bore me with that financial drivel this time. This gentleman's not here to talk about investments," said Mrs. Thompson. "Can we get the game started already?"

"Hold on, he just got here," said Mr. Bradford. "I'm just tryin to help him out, give him a little sound advice."

A young Latino woman came up to the table holding a small pleather booklet and pen.

"How bout we order first," said Fergus. He ordered himself a Gin Rickey, double. The server went around the table, took the other orders, a series of gin drinks. "And get this young man whatever he wants, Mary. Put it on *my* tab." Mr. Bradford said, sending her over to me.

"For you, sir?" she asked politely.

"Whiskey. And a cup of coffee." I said to her. She gave a slight nod, customary smile. I noticed the embossed nameplate on her shirt. "And, thank you, Maria," I added sincerely, trying to convey an empathy for things done without joy.

The drinks were brought out and they all chased the straws around the rim of their glass, sucking them down like bottle calves. As the gin loosened up their tongues, they turned to me, holding my pen and paper, an excuse for dispensing little pills from their prescripted life stories. I held the notebook in front of me, scribbled once in a while, sipping my whiskey, my mind drifting in and out of the conversation.

"...and that's when I shifted over to the derivatives market. Mortgage-backed securities, that's where the *real* money can be made. Are you getting all this?" Mr. Bradford asked, noticing that my pen wasn't moving.

"Of course," I said, putting pen back to paper, circling around with continuously lapping lines, automatism in ink. He continued with his story. I flipped the page, started sketching Fergus with his big, grayscale teeth.

The article would appear across from a quarter page ad for Fergus Thompson's private investment firm. I was asked to do a story any time the paper could angle for advertising dollars. If a person wanted to see their name or business in print, it was usually followed by a phone call from someone at the paper asking if they would like to parlay that into a bargain-rate advertising package. Every page was up for sale.

The drinks kept coming, cards dealt, played, shuffled, dealt again. I kept sipping my whiskey, letting my pen wander the page.

I was collecting a pile of clips that would be useful when I moved on and tried getting another job. I had already written plenty of articles for the *Telegraph* and knew the formula they were looking for and could do it without much thought. A few basic facts, some new adjectives found under the thesaurus entry for *exciting* or *momentous*, check the names and spellings. This was how it worked, I figured. This was a foot in the door, cutting my teeth on a wrinkled old card game.

# Pat's Place

After dark, when both jobs were finished, I took my cigarette for a walk through the back alleys downtown, stopping here and there to scribble in a pocket notebook. Wind whipped through the canyon of buildings, blowing sheets of unread newspapers off the stands, cartwheeling them down the empty streets in a narcotic, American night.

I coursed the walkway around the proud capitol building, running my hand across a frozen bronze sculpture of a Greek centaur, surging violently out of an emptied water fountain.

I passed by Central Bank. In the front lobby, above the teller counter, was one of Warhol's *Flowers*. I pressed my face to the frigid glass and peered down the hall to the conference room, barely able to see the Hans Hoffman "push/pull" piece hanging above the table, its vibrant colored rectangles singing with purity. I'd never seen it up-close. They only let you back there if you were able and willing to sign up for a compound interest rate.

A little farther on was Pat's Place, where I knew I would find Travis. I walked into the narrow bar, a thunderhead of cigarette smoke hovering below the ceiling. The interior was smothered in an affected Irish decor. A shillelagh hanging from the leather strop. A polyester tricolor flag. A tapestry with a Celtic cross. Bagpipes. Pennywhistles. Bookshelves with selections of Dylan Thomas, Seamus Heaney, Yeats. A Cranberries song playing on the Muzak channel. A map of Ireland painted on one wall, thumbtacks punched into all the places visited by Arvin, the owner of the pub. Arvin was mostly Dutch, but somewhere down the line one of his ancestors was fucked by an Irishman, spurting one thirty-second's worth of Gaelic blood into the line. He was Dutch through the afternoon, and Irish every night, after a few pints of Guinness tuned up his accent.

Arvin was standing in front of the window looking into the kitchen, eyeballing a plate stacked with a burger and fries.

"How much does that patty weigh?" he barked at the cook. He reached in and pulled the sweaty, marbled burger off the plate and set it on the scale. "Look here, two thirds of a pound. We don't sell burgers at two thirds of a pound, we sell burgers at half a pound. Its called quality control!" He slammed a fist on the counter after each sentence, punctuating his rising anger. "I guess I need to be in there watching over my kitchen. No one ever thinks about the consequences!" He raised his meaty fist and brought it crashing down onto the scale. "I'm the fucking *consequences*!" The scale shattered, sending metal and plastic parts flying into the kitchen.

He walked away in a quiet rage, standing behind the bar, shaking his head, arms crossed over his inflated chest. His point was driven home.

I walked up to the bar. There was an old man at one end, a regular. Combing his long white beard with petrified fingers. Wearing dirty blue overalls from a lifetime of labor, his body now bent and split like weathered wood. Signing over social security checks for well whiskey and sitting on his peanuts. This was his retirement, his health insurance, his final vacation. I saw Travis dosing himself at the other end of the bar and took the stool next to him.

"Make that two beers, Arvin," Travis said when he saw me.

"Guinness?" To Arvin, there was only one beer. He walked over to the taps, his head still shaking, gray hair curling out of his blended poly-cotton tam. He chewed vigorously on the end of a Dublin basket pipe, sputtering little curls of smoke into the air.

I hadn't bothered to change after work, the drywall mud still encrusted in the hems and patched knees of my Carhartts. Travis, on the other hand, had on a fresh change of clothes, even though he always managed to stay pristine at work. He spent half the day washing and preening. He refused to let the trade sully him, to become a part of who he was. Sometimes I wondered why he didn't look for another job to make his life easier. But drywall paid well enough. He always had a wallet choked with bills and a bone-dry bank account. He enjoyed throwing money around. Casting it into the wishing wells.

"If you see that bastard with the black goatee walk in here, let me know," Travis said to me, casing the bar for his probation officer, eyes darting to the front and rear exits like a metronome.

He often got into legal trouble, which was part of why he never left the town. And it was never hard crime that plagued him, just a slow accumulation of minor infractions. Bar fights. Drunk driving. Possessing a night's worth of schedule-1 drugs. Now, as part of his probation, he wasn't even allowed in public bars.

"Can't believe you're still dealing with that guy," I said. Travis had been on probation most of his adult life.

"That rotten bastard has it out for me. It's like he's got nothing better to do than track my every move. Like he *wants* me to fuck up. He can't bear the thought of letting me go."

The door flew open, letting in a draft of winter air. Travis peeked over my shoulder nervously. A strange, Nordic-looking waif drifted in carrying a rucksack and wandered over to the bar next to me. He pulled out a handful of change from his pocket and sorted dollar stacks on the bar. He was wearing threadbare jeans, flecks of bright acrylic paint saturating the fibers. Red handkerchief waving out of one back pocket. Thick callouses on the fingers of the fret hand, peeling back at the edges. Physical indictments of artistic struggle. He paid for his beer and lumbered to a table near the back. He acknowledged no one around him and seemed a little out of place. Like the wilderness brought indoors.

"Two shots, Arvin," Travis said. Arvin poured out a little whiskey from the well. He set them down and Travis grabbed his, clinked it against the other on the bar. "Cheers." He knocked it back before I picked mine up. "Ah," he cringed, breath hot, then made a banner in the air with his hand. "Sub-bourbon: For the gentleman who can't afford to live in the city, but wants to drink like he's still master of his domain."

"Here's how." I turned up the shot glass mechanically, drank it off, slid it empty down the bar, then turned to the back of the room again, the strange Norse still curious to me. I watched him shuffle through his bag, pulling the contents out onto the table. Clothes. Ratty paperback. Guitar picks. He finally dug a loose cigarette out of the bottom, pulled a fist of his long blond hair into a ponytail, held it back with one hand as he leaned over to light the twisted cigarette off the candle on the table, head canted away from the flame. Then he looked straight up at me, punching through me with his blue, barbarian eyes, breathing a cobalt cloud of smoke in my direction.

I realized that I had been staring at him since he came in. I turned uncomfortably back to the bar.

"You know that guy in the back?" I asked.

Travis turned and looked over my shoulder. "No, can't say that I do."

"You ever seen him here?"

"Never, and we're here every goddamn night."

"Fuck, don't remind me. Every day it's drywall, then here, then more drywall."

"Whatever. It is what it is."

"It's a vicious cycle. I'm ready for a change."

"So what are you waiting for?"

"What do you mean?"

"You keep saying you're ready to quit. So quit."

"I'm going to. I'm just waiting for the right time."

"Do you even know where you're going?"

"No...I mean...I have some idea. I don't know, New York? San Francisco? Portland, maybe? I just need a place where something's *happening*."

I looked over my shoulder and recognized Bohinky rolling by in his wheelchair. He parked at the table across from the Norse, a blanket on his lap, draping down over the wheels. He pulled out a vinyl roll and bag of chess pieces from under the blanket and set them on the table. Bohinky came in all the time to find chess partners. This was his one passion in life, and he was very good at it. Despite many attempts, I had never won against him.

"Good luck with that," Travis said. "Let me know if they pay drywall monkeys better out there."

"I'm not going there to fucking do drywall," I said.

"Of course you're not. They're gonna sweep you up and make you a writer. I'm right behind you, as soon as I pay off my lawyer's mortgage and get off probation."

"At this rate, you'll probably never get out. You'll be stuck in the system forever."

He grinned. "That's fine, who cares. One thing I don't want is to be bored. I have to keep myself entertained. Unfortunately, not all sources of entertainment are legal. Your problem is you keep trying to find some kind of deeper meaning. Always talking about art and writing and the movement of a bunch of corpses."

"Art can be a form of entertainment." I lit a cigarette and took another sip of my beer. "You just don't have the attention span for it."

I turned again to see the chessboard was set up, the Norse scratching the hair on his chin, ruminating on his first move. He hesitated, then moved a piece. As he sat back, Bohinky's hand fluttered out from under the blanket like a sparrow, pushed a piece forward, then disappeared under the blanket again.

"I don't give a shit about art," Travis replied. "You have to stay on the surface if you want to be happy, that's my idea. Eat as much as you can, sleep as much as you can, and fuck as much as you can. That's what life's about. Don't waste your time trying to sort it out with art."

"But that's the only thing I want to do." I took another sip, watched Arvin carefully pour another Guinness, then put a spoon over the rim, topping it off at the appropriate time. Thick, rich foam flowed over, leaving a perfectly domed head. "I started writing a book. That's what I want to be working on. Not drywall."

"Oh yeah, what's the book gonna be about? I better be in it, and don't make me out like some kind of hedonistic asshole."

I started to answer when the front door opened again, letting in another black blast of air. A portly, middle-aged guy walked in, wearing a dark polo shirt and pleated slacks, a jet-black goatee carved to a point on his chin. I turned back to warn Travis, but all that was left next to me was a drained pint on the bar, thick foam still sliding down the inside of the glass.

## Self Portrait

The predawn hours were the sweetest part of the day, while the rest of the town slept and I had time to myself. Just before the sun peeled back the night, the Big Screw wound back on the clock and reset to a fat, global zero, and the world set itself to work again, marking time in the void.

On the desk in my apartment were a coffee cup, a pack of American Spirits, a half bottle of Evan Williams, a manual typewriter, a copy of *The Death and Life of Great American Cities*, and a two-volume history of twentieth-century art. The desk was the only piece of furniture I had. Across the room was a mattress on the floor. Construction tools piled in one corner. Books stacked all around the walls. Several of them lay open in the middle of the room. Art books. Varied paperbacks. Norton Anthologies, the remnants of an uncompleted literature degree. One of the many things I'd never followed through with. Next to these were ink pens, pocket notebooks full of scribbles, typed pages of false starts.

I rolled a page through the typewriter, filling it halfway before ripping it out and throwing it on the floor.

I squared up another page. Torqued on the keys with heavy, bruise-blood hands, sickles of dirt under my nails, knuckles scuffed into a white patina of scars. Workman hands, but hinged on tiffany wrists, like filaments almost too slender to hold them.

There was a knock on my apartment door. I opened it to Ms. Krutzwaller, the implacable woman who owned the building. She lived in the unit right above mine.

"Good morning, Ms. Krutzwaller." I tried not to get too close. Didn't want her to smell the whiskey. I left the door half closed, half standing behind it.

"Morning?" she snapped. "Do you have any idea what time it is?"

She was eighty-something, slight, gray skin hanging from her bones like plastic hospital sheets. She spent most of her waking hours blending peptic drinks, smearing cold cream and vitamin E into her corrugated skin, and sweeping the floor. I always heard the *swick swick swick* of her broom coursing above the plaster ceiling.

"Why are you tormenting me?" she asked. This was a rhetorical question. She was always tormented. Projecting this was what kept her going.

"I'm sorry, Ms. Krutzwaller, I'll try and keep it down," I replied.

"Are you smoking in there?" I shook my head, but before I could come up with something she started in again. "No, I know you're smoking in there. Did you even read the terms in your lease? Do I need to show you where you signed? That you agreed you wouldn't smoke in this apartment?"

"I don't—"

"I'm right above you, I *know*. My whole place smells like a jailhouse. Of course you didn't think about that." She sighed with exhaustion, then dialed it over to pity. "You shouldn't even be smoking in the first place. When I was younger, we didn't know anything about cigarettes. But now you have medical proof, you know it's bad for you. You're only what, 23?"

"24."

She reached up and took hold of my shirt collar, pulling me close to her furrowed face. "It makes me *ill*." She rolled back her upper lip, exposing purple gums. I could feel her hot breath, words sticking in the air between us as I tried not to inhale.

She let go and pushed past me and through the door into my apartment.

"Another thing we need to discuss," she said, examining the place, "is the typewriter you're using. You have no idea how loud that is in my apartment. I can see why. You don't have any furniture. There are no rugs, no curtains. This entire place echoes every time you type on that machine. Don't you realize it's the middle of the night and I'm trying to sleep, what with my arthritis and rheumatic hips and heart palpitating every time that thing clacks—" She threw up her hands like salt-boiled pincers.

"I'll try and—"

She was poised for me to say something, just waiting to cut me off.

"Don't say you'll *try*. I've asked you before, and you didn't listen."

She was right. The whole scene was a carbon copy of three nights earlier.

"If you want to continue living here, you'll have to abide by the rules, and I absolutely forbid you to use that typewriter in this apartment anymore." She gave me a stern look, letting me know she would not compromise. "Don't forget, I *own* this building."

She turned to leave, then paused to let me know just one more thing.

"Just one more thing," she said. "No smoking!"

The door shut behind her, hard enough to make her point, but not enough to be a disturbance to the other tenants.

I went to the bathroom and filled the sink with soap and water and buried my face in it. Time to sober up for work. I lifted my head and stared into the mirror, soap streaming through the hair on my face. A diluted phenotype stared back at me. Brownish hair, blueish eyes. I, along with everyone else, was slightly above average in a majority of things. An accumulation that, unapplied, proved absolutely worthless. I watched the water fall off my chin and reappraised the situation. Attempting to work up enough courage to follow through, to reach escape velocity, decoupling from the dailiness of the town as I knew it. This was all part of the morning routine.

*Let the job go to hell,* a wild goose whispered in my ear. *Pack your things and go.*

## Boomtown

Like the rest of the country, the town was in a boom market. An economic bubble, swelling with easy credit and cheap materials, swallowing up the land for development, pushing everything farther out, indeterminate as the growth of fish. Business was good for contractors, realtors, bankers. They were building quickly and stepping out a little more each time. Laying houses down in succession like rail tracks through the American West, trying to stay out in front of the locomotive of progress, not stopping until they'd made it all the way. That great day when they hit another subdivision oozing out of the next town. Last house connecting the two streets like the golden spike at Promontory. The contractor proudly driving the final 16-penny nail.

It was early in the morning. The subdivision was full of work trucks, ladder racks on top, magnetic company placards stuck to the doors. With all these homes being clapped together, anyone with a tool belt could go down to the Sign-O-Rama, pick up a shingle, and be in business.

Travis was sitting on the tailgate of one of the trucks drinking coffee, a row of lottery tickets across his lap, vigorously rubbing one off. Trying to scratch out a better living with the side of a hard-earned dime. He was wearing pinstriped pants, v-neck sweater, and plaid scarf, loosely tied.

I took a seat next to him on the tailgate, and we watched the other work crews swarm the job site, cycling through rote conversations.

*Whattaya know Charlie?*

*Oh...you know...same shit different day...*

"Look at all these people," Travis said. "Put them on a payroll and they'd do anything you want." He wadded up a lottery ticket and pitched it into the yard.

"Another dud, huh? One of these days you'll get lucky."

"Whatever. I don't even care. You know what I'd do if I actually won the lottery?" This was one of his favorite games. He could spend hours following this train of thought, adding to it all day. By quitting time, he'd have an elaborate scheme worked out to the atomic detail.

"You'd start acquiring expensive tastes?"

"I'd create a monarchy."

"Of course. And where would you establish this monarchy?"

"Right here. All around us. You'd be sitting in my kingdom right now. All I'd need is, say $100 million. I'd start by buying up all the real estate around these subdivisions. Not the houses though. They could keep their shitty houses. I'd buy up every gas station, every bank, every grocery store, every restaurant. I'd create a monopoly, so they'd have to go through me for everything."

"Okay, say they get savvy and start shopping in the next town."

"Well, commerce would only be phase one. If I wanna put the squeeze on, I'd have to have my hand up the ass of the entire political system. Every city council member, the mayor, the sheriff, the prosecutors, they'd be hand picked and paid for by me. On a local level like this, $100 million should be plenty. I'd have my own private ruling class. Any time I wanted a new law, I could have one of my puppets make it so."

"For example?"

"For example, we'd need official city holidays, like ones that celebrate me at the expense of everyone else. My birthday would be one. The day I achieved greatness would be another. Parades would be held, starting around midnight on a weekday and marching by every house in town, doing drugs, playing music at full blast, fornicating in the streets. Anything goes."

"What if they got tired of it and moved away? You'd have a mass exodus."

"Ah, now you're at the crux. If they wanna leave, fuck 'em. The real trick is to *compel* them to stay. I'd eliminate property tax, sales tax, everything that costs money. I'd own the hospital and order the doctors to treat them for free. The grocery stores would be free. Keep them healthy and alive for as long as possible. That way they'd have to decide. They could pack up and go, but they'd miss out on the lowest cost and highest standard of living ever. Or they could stay, but they'd have to endure *me*, and I'd strip away every personal liberty from them I could."

"You think they'd go for it?"

"Look around," said Travis. "Take these people as a cross section of this great experiment. What choice do you think they would make?"

Workers were filing out of the trucks, scattering in all directions to set up tools, hump lumber, and move, move. Time was money. A long Town Car pulled up to the house, and a realtor stepped out, putting little plastic covers over his shoes before crossing the mud to the front door of one of the homes. He showered before work, not after.

"What about crime?" I asked. "If people had their needs provided for, and they didn't like the situation, it would be a recipe for an astronomical crime rate. Or a revolt."

We hopped off the tailgate and walked up the driveway toward the house. "Now you're getting to the fun part. I'd have a ruthless penal system set up. They wouldn't have guns, of course. Those would be taken away. But, if they did try to revolt, the law would step in. Public beatings, for one, just to set some examples…labor camps…solitary confinement… waterboarding, that seems to be popular. We'd have to be mindful of federal laws, of course. Wouldn't want the Guard interfering. But, then again, my mule team of attorneys would handle that…"

He trailed off as we walked into the house, a 4,000-square-foot box with a cheap comb-over of polyvinyl, composites, and drywall. Inharmonious lines, unnatural angles. No attention to design, no consideration for the land, because the land itself was disappearing below the crust of pavement. Everything about the house was affordable, cut-rate. I knew exactly what it would look like when it was finished. There's no place like home, except the one next door. It had a way of draining out all of my personality, spine, spleen, leaving nothing but an empty veneer.

This was where I worked, every goddamn day.

We pulled out a few tools. Travis was still thinking about his kingdom. He would be building his castle in the sky the rest of the day. Working with Travis almost made it worthwhile some days.

I turned on the radio, started cleaning off my pan and knives. Classical music was playing on the public station.

"Great choice. I love this shit," Travis said.

"Really? I didn't know you were into it."

"I'm not, but something about hearing it makes life feel more *cinematic*." He dropped his tools and turned to the picture window overlooking the neighborhood, the workers, waving his hands in the air like a conductor. "When I win that lottery, instead of a radio I'll hire a full live orchestra to follow me around at work all day…"

"Travis, you're my closest friend in the world." I shook my head, laughing a little. "And sometimes that depresses the hell outta me."

Travis grinned, hands arcing wildly before the window. "Welcome to the boomtown!"

# Telegraph

The *Telegraph* was headquartered in an old office building on Madison Street. I found Jenny behind the front desk cutting ads out of back issues, stapling them to pink invoices, stuffing them into envelopes.

"Back from the beat, eh?" she said. Jenny was a kind, younger woman, short hair, ameliorating sense of humor. She and I often joked about the work we did there. She had been hired as the receptionist, but in reality she was the design assistant/proofreader/accountant, who also answered the phone. From what I could tell, she was the one holding the paper together.

"What's the mood like today?" I asked.

"End of the world, as usual," Jenny said, meaning it was deadline.

I handed her an article. "Here you go. This could be my finest work yet."

"Ooh la la," she said, reading the headline. "Looks like city council is at it again."

"Make sure my name's spelled right. I'm blowing the lid off this entire traffic signal scandal, exposing the underbelly of corruption. This is Pulitzer material."

Jenny flipped through the pages and made a generous estimate of the word count. She dropped the article into the overflowing tray on her desk and pulled the petty cash box out of the drawer. "Here you are," she said. "The going rate for hard-hitting local journalism."

She handed me $30.00, which I wadded up and stuffed in my pocket. "It's not about the money," I said on my way past Jenny's desk. "I just want to make a difference in a child's life…"

Scott and Gary were at a drafting table in the main room of the *Telegraph*. They moved around frantically, assembling the paper by hand on blue-line wax plates, a technique at least 20 years outdated. Triangles and rulers to measure picas and points. Cutting and pasting with actual scissors and wax. Ribbons of onion paper snowing to the floor around their feet.

"It's gonna be close this week," said Gary hurriedly. He had a kind, effeminate look, thin combed-over hair, patent leather shoes. "I don't know if we'll make it. We still have to get these to the printer tonight, and we're waiting on more content, and there are these accounts out, so even if we do get it there in time, I don't know how we're gonna pay for it. This might be the last issue."

"Pffft," was Scott's only reply. A silent fart of breath and wave of his hand, his usual disregard for anything Gary ever said. Scott was a rough old man, thick glasses, white hair under his tweed hat, a mattress of scribbled notes in his front shirt pocket. The two of them were hovering under the drafting lamps, communicating through guttural monosyllables. The only other sound in the room was the repetitive slice of scissors through paper.

Gary was the publisher. Scott was the editor. At least, that's what it said on the masthead. The whole endeavor seemed like an impossible task for having almost no staff. But somehow, every week, the paper came together. As they got closer to the week's end, they usually worked through the night to make deadline. Around three in the morning every Tuesday a van would show up to collect the wax plates. The driver/circulation manager/delivery person took them to the next town where the plates were photographed. Then they took that negative to another machine, where it was burned into the light-sensitive emulsion of the actual press plate, run through the press, loaded in neatly stacked and tied bundles, driven back, and finally dispersed through the town. Like most people at the paper, he worked on a freelance basis. In this way they cut costs on taxes, payroll, benefits.

Gary finally spotted me standing in the doorway. "Hellohellohello." He spoke in a rapid clip, his tongue always piling up against the back of his teeth. "Look Scott, just in time. Content!"

Scott looked up from the drafting table and pushed his glasses tight to his face, eyes squinted, gray wires of hair purling from his brows over the thick rimmed glasses. "Pffft," he said in my direction.

"Comecome, let's go to my office," Gary said. "I have some more assignments for you. Did you finish the City Council article?"

"Just turned it in," I said.

We walked down the hall, past vacated offices now stacked with old furniture, broken swivel chairs, boxes full of back issues. In the middle of Gary's office there was a desk buried under a mound of paper. On the wall behind the desk hung a faded photograph of Hemingway during his days with the *Kansas City Star*, slightly crooked inside a dusty old frame.

"Did Jenny pay you already? Goodgoodgood, now I suppose the first thing we should discuss is your uh, shall we say...honorarium. Remember that I promised if you stayed with us we would be sure to increase your rate, and well I believe it's about time, don't you? After all, we want to keep you around."

"Sure," I said, a little shocked.

"Let's see then, how much is it we're paying you currently?"

"I've been getting three cents a word," I said.

"Well, double it! From this point forward your rate will be six cents per word." He beamed at me, but my expression didn't change. "I know, I know before you say anything this is not a significant amount, but you must understand that times are tough right now for print media, and if you stick with us we'll get through it and pay you more to be sure, but for now this is all we can afford. You see this is the unfortunate position in our society as we lay idly by watching our venerated newspapers putting chains around the doors..."

As he talked his lungs steadily deflated until there wasn't enough breath to pass over his voice box, the last couple of words wheezing out, spittle building up in the corners of his mouth. He sucked in another breath and continued.

"...and all these mergers mergers mergers soaking everything up, and pretty soon we won't have anything left but one big wet sponge. Do you think that's best for the people? What about the Fourth Estate? On top of that, everything is going online, if you can believe that, although I must say I can see the advantages in reducing the printing costs, but try and make a living selling intangible ads on a screen and tell me how because I would love to know." He paused for a second and looked forlornly at the portrait of Hemingway.

"Anyway," he continued. "I have a couple of assignments for you here, let me just find them—" He rifled through the piles on his desk. "Aha! Here we are now, let's get you lined out. Looks like we've got a chamber of commerce meeting coming up that I'm sure our dear readers will be interested in, and here we have a new restaurant opening up, do you like Korean barbecue? Suresure it's very good, and most likely they'll treat you to a little taste while you're there, you see this job is not without its *perks*. And here we're inaugurating a new chaplain of the State Senate, a real slice-of-life kind of story. I want you to be sure and catch him, he's a Presbyterian, and I've already had a chat with their uh...minister of finance if you will, and I have all but assured a half-page ad. You see," he leaned forward in his chair and cocked one eyebrow, "It appears ours is not the only occupation dealing with *extraneous circumstances*."

After a short pause he hopped out of his chair, stuffed the notes in my hand, ushering me toward the door. "Off you go now, off you go, no time to waste!"

He went back to his desk and buried his head in the mound of pulp like an ostrich, preoccupied with the terror of getting this week's issue out the door. I walked down the hall, back into the main room where Scott was still gluing the next issue together. When I started working there, Scott was the one assigning the articles, but the guard changed when the paper was about to go bankrupt, and Scott relented to Gary's new business model.

"Off already?" he said. "What's he got you on this time?"

I looked through the notes. "Chamber meeting. Korean barbecue. New Senate chaplain."

"Pfffffft." He shook his head, went back to work.

"Sounds like you're on a tight deadline again," I said to him. "Can I help with anything?"

"Can if you want. It's not your job though. You're giving plenty of your time as is."

"I don't mind," I said. "I've been curious how you lay the paper out. Why do you still do it this way?"

"Gary and I have been in the newspaper business for over forty years. This is the way it was done when we started out. He's been pushing for us to learn some new tricks, but I'm too old for that. We're probably one of the only papers still doing this. Want me to show you how it works? Come on over."

I gave him a hand. Cutting up paper, gluing it on, proofing the pages. Scott mostly gesturing and grumbling a few words about where to place the copy within the grid lines, the most conversation we had ever had. Together, we methodically assembled the paper, like filling in dimensions on a blueprint.

# Station of the Cross

After the inauguration ceremony, I found the chaplain in his new third floor office of the capitol building, unpacking and arranging his personal effects. He was much younger than I expected. The first thing he did was take off his vestments and hang them behind the door. He was wearing blue jeans, rolled up sleeves, his face pensive but handsome.

"Go ahead and have a seat." He motioned to a chair. "I'm going to unpack while we talk, if you don't mind."

I started in with the usual questions, where he came from, how he got there, how he felt. He gave a series of glib responses to my series of facile questions. I took down the facts, some quotable lines.

Meanwhile, he opened up boxes, arranged his things in neat order. A little ceramic statue of St. Anthony. A small gilded cross. He lined up a symmetrical row of pens on his desk. Opened a large crate that contained a stack of canvases. Pulled them out and leaned them against a wall, one at a time. Each painting a field of white with a variation of black vertical stripes.

He began to hang them around the office. He was still talking about the experiences leading up to his appointment, but I was too distracted to write anything down. I watched as he hung the paintings, examining them closely, suddenly interested in the new chaplain.

"These paintings," I interrupted him. "They're not the usual sort of decor for—"

"For a chaplain? I know. Most pastors have a more traditional homage to Christ. I prefer the abstract. These are among my favorites. Do you know them?" He hung another one and carefully centered it, then took a step back to make sure it was straight.

"Barnett Newman, right?" He nodded. I had recently been to an exhibit at the Nelson-Atkins Museum of Art and seen some of Newman's other work. I walked up to the closest one. "At first I thought these were prints."

"No, I painted them myself. Don't underestimate a pastor. I studied art while in seminary." He tacked another nail into the wall, lowered the canvas down onto it, adjusted it slightly.

"Perhaps it's sacrilegious to someone in the painting world," he continued, "that someone should recreate the work of others. I made them because these paintings inspire me, and I want to surround myself with inspiration. There's nothing wrong with that, is there? Maybe there are copyrights, but who'd come after a man of the cloth, right?" He shifted around to the center wall. There was a framed print of Warner Sallman's *Head of Christ*, left by the previous chaplain. He lifted it off the nail, turned it around backwards, and leaned it against the wall. He then used the same nail to hook the next of his Newman recreations.

I walked up close to one of the paintings, then stepped farther back, taking in the fastidious detail.

"These are really good," I said.

"Thanks, most people aren't that interested."

"I have to ask though, if you're painting, why not make something original? Why copy what's already been done?"

"This doesn't take away from the originals," he said to me over his shoulder. "It celebrates them. Technical skill isn't what makes them art. These paintings are an old idea made new again, given more freedom, more room for the imagination. Besides, I like looking at them."

The chaplain hung the last of the paintings on the wall and walked to the center of the room, looking around, five to a wall on either side of his desk, four in front. I grabbed the pen and notebook and started writing again. I knew none of this would make the article, but I wanted to know more. I asked more questions.

"To some, these are a meaningless alternation of black and white stripes," he said. "To me, they're much more. They're vivid reminders that this life is very brief. That your friends will help you through difficulties. That sometimes there are things we are called to do, impossible or painful as they may be."

"All of that, right here in a few simple stripes?"

"I think so," he said.

I looked around and could see it all in a way I never imagined, through his eyes, and it took on new meaning, new depth. As he continued talking, I was moved the way he was moved, more reverently, eyes fixed on the paintings, the entire passion playing out in the holiest contrast of color.

# Time and Material

After leaving the chaplain's office, I walked down the marble halls of the capitol, into the House Lounge. The entrance to the room was a set of large, oak pocket doors. No handles. I stepped onto the black mat in front of the doors, triggering an electric motor that slid them apart and into the walls. I crossed the threshold. The motor drew the doors shut, closing me into an immense silence, a hidden room, a place I often escaped to admire the mural painted by Thomas Hart Benton that filled the walls. This was a man who taught during the New York School. From his sinuous, regional style, Jackson Pollack rebelled, and was born. The panels included a mother wiping the naked ass of an infant in the middle of a campaign rally. Native Americans trading booze and blankets. A black man being lynched, silhouetted by the fire and smoke of a town being burned to the ground during the Civil War. Benton was smart, insisted on free reign in his contract, he could paint anything. So he filled it with the iniquities, horrors, hypocrisies of the population. Images that drove the town crazy. They couldn't stand looking at their own filth and follies. He was an iconoclast, and my favorite painter. In the side panel I found what I was looking for, a depiction of the Nelson-Atkins Museum of Art. Below the front steps there was a burn barrel, three people standing around it, trying to warm their hands over the fire.

It was getting late, so I left, still thinking about the chaplain. I wanted someone to talk to about it, but I knew Travis wouldn't be interested. I passed by Pat's Place and went home.

I gathered up my typewriter and a few supplies, carried them down to the dingy, one-room cellar below my apartment building, where I wouldn't be a bother to Ms. Krutzwaller. It was unpleasant, but better than nothing. One ceramic light hanging by the wire nuts, flickering overhead. Wet earth heaving freshets of moisture through the pores in the foundation. The smell of mildew.

I made a desk out of two sawhorses and a half sheet of plywood. I grabbed a cup, poured in four fingers of whiskey, lit a cigarette, loaded the typewriter with a crisp sheet of paper, the noise and smoke absorbing into the subterrane around me.

I watched the typebars hammer against the platen, driving each letter like a nail into the joist. Pure, simple, mechanical force. But after a while, there were only a couple of bruised pages laying next to it. False starts. This happened a lot, a symptom of the perpetual cycle taking hold. Blanked out. Because I wasn't living, I had nothing to nail down. I was empty.

I leaned back in the chair and blew smoke into the air above, staring at the rough-hewn undercarriage of the building. There were rusted water lines and gas pipes and electric wiring snaking through the joists. Dust flaking from the stone walls. It was cold, solitary.

An old HVAC unit in one corner sputtered and rumbled like the rusted Ford, wheezing heat into the units above. The whole apartment complex reeked of cheap construction. I knew the smell, working in it every day. I could tear this whole thing down and build it back up again. All I would need was time and material.

I went over to the furnace, found the vent leading up to Ms. Krutzwaller's unit and disconnected it, pointing it toward the middle of the room. Then I brought down the easel from my apartment and set it up in front of the desk, put a 3x3 sheet of drywall on it, salvaged from the jobsite. I couldn't write anything, so I took out some tubes of unmixed oil paints and palette knives and went to work on a painting. They were similar to drywall knives, only smaller. Even using the same method as drywall, putting paint on, wiping it flat, the same wrist motion learned through the trades, the cellular memory.

Painting was a diversion. I enjoyed the way it tasted. The way it smelled. I respected painting and people who did it well. I thought about the chaplain. He went straight for imitation, but he was still painting. He was doing *something*.

I put more paint on, took it off, put it on, took it off, blending and sculpting the thick, rich colors, full of life, my back turned to the typewriter, blank page still sticking its tail out of the roller. I would get back to it soon enough. I painted to keep the electricity in my right brain firing until I could find something that was true. All I needed was time and material. Then I could go back to the typewriter and post holes in the snow.

## Blue Period

Time passed by in an overarching yawn. Push the button, get the pellet. Routinely uneventful. Destroyer of vigor. We were working even though it was a Saturday. Weekends were supposed to be optional and only when things were busy. But it was always busy and never really optional. The boss didn't cut paychecks until Saturday, and it was implied that if you wanted to get paid, you had to give the company that day, too.

"So I was watching TV last night," Travis started in. "And I came up with a million-dollar idea."
"Uh huh," I barely replied. My head wasn't in it that day. I found a blank spot on the wall, wrote another line.

*Getting and spending, we lay waste our powers*
—*Wordsworth*

"I keep seeing all these prescription drugs, like Zoloft, or Viagra, or Abilify," Travis said. "We have a prescription for just about everything." He did a pirouette in the center of the room as he was talking, flinging his drywall hammer as he spun around, burying the hatchet side in the wall a few feet from me.

"Yeah, so what, you'll be a pusher for the pharmaceutical companies?"

"No, I came up with my *own* drug. Well, the idea, anyway." He walked over and pulled the hammer out of the wall, picked up his pan and knife, patched the hole it left behind. "I still need to hire a lab to come up with the chemistry for it. I call it *Abolix*. Take one pill at the beginning of the work day, and you black out for eight hours. Just your brain, though. Your body'll keep going. But when you come to at the end of the day, you'll have no memory of exactly the last eight hours. It'll be like you weren't even there."

"Doesn't matter, you'd have the muscle memory. You'd still feel it in your bones."

"True..." he said, pausing in the middle of the rom. "But they already came up with drugs for that."

Riley, the boss, pulled up in a white, extended cab truck and honked the horn. Travis and I put down our tools, walked out to meet him. Riley had worked construction all his life, starting at the bottom, climbing the trade ladder. Now he was a contractor, top of the food chain in that little ecosystem.

He rolled down the window, a cloud of cigar smoke exhaled out and over the cab. "What's it look like in there boys?" he asked. At one point, Riley was made of iron. But those who take up the sword, perish by the sword. His body paid the heavy price for it all, took the simian shape of hard work and hard drink. His arms and back were slabs of gristle, abdomen calcified by the drink into a smooth, round viscera. His hands were a biological history of the working class, written over the years in cuts, calluses, tissue that no longer regenerated, dull arthritic pain. His veins were so constricted he could barely walk, had to have his legs wrapped all the time. Now he rarely ever got out of his truck. It was like an enormous, 4x4 wheelchair.

"Fine," Travis answered. "Putting on the final coat, then we're done."

"What?" Riley snarled, his eyes doubled by his quarter-inch-thick glasses. "Speak up boy." The high whine of power tools had drilled holes in his ear drums over the years.

"JUST FINE," Travis yelled.

"Good," Riley said. "You'd better be putting the last coat on today and then be done with this job. I have another one ready for you boys on Monday."

Travis rolled his eyes in my direction. Riley reached down and pulled his distended belly back where it was wedged into the steering wheel so he could pull open the lapel of his coat. He reached to the inside pocket and pinched out his checkbook, opened it on on the center of the steering wheel, one eye squinting, thick wet tongue rolling to the corner of his mouth. He was doing math.

We waited for him. Travis smiled and rubbed his hands together. "The best part of sucking his dick for six days," he said to me, "is watching him blow his wad on you."

"What's that?" Riley asked through the cab window.

"I SAID, IT'S THE BEST WORK WE'VE DONE THESE LAST SIX DAYS. CAN'T WAIT TO SHOW THE WALLS TO YOU."

"Hm," he peered over his glasses at Travis, then the tongue rolled back into the corner of his lips. He tore out two checks, thrusting them toward us through the window. "New job site on Monday." He put the fat cigar in his mouth, started the truck, and rumbled out of the subdivision.

"We give it all away for this," Travis held his check up to the sun, like he was searching for a watermark.

"Wasted kinetics," I said, folding my check in half.

"It's not so bad. Beats minimum wage, at least. We'll go out and celebrate and forget about it. I'll see you at the bar tonight."

It hit it me right then and there. Something clicked free, finally decoupling within my brain. "I'm finished," I said.

"What do you mean finished? Day's not even half over."

"I mean I'm finished. I can't fucking do it anymore. I'm not gonna start another job site next week. In fact, I'm never touching another sheet of drywall again. This is it."

He could see that I was serious. "So you're really gonna do it? You're gonna take off?"

"Yes, I mean it this time. No more blue-collar work for me. Can you finish up? I need to run to the bank before it closes."

"You're leaving right now?"

"Right now."

"Sure, I guess."

"Thanks, gotta go."

"What about your tools?"

"Keep them. I won't need them anymore."

"Whatever. Good luck," he called after me.

I jumped in the truck. Travis stood in the doorway of the house. I gave him a final wave and started the motor. He raised his hand in a mock salute, then turned up his middle finger as I sped out of the winding subdivision for the last time, back into town.

I stopped at Central Bank. Stood in line, anxious, waiting, looking up at the Warhol painting hanging on the wall behind the tellers.

"Next!" I was called from behind the marble countertop by a powder-faced young woman, artificial tan, soft flesh marking dimples around her elbows.

"I'd like to make a withdrawal," I said excitedly.

"How much?" she asked with a glib, rote smile. I could almost see the boredom coursing through her veins.

"All of it," I said proudly.

She turned her eyes down to her computer. Before she could authorize the transaction, I had to show her multiple forms of identification, answer account security questions, assure her that I did in fact want to withdraw everything. Then she called the manager over, and I had to go through the entire process again. I was getting impatient, just wanted to hurry, go, go.

Finally, she coldly punched it into the computer and counted out the bills. "Six thousand one hundred thirty-one, thirty-two, thirty-three, and seventy-six cents. NEXT!"

I pulled up to my apartment. Ms. Krutzwaller was in the hallway with the broom, *swick, swick, swick,* around the baseboard. She always swept the hallway around the first of the month, an excuse for rent-seeking outside my door.

"I was just cleaning the house, trying to get rid of all this dust. You have to stay on top of these things or this place will attract dust mites. Even in this tiny little apartment, I can see it building up if I don't sweep and mop. I don't know how they do it in those big houses you're building. People don't think about that when they buy a big house, how much time they'll have to spend just cleaning it. It never *ends*."

I still owed rent for last month, so I peeled off some of the cash and gave it to her. "Here you are, Ms. Krutzwaller. Thank you for being such a gracious landlord." She glared at me, but I immediately turned and went through my door.

I went over to the bookshelf, pulled out a copy of *Ulysses*, tucked the crisp bills between the pages. Then pulled the rest of the books off the shelf and dropped them into boxes. Threw the clothes in the closet into a duffel bag. All that remained were the things I'd left down in the cellar. I didn't care about the furniture or the rest of my tools. Krutzwaller could deal with that.

Then I remembered I still had one more article I hadn't finished for the *Telegraph*. The one about the chaplain. I already had the interview, I just needed to type something up. Wouldn't take long.

I looked around my apartment. Most everything was packed, and if it wasn't packed, it didn't matter. So that was it. I pulled the copy of *Ulysses* back out, peeled off a couple dollars. I would get a cup of coffee, finish the article, drop off the work truck, and buy a ticket out.

# Coffee Zone

Taisir was the owner of Coffee Zone and the only person I ever saw behind the counter. Because he came from Jordan, and because he was Muslim, he was suspected by some of being connected with Al Qaeda, or the Taliban, or some other terrorist organization. When the twin towers went down, Taisir's shop was vandalized. The front of the building spray-painted with slurs. One of the windows opened with a brick. Taisir, however, didn't hold this against anyone.

"Hala hala, my friend! It's almost Friday, yes?" Taisir said, smiling as usual.

"It's Saturday," I said. It didn't matter the day, he always said it was almost Friday. "Are there any days you don't work?"

"Oh no, my friend, I never work," he smiled. "You want Rocket Fuel?" This was his signature blend. A thick, black, jet sludge, bitter as roots, exponential in its caffeine, a liquid that could fuel a nuclear submarine. I ordered a cup to go.

"That will be two dollars my friend."

I paid and grabbed a table near the front, pulling out my notes for the *Telegraph* article. I sipped at the Rocket Fuel, wrote up a piece about the chaplain, including his art background and the Newman paintings, taking all sorts of liberties with the article, knowing it was my last.

That's when I saw the Viking character from the bar the other night, standing on the street corner outside. Something told me to forget about it when he walked past the window. The article was finished. I just needed to turn it in, get on my way. But instead, I got up from the table and followed after him.

# Workshop

I stood inside 124 High Street, in the middle of the large, unfinished space, wondering what to do. I wanted to know what was happening, but the Viking was long gone, and the only other person there was still unconscious. I turned, started to walk out. I didn't see the empty bottle in the middle of the floor when I kicked it, sending it flying across the room, where it cracked against the brick wall.

The person lying on the booth seat jerked his head out from under his elbow, glowering as the light pierced his shattered eyes.

"What the—?"

"Sorry to wake you," I said, caught off guard as much as he was.

He struggled to an upright position, took a moment to re-engage his cortex. "It's fine," he said finally. "What's up?"

I hesitated, trying to think of something. "Uh…I'm with the *Telegraph*. I'm here to maybe get a story."

"A story?" There was a fume of alcohol oozing from his pores, smoke breathing from the hair follicles, sweat ringing the joints of his clothes. He leaned forward, hocked up a white tonsil stone, spit it onto the floor, then ground it out with the heel of his ragged, black boot. He was rubbing his eyes, still coming to. "What place are you looking for?"

"They like to do an article on any new businesses downtown. I was just checking to see what was going in here."

He laughed, a throttled whiskey wheeze, coughing it out. "You got any cigarettes?" he asked.

I handed him one, and he pulled a lighter out of his pocket, narrowing his dark eyes to the flame. People passed by on High Street, casting shadows through the window that crossed from one side of the room to the other.

"I'm Steven," he said, his large frame sinking back into the seat. He was starting to pull himself together, the pallor slowly relenting as the blood cells returned to his skin.

"Mark," I said.

"So you're a writer." Steven said. "I don't really read the *Telegraph*, to be honest with you."

"That's alright, neither do I."

"You wanna do an article on this place?" He turned the cigarette up and swished it in the air, admiring the skylight beams striking the whorls of smoke. He lifted one leg up, both hands under his thigh, and manually crossed it over the other. He took a long drag, leaned forward, scratching his scalp through a shock of black hair. A slight dander mixed with the dust in the air.

"Maybe." I looked around at the piles of scree. "What is this, exactly?"

"It's kind of a long story. Gimme a second, I'll find us something to drink." He struggled to his feet, tromped over the rubble toward the front of the building. "Then we can talk about whatever you want," he said over his shoulder.

"Sure thing."

Just inside the storefront window there was a low, round wooden table with rings of acrylic on the surface from dripping paint cans. Steven sat near the table, back to the window, on an upturned five gallon bucket. He took two coffee cups off the table, swished the dregs around, spilled them out on the floor, then wiped them out with the tail of his shirt. He produced a half bottle of wine from a row of empties, filled the cups, handed one to me. He turned over a milk crate and kicked it my way.

I sat facing the storefront window, looking out onto the street, but no one passing by could see in. I looked around the interior again. "You have some tools lying around," I said. "Are you fixing this place up?"

He exhaled two wan tusks of smoke from his nostrils. "Something like that. It used to be a deli. The last tenants moved out three years ago, and the place has been empty since. I did some construction work for the landlord, and I started talking to him about architecture, and the beauty of these old, unappreciated buildings downtown. That's when he told me about this place and all the character that's been covered up and forgotten over the years." He motioned for another cigarette. I took one out for each of us, left the pack on the table. Steven lit one cigarette with the other. "I know it looks like shit in here, but underneath it all, this is a great building. Below us is the original cross-hatched wood floor." He swept the side of his boot across the floor a couple of times to move the bed of debris. "And if you stripped the layers of paint off that ceiling, underneath are these iridescent pressed-tin panels. Behind the plaster on this wall is the original brick." He pointed to a section that had the plaster broken off. Just enough to see that there was in fact something behind it.

I looked around the space. It did have charm, history. Certainly better than the clapboard houses being thrown up on the perimeter of the town.

"So you were hired to remodel all this?" I asked.

"Not exactly. We made a deal with the owner to trade some labor for use of the space. He couldn't find anyone to rent it like it is, so as long as we fix it up, he doesn't charge us anything."

"How long is that gonna last?"

"I don't know. As long as there's work being done. At this rate—" He waved his cigarette into the abyss at the back of the building.

"What's it even for? Why put all that time and effort into it?" I thought about work in the trades, the dull, boring anguish. And here, apparently, were people doing it voluntarily.

"It's a place for art, more or less."

"How do you mean? Like a gallery?"

"Not exactly," he said. "More like a sort of workshop or studio. A place for us to paint, write some music, that kind of thing."

"Who is us?" I asked, still trying to piece it together.

"That's a hard one to answer," he said. "New people show up all the time. I'm not even sure how anyone finds out about the gallery."

"Wait, but I thought it wasn't a gallery?"

"Oh, it's not, I just call it that out of habit. We've talked about opening and actually showing work. But as you can see by the state of things, that's pretty much impossible. We really just wanted a creative space."

I looked up at the window, the painted writing, the long, high-ceilinged space. "You have a storefront and all this wall space. You have the building of a gallery, not a studio."

"That's just a coincidence. We just happened to find this place. It could've been anywhere."

"Anywhere in *this* town, or just anywhere?"

"What do you mean?"

"I mean, why here? Why not somewhere else where it might go over better."

"Let me guess, you wanna move away."

"Of course, there's nothing here. I'm actually getting ready to move, right now."

"Not surprised. Most people wanna leave this town. How about you, where you going?"

"I don't know. I was leaning toward New York."

"Good luck with that," he said. "I have some friends there. All of them work two or three jobs just to stay on their feet. I have no interest in that. What's the point of being there, if you never have time to do anything? Anyway, that's just me."

"Yeah...I don't know." I hesitated. "Whatever, tell me some more about this place, I'm still trying to wrap my head around it."

We talked more about the space for awhile, every question raised a thousand more questions, all piling up in my head. We drank off our wine, smoked a couple cigarettes.

Steven grabbed the bottle off the table to refill our cups, but it was empty.

"It never lasts long around here," he said, slumping back against the window, letting his cup fall to the floor.

I wanted to keep the conversation going and could see it flagging without more drink. I stood up. "I need to run to the *Telegraph* real quick. If you're gonna be around, I'll pick up some wine on the way back. I wanna know more."

He nodded. "Sure, I'm not going anywhere."

I stepped back outside, into the unchanged town on High Street. But everything seemed very different, knowing there was something there, something that's been there all along. I glided down the sidewalk, a current of air under my soles, low pressure passing over high pressure, generating lift. Art, real and alive, a place, people who are creating and living it, right here.

I decided I would wait, leave tomorrow. What's one more day?

# Telegraph #2

Tolson's Drug Store was a couple of blocks down High Street. They sold wine and cigarettes, but I had left all my cash back at my apartment, so I stopped into the *Telegraph* to submit an article and get paid. And to let them know they would need a new writer after tomorrow.

Gary and Scott were sitting on the couch in the main office, relaxed for a change, deadline now past. Scott was squinting over the bridge of his glasses at a *Washington Post*. Gary was leafing through the local business journal with a pen in hand.

"Wellwellwell what are you doing in here on a Saturday, come in come in have a seat." Gary reached over to the chair across from them that was full of newspapers, cleared it off with a single sweep of his arm.

"Finished the chaplain article," I said, handing it to him. "I was hoping Jenny might be here—"

Gary snatched the article. "Uh huh, uh huh." He scanned very quickly. "Suresuresure." He flipped the page. I didn't know how he could be reading anything that fast. "I see I see." He picked up a red pen and started crossing things out. Whole lines, sections. He cut every unnecessary part of the story, skinning it, removing the meat and guts, leaving only a dried skeleton of facts.

"We were just discussing what to have you cover in the next issue," Gary said, putting the article aside without commenting.

"I wanted to talk to you about that—" I started to explain.

"It's damned hard business trying to come up with content every week. I've been racking my brain all afternoon trying to find some news."

I thought about all the articles I had written for the *Telegraph*, what was being called news.

"Actually, I just ran across something today," I said. "An art space downtown. I think it might be a great thing for you to do a story on."

"Looklooklook Scott we have some initiative here, our writer is pitching story ideas. So tell me more. Is it an art gallery you say?"

"Well, not exactly," I didn't know how to explain because I still had no idea myself.

"Okay well when is this art space planning to open up? Maybe they need to do a little promotional advertising to get the word out there. You know it can be hard starting a new business and they'll need all the help they can get."

"I'm not sure about that either," I said "I can find out though and get a story today if you want. Tomorrow I'm—"

"Yesyesyes." Gary's eyes lit up. "This could be a great opportunity here in fact you could even take the lead on getting them some advertising while you're doing the interview…"

"I'm not sure I can—"

"Maybe you can even make a little commission on the ad along with the article…"

"I really don't—"

"Yesyesyes there's an idea, maybe you could supplement your income a little if you want to start drumming up your own material and dovetail that with a nice little ad, double dip so to speak. This could be great for the newspaper and for you too, right Scott?"

Scott rolled the unlit cigar around in his mouth. Without looking up from his paper, he leaned to the side, lifting the weight off one leg, releasing a slow mmmmph. He turned to the next page of the *Post*.

"Okay then if you have questions on how to pitch the ad or want any tips don't hesitate to ask but I think you'll find that it's all pretty natural." Gary stood up so I stood up, he shook my hand vigorously to seal it, send me on my way. "I'm glad you came in with your ideas today because that's what keeps this paper running, fresh ideas."

"Right. Well. I guess I'll be going then." I had no idea what had just happened. I turned to leave.

"Waitwaitwait before you go." Gary stopped me, went over to the desk drawer and pulled out a twenty and a couple of ones. I had almost forgotten. "Normally Jenny handles this but let's see here you are, some petty cash." He handed me the bills awkwardly, gripping in a sort of handshake around the thin paper.

# Framing

I scanned the shelves at Tolson's, arranged in descending financial order, quality on top, quantity on bottom. I reached to the lowest shelf, selected what I hoped was the least cloying, pulled off three bottles. At the counter I got another pack of smokes, then walked back to the gallery, or whatever it was.

Steven was still sitting in the front, leaning over the wood-worn parlor guitar, strumming lightly, percussive chuck, faint hum of formless lyrics.

He was not the same as the person I found on the booth seat earlier. He was awake, alive. His stature large and commanding, strong without muscular definition, making the shallow-bodied instrument look miniature. His face had a sheen, an unhealthy sort of glow. Carelessly dressed in jeans and blue t-shirt, the neckline fabric stretched and hanging loosely. Thick wave of black hair swelling out of the sharp receding point over the left eye, breaking somewhere over the back. Eyes closed while he strummed. Brows lifted high on the forehead. He was magnetic.

I pulled the plastic ring around the new pack of smokes and set the wine on the table. Steven came out of it when the bottles hit, putting down the guitar.

I was about to start asking more questions when we heard a noise. A light poured in from the depths of the building, the back door thrown open, silhouetting a tall figure. It slammed shut again. Someone stomped through the dark, over the rubble piles toward the front. The big, blonde Viking emerged from the chaos into the half-light of the window, stopping in front of us without saying a word.

Steven paid no attention to him, instead picked up a screwdriver and rooted around the floor, found a long phillips screw. "No corkscrew," he explained.

"Sorry, didn't think about that." He used the screwdriver to twist the screw down through the cork, then grabbed a hammer and pried the cork out with the claw.

The Viking walked over to a pile of tools in the corner. Pulled back his long hair into a knot. Slid a leather tool belt around his waist and dropped a hammer into the loop. Opened a nearby water jug and dumped the last bit over his tanned face and still-bare chest, shaking off the excess like a wet antelope, the pearls of water pulling dust out of the air.

He walked toward us until he was standing right in front of me, looking straight through me with wolfish eyes. He grabbed the empty pack of cigarettes on the table. Swirled it close to his ear like a gold pan, listening. He tossed it aside, grabbed the pack I'd just bought. Flipped it open and pulled out a stick of sediment, tucking it in his pink lips.

"This is Pederson," Steven finally said. "Pederson, this is Mark. He's a writer."

Pederson gave a small nod, then made a flicking motion with his thumb, indicating a need for fire. Steven pulled the lighter from his pocket and tossed it to him.

Still without a word, he went back into the depths, over to the plastered brick. Cigarette dangling from his lips, the hammer drawn, he began to swing. Making wild chopping motions, bringing more of what was still upright down to the floor.

"I've seen him around," I said to Steven. "What's his story?"

"Don't mind him," Steven said. "He doesn't say much right now."

"I've noticed. Is he part of the gallery?" I watched as Pederson swung frantically, plaster chunks careening all around and at him, a cloud of dust rising around his feet.

"He's one of them, yeah. He does sculpture."

A large plate buckled from the wall and fell intact. Pederson leaned over and hammered away at it until it was shattered into dust.

"I see," I replied.

"He took a lot of acid. We're still waiting for him to come out on the other side."

"He's on acid right now?"

"Not right now, no," Steven laughed. "That was almost a year ago. Might have been a little too much. He's been dramatized ever since."

Pederson was still tearing at the walls like a trapped animal. We lit another cigarette and watched him, the beastly movements, destroying rather than disassembling, brick coming down with the plaster, piles mounding in the angle of repose.

"Is this part of paying rent?" I filled my cup from the bottle of wine.

"Yeah, right now we're just clearing the place out, getting rid of all the old stuff. In fact, I should probably help out." He shuffled to his feet, stretched out his spine. "You're welcome to stick around if you want. Up to you."

"This seems like a great endeavor, everything about this space, about what you're trying to do, but I gave up this sort of work not long ago."

"I know what you mean," Steven said. He grabbed his wine and walked back into the gallery toward Pederson. "I've done that too," he said over his shoulder. "Dozens of times."

Together they broke down a section of wall, leaving the scraps where they fell. The more they brought down in the deconstruction, the bigger the piles on the floor. I surveyed the scene. Still had a thousand questions I wanted to ask.

As Pederson got wilder and more careless, Steven stood back, trying to dodge the falling debris. I tried to imagine the place if none of the waste were there, if it was totally empty and clean, even finished. I began to see all the potential that

Steven was talking about. I looked around, thought of all that could be done. Not to mention how incredible it would be if this were an art gallery.

I was feeling guilty for watching while they were busy working. I thought about leaving and maybe stopping by again later. The two of them had their backs turned. Steven was scraping up some old linoleum glued to the hardwood. I wondered if that had been all the progress thus far, the demolition. Eventually, something would have to be reconstructed. Especially if the rent and the space depended on progress.

"You know," I said on my way out. "If or when you ever do open this up as a gallery, you could finish a wall over here to hang paintings."

"What's that?" Steven looked up from what he was doing.

"Over here, along this stairwell." Steven looked over. "This is the only thing breaking this side of the gallery up from the rest of the space. Instead of having a set of stairs coming down into it, you could build a wall across the front of them and leave an access at the bottom. Then you'd have this extra space for hanging your work. It's just an idea."

"That's not bad. We do have some boards here that we pulled out of the upstairs," Steven said. "We could re-use those, they're straight enough."

"I could give you hand with that, at least."

I picked up a hammer off the floor, and before I knew what has happening, I was committed. We gathered up some of the old lumber to build a frame for the wall.

Somehow, it didn't even feel like work. This was for something valuable. The three of us worked alongside each other, hammering nails into the frame, Pederson's wild eyes staring into the cosmic void, Steven smiling a Tom Sawyer smile.

# Work in Progress

Steven, Pederson, and I took a step back, finished. We went to the table in the front.

Pederson was drenched, sweat streaming down his body, soaking into the leather on his tool belt. He took it off and flung it into the corner. He sat down, still with that blank stare, gazing into the black lettering on the front window, searching for meaning.

"Well, not bad, I suppose," Steven said. "A solid two hours of work." His feet were up on the table, apparent closure.

"Are these the normal hours around here?" I asked. Much different than the working-class schedule. I wondered what Travis would think about this. How he would love to work only two hours a day.

"We're lucky if we can get that," said Steven. "But we need to keep the landlord happy. He's been getting edgy lately, wondering when we would start putting something together instead of tearing it apart. Now we have a wall to show him."

We looked at the crowning accomplishment. Stud frame, sixteen inches on center, closing off the stairs, completing the wall as one continuous stretch. Now the building was a brick wall down one side, framed wall down the other, heap of garbage in the middle.

"What happens next?" I asked.

"Next? We've secured the space another day," Steven said. "Now we do whatever we want."

We each poured some more wine, lit a cigarette. I looked down at my hand and saw a small cut on one knuckle. Must have happened while raising the wall. I wiped it off on the bottom of my shirt.

"I'm still a little confused," I said. "Is this going to be a gallery or isn't it?"

"I don't know," Steven said. "It depends on how you look at it. But that's not the question that really matters. In fact, the question itself is all that matters."

"I don't follow," I said.

"Asking questions. Searching for something, looking deeper into things and trying to find the answers. That's what this is about, and to me that's what art is about. We're all made up of questions more than answers. You keep asking and searching and if you find the answer, or think you found the answer, you ask more questions. Out of that you produce your own work, and that's what this gallery is for. Whether or not we actually open it up and display anything, it's still a gallery."

The more we talked the less I could nail down. Steven always maneuvered around anything definitive, anything absolute. Instead he steered toward the open-ended, undetermined, flexible, evolving. This allowed our conversation to go on indefinitely.

"What the fuck are you guys talking about?" A new voice came through the front door.

"Bradley!" Steven replied. "Come check it out, we have a wall now."

Bradley came in shouldering a large canvas bag. He gave a cursory look at the new wall, unimpressed, then turned to me. "Who's this?" he asked.

"This is Mark. He's a writer." Second time I was introduced as a writer at face-value. It felt odd, like I hadn't earned it yet.

"Tell me you haven't copped on to this sinking ship," Bradley said. "The fact that you're sitting here sweating with these two jackasses tells me you've been helping out. Let me give you a piece of advice that may help your writing career: Don't waste your time here. This place is a black hole of creativity. It's full of great ideas and conversations, but this front door is the event horizon. Nothing artistic can escape it."

"I just came here to get a story for the paper," I said. I had forgotten all about the newspaper.

"We have a little bit of wine if you—" Steven picked up the bottle and turned it upside down. A couple of drops slid out and hit the table.

"Of course you're out!" Bradley laughed. "Don't worry, I brought more." He opened the canvas bag and fished through some paintbrushes to produce two more bottles. "There's never enough art supplies around here," Bradley said to me. "You'll learn that right away. Drinking is the only thing these charlatans do with any kind of dedication." He threw a bottle to Steven.

"How about you?" I asked. "Are you involved with the gallery too?"

"Fuck no. I would never attach my name to something that I know is going to fail. No, I'm only here because I need a place to paint."

"How do you know it's gonna fail?" I asked. "There's nothing else like this in town."

"Did they tell you what happened with the last space?"

"I didn't know there was one." I looked over to Steven, who just laughed a little and waved off the comment.

"Of course not. No one wants to mention that disaster."

"Don't listen to Bradley," said Steven. "He tries to come off hard. He's a hell of a painter, so we forgive him for being such an asshole. He's got some paintings upstairs if you wanna see them."

"I had a look when I first came in," I said to Bradley. "I saw the one drying in the middle of the room. It looks like you were using silicone caulk?"

"That's Bradley's newest theme," said Steven. "Inspired by the factory across town where they make prefabricated panels for trailers." He grinned, making a jab at Bradley.

"You work in a factory?" I asked.

"For now." The blood rose through the capillaries of his high cheeks and into the the tips of ears. His aquiline nose had a tiny gutter running through the tip. Face clean cut, hair short, brown. In fact, Bradley seemed generally more healthy than anyone else in the room. A lean mixture of crude oil and gasoline. "I only took the job so I could rip off materials. I can't afford this crap on my own. I've been stockpiling a little every day, and as soon as I get what I need, I'm out of there."

"Well, the paintings I saw upstairs were good," I said. "You gonna be showing them here when it opens?"

"Opens? You're not hearing me," Bradley said curtly. "This place is never going to open. And even if it did, I'm not hanging anything of mine in this dump. I'll let Joey have that. His paintings are far too good to be here, but he doesn't have sense enough to know better."

"Who's Joey?"

"You haven't met Joey yet? He's a great painter. He's the only one I know who's better than me." He turned to Steven. "Don't tell him I said that. Anyway, if you're foolish enough to stick around, you'll find out. I'm going upstairs now to get some real work done."

He picked up his bag and walked to the stairs. "Nice job putting a few boards together," he said, looking at the newly framed wall. "It'll probably never get finished beyond this point." He disappeared up the stairs.

"It'll get finished, one of these days," Steven said to me, leaning back against the window, puffing his cigarette. "As soon we can afford some drywall."

I thought about this for a second. "I know a place where we can get drywall right now."

"On a Saturday night? Everything's closed."

"Yeah, now would be the perfect time."

## Minor Key

We drove out to the suburbs, back to the job site, slipping in under the cover of darkness. No one lived on the street yet, so there was no danger. We quickly loaded up a few sheets of drywall and some mud that was stocked there, and I grabbed the pan and knives I'd left behind earlier that day.

We brought it back to the gallery. Bradley was still painting upstairs and Pederson had wandered off somewhere, so it was just Steven and me. We hung the few sheets of drywall and I got out the pan and knives, cleaned them off again, and put on a coat of mud. It didn't take long.

Steven and I sat down again at the table in front of the gallery and lit a cigarette.

"This is way more than I would have done," said Steven. "That should keep the landlord content for a while."

We started talking, going back and forth about the artists we admired. The writers, the photographers, the musicians, films, books, paintings. Everything. We talked for hours on end, into the night, an argot of form and line, field and figure, rhythm and color. The sort of long, emphatic conversation that I hadn't shared with anyone for a long time. Steven could hold court on any subject, any medium, and speak with charismatic authority. If the topic was literature, then the entire canon was defined by the books he had read, which was no small amount. But outside of that, nothing existed. In some cases he hadn't even read the book, he only talked about it with someone else, absorbing it through conversation.

"What about you?" I asked after a staggering treatise about musicians. "Where are you trying to go with your music?"

"I don't know, right now I'm just intent on writing songs," he said.

"You don't really need to have a space for that, right? At least, not a gallery. You could do that anywhere."

"That's true, but there's more to this place than that. If it were only writing music, I would still be sitting on the edge of my bed with a guitar, the way I did when I was thirteen and learning how to play. But this place is inspiring, despite all the squalor you see around here. Maybe even more so because of it. And there are some great artists involved who are struggling to do the same thing in their own way. There's something about being surrounded with all this that's enriching."

"It still baffles me that yesterday I didn't even know this existed. I don't know how many times I've walked by here without the slightest idea."

"What about you?" Steven asked. "What kind of writing do you do outside of the *Telegraph*?"

"I've been working on a novel."

"Really? What's it about?"

"I don't really know yet. I'm sort of figuring that out as I go."

"Where are you doing your writing?"

"I have an apartment a few blocks away." I thought of that filthy, poorly-lighted place below ground.

"How'd you like to have a space to write? There's an office upstairs, or at least we're calling it an office. It has a big six-drawer desk. You're welcome to take it over if you want."

"Isn't someone using that?"

"Not really. We'll probably need to clear out the drawers and clean it up a little."

A space to write. A workshop. An office. Something I had never thought possible. "I don't know what to say."

"If you can stand the chaos, it's all yours. Besides, you're a part of the gallery now. Your blood is even in it." He motioned to the tiny, painless cut on my knuckle, dry blood flaking off. He reached into his pocket, fished out a key and threw it onto the table. "This is my only key, so make a copy of it and give it back to me. Now you can come and go as you like."

"Just like that?"

"Of course," he shrugged. "How else?"

*Not a poet but a poem. Not an artist but a work of art. Not a workshop but a gallery.*
—G.K. Chesterton

# PART 2

# Woodshed

I was going to stick around for a couple more days, just see what came of it. A couple days became a week, then another week, then a month, then another month. Winter finally came to an end, refilling the flora all around with color, vibrance, life.

    Before long I forgot all about leaving. I was settled into the office in the gallery, absorbed in the space. I fed pages through the typewriter, spinning, spinning, a long and delirious intoxication. The ashtray overflowed with cigarettes. There were pages and pages everywhere, cascading off the desk and onto the floor, lying like autumn leaves at my feet. Some of them crushed and tossed in the corners. I didn't sleep much. Everything else fell by the wayside as I became more wrapped up in the gallery. Time became distorted. We'd stay up all hours of the night talking, drinking whiskey and wine, playing music, pulling books off the shelf to read passages aloud, firing canons of literature into the air. Feeling the texture of life.

    My only job was writing the few paltry stories for the *Telegraph*. When I set the articles aside I kept writing, writing.

I had all the free time in the world. I could have gone back to work, back to doing drywall, but I didn't give it a thought. The feeling of being perched at the forefront of a microscopic cultural revolution. The headwaters of inspiration. I was writing more than ever before, sitting for hours, pounding on the keys, reeling in the space. I had a dedicated office, right in the middle of an art gallery. Maybe it wasn't actually a gallery, but it was something burgeoning, artistic.

Some days work was done on the space. Most of the time work wasn't done. It didn't matter. We just had to make enough progress to appease the landlord.

Over time I came to know the other affiliates. Individuals, artists to the marrow. Each of them possessing incredible, raw, honest talent. Steven was the de facto bellwether, but there was no real leadership. It was cored on the freedom of artistic expression. I immediately had the feeling that it belonged to all of us and, at the same time, none of us. Steven was simply the dark charisma that landed the building in the first place. He and I spent hours talking about what we could do with the space. How we could make it more than a gallery. A music venue. Or have film screenings. Or throw big opulent banquets. This could be anything and everything.

Our ideas were all conditioned in the bottle, never making it any further than that, because we had no resources to fix up the building and actually bring them to fruition. Ideas, that was all. Dreams. Like writing Christmas lists in the trailer park.

We had a space, that was all that mattered. What the gallery did, above all else, was drag a net through the town and scoop up these artists, bringing everyone together under one roof. It was a forum, a gathering place. A place to get away, to work out ideas, to work on your own projects. A place that reassured you that while the bottom fell out of everything else, you could always find refuge here.

# Fugue

Steven, Bradley, Pederson, and I were in the gallery, shoveling the debris to the side, trying to clear a walking path. We had been working on the place, but you couldn't tell. All you could see was trash, material waste. We were motivated to do something about it.

"What are our options?" I asked. "We need somewhere to dump it all."

"We can leave it right where it is and wait for it to decompose," Bradley said.

"How about hauling it to the dumpster in the alley?" I suggested.

Joey walked through the door carrying a paper bag. "Hey, man. How's it going here?" He pulled out a bottle and set it on the table. Naturally, everyone put down whatever tools they were holding and migrated over, forward momentum gone, the sails luffed by a little whiff of whiskey. I wanted to keep working, but I was the only one. I tossed the shovel aside and joined them.

"There's no way all this would fit in a dumpster anyway," Steven said, filling his cup with whiskey.

"We could spread it around, put a little in every dumpster back there," I said. "At least it would get rid of some of it." I sat on a bucket, poured myself a drink, grabbed a newspaper lying on the table.

"We could fill every dumpster and it would barely make a dent," Steven said. He picked up his guitar and started strumming.

"What you need to do is haul it off," said Bradley.

"That would require a truck," said Steven. "Or a trailer. We don't have any of that."

I thought about the old Ford I had before. It would have worked, but it was a company truck and after I quit I had to give the keys back to Riley.

"Or you could rent a dumpster," Bradley said. "You can have them drop it off right out front and then come pick it up once we fill it."

"Who's gonna pay for it?" Steven asked. No one spoke up. I turned the page in the paper, keeping quiet. "Exactly."

We let it go at that. Maybe some other day, not this one. We sat around the table, figuring out our next move.

Pederson cut the top out of an empty Stag can with his pocket knife, poured himself a little whiskey. He was sitting with his back against the window. I felt like I knew everyone else pretty well, but I still didn't understand him. They said he was a sculptor, but I never saw any evidence of this. Although, he did most of the deconstruction of the space, so I guess in the way painting is more an addition of medium and sculpting more a subtraction, he was doing something. That's all I could really tell about him. If nothing else, he made an interesting human sculpture, often standing catatonic, staring through distant time, a reversion to primordial man, the noble savage, struggling every day to relearn the world around him.

As I was looking through the paper, I found a listing for a free piano, an old upright. I knew how to play somewhat. I had taken a few lessons but stopped going after learning the basic chords. But now there was a piano available and a place to put it. I showed the others.

"What do you guys think?" I asked. "Says it's free, just need to pick it up."

"Up to you," said Steven.

"How you gonna get it here?" asked Bradley. "You don't have a truck, remember?"

I looked at the address in the listing. "It's not all that far. We could just wheel it."

"You serious?" asked Bradley. "You're just gonna push it down the street?"

"Why not?" Steven said. "Let's do it. Come on Bradley, you're coming too."

An hour or so later we were thundering down the middle of High Street behind a big upright piano. Joey held the door open while Bradley, Pederson, Steven, and I heaved it over the threshold and into the gallery.

We cleared away a space along the brick wall and wheeled the piano up against it. I stacked up two empty milk crates in front of it and tested the keys. Most of the important ones still worked well enough.

We pulled out the rest of the instruments and used whatever we had for seats. Upturned buckets. Pallets. Paint cans. The gallery was strewn with these things. We circled a few of them in the open middle. I ran down to Tolson's and bought some more supplies. We were bolstered, happy, without care.

Instruments made the lap around the circle behind the bottles of wine, and everyone played a song or strummed out the rhythm to whatever else was happening. We all had a varying level of ability, but there was only one person with any real talent, and that was Steven. When a banjo or guitar came his way, he was reluctant at first, preferring the bottle. But after a few laps he took the guitar and started playing a melody.

"Which one is this?" Bradley asked. "I haven't heard it yet."

"It's new. Steven mumbled through his cigarette. "It's not finished yet." His head tilted slightly back to keep the smoke from rising into his eyes.

"They're never finished," Bradley said. "I don't think I've ever heard a completed song." It was true. He was writing a lot, but for some reason all of his songs had a chorus and a verse or two and then just stopped abruptly without coming to an end.

Steven switched to a blues standard, simple rhythm, easy for the rest of us to follow. Me playing chords on the piano,

Bradley blowing on the trumpet, Joey drumming on an upside down bucket and whatever else he could reach with a pair of paint sticks. Pederson stood along one wall with a piece of broken soapstone, drawing petroglyphs on the brick. Everyone stomped their feet on the floor, the volume picked up and we were all singing along, song after song. Sometimes it skidded out of control, turned into a hot mess of music. Punk drumming, blues guitar, country piano, Bradley blowing whatever he could. But when you were inside and playing along it didn't matter, all that mattered was you were making noise, adding something.

Pederson put down the soapstone and walked out the front door. When the song we were playing ended, Bradley and I went out to take the air. We stood in the alcove smoking a cigarette, watching Pederson climb up the tree in front of the gallery, the bark scratching lines into his pink belly, the top limbs swaying in the street lights.

Two girls walked by, and right as they passed below the tree he dropped out onto the sidewalk in front of them and fell over. They screamed and flailed at him as he tried to stand up, but he was laughing too hard. One of them kicked Pederson in the ribs, and he finally got up and ran off down the street. They heard Bradley and I laughing in the alcove after he was gone.

"You think that's funny?" said the first girl, a baudy woman with short brown hair and a thick Ozark dialect.

"Don't worry," I said. "He's harmless."

"I shoulda kicked his ass," she said, slurring a little.

"You wouldn't wanna do that," Bradley said. "He may not look like it, but that man is actually Norwegian royalty." Bradley loved to put on a front, always messing with people.

"Bullshit," she said. "If he's royalty then why's he living here and not in Norwegia?"

"It's true," said Bradley. "He's 27th in line for the throne. There was some political turmoil and the whole family was exiled. He's just here to lay low and bide his time before reclaiming his divine right."

"Really?" asked her friend. She turned to me. "Is he being serious?"

"Sure," I corroborated. "That's why he picked this place. It's the perfect location to go unnoticed. And we're on the river, so he can sail from here all the way to the ocean when the time comes."

The first girl shook her head. "Don't listen to them, they don't know." She looked into the open door of the gallery, noticing the wine bottles and cans of Stag on the table. "What're y'all doing here, anyway? Got anything left to drink?" She pushed past me and went inside, helped herself, grabbing an open bottle, swirling it over one of the cups, trying to dial in her aim before she started to pour. Wine spilled over onto the table.

Steven looked at her, a little confused. "It's fine," she said. "Your friends owe me a drink for listening to their bullshit." She sank into one of the seats across from Steven. "Go on," she said, waving her cup, spilling more wine. "Play me something."

The rest of us walked back inside and the two of them joined us around the circle, drinking and talking and smoking cigarettes. They had come from the bar down the street where Marcy, the first girl, was draining pitchers of beer. Her friend Heather was more subtle, sweet, dark hair and eyes, innocent laugh. She didn't say much because Marcy was doing all the talking, loud and obnoxious, trying to focus the limelight. She sat next to Steven, occasionally looking over at him as he sang.

"What are you guys doing here anyway?" Marcy said over the music. "This place is a dump."

"It's not a dump," said Joey. "I think it's beautiful."

"It takes a shift in perspective," Steven added. "Like the Japanese wabi-sabi, you come to accept the imperfections."

The two of them looked around at the wreckage. "I don't know what y'all are talkin about," Marcy said. "It looks like hell in here."

"Where are you from anyway?" Bradley asked her, changing the subject. "Why do you talk like that?"

"What's wrong with the way I talk?" she asked.

"Nothing. Just that it's the inflection of ignorance," he said.

"Fuck you," she said. "What's your name?"

"Huckleberry."

"What's your real name?"

"That is my real name. My parents were big Mark Twain fans."

"Who's Mark Twain?"

"What! He's a local hero. You really don't know *Mark Twain*?"

"Nope."

"Oh, well he was the mayor of this town for years. He's the one who campaigned for the after school reading program. Now he owns the bowling alley across town."

"You're so full of shit!" She slapped his shoulder hard but playfully.

Steven was strumming through a couple of chords while listening to Bradley. I wanted to keep playing music.

"Do you have another song?" I asked Steven.

We started playing again while Bradley and Marcy kept talking. The louder she talked, the louder the rest of us played. Eventually it became too muddled, useless. Marcy got up and walked outside, and Bradley followed after. From where I was sitting at the piano I could see through the open door, the two of them on the other side. They talked for a while, then disappeared together.

Steven stood up to get two cans of Stag and handed one of them to Heather as they talked, leaning against the brick wall on the other side of the gallery. Joey was still drumming but it didn't sound right with just the piano.

"Has anyone seen Marcy? Is she still outside?" Heather asked after awhile.

"They left," I told her. "She went with Bradley."

"Fuck. She was my ride home," said Heather. She glanced over at Steven. "Can one of you give me a lift?"

"I would," he said. "But I don't have a car."

"My car is downtown, I was just planning on leaving it here. Are you okay to drive?"

"Sure." He set his beer down and they walked out together.

"Just you and me then Joey," I said.

Joey stood up. "Actually, I need to get going too, before Carly finds out I'm here," he said. "You and Steven should come by the studio tomorrow. I'll show you the new paintings."

"Yeah, sounds good. See you later."

Joey was the last one to leave. Everything dropped down to an acute silence. The violet glow of streetlights filtered through the painted storefront window. Faint sound waves of overnight industry breezed through the open door. Street workers cutting through concrete several blocks away. A garbage truck backing into an alley. A wet spring smell on asphalt from an earlier rain.

    I poured out the remainder of a bottle of wine into my cup and lit a cigarette. The piano was lit by the warm incandescent shop light, made small by the enormous emptiness around it. One floor above and one below, the whole building hung in silence. It was a rare moment to have the entire place to myself. A feeling of possession, like I could do anything I wanted here. I was alone, but not at all lonely. I drained off the wine and scooted the milk crates closer to the piano. For the next couple hours I filled the air around me with the piano sound and cigarette smoke. Sometimes we made music together, and sometimes we didn't.

# The Great and Savage Artist

Through the door at the end of the long hall at Joey's house, we entered the nursery. Joey and his wife had no kids, but he still called it the nursery, because the last tenants had decorated the place with baby-blue wallpaper patterned in monkeys and carousels. You could barely make them out, since Joey bubbled the entire room in translucent thin-mil plastic.

He never worked at the gallery because of Carly, his wife. Carly was also a talented artist, but for reasons of her own never wanted anything to do with the gallery. She thought it was ruining Joey, that we were stifling his art, his life, his marriage. Anyone who got close to Joey was either trying to use him or lead him down a path of destruction. It was her duty to protect him, especially from us. She convinced him that his paintings weren't safe there, knowing that Joey would heed anything that involved his work.

Joey had just gotten off from Kinko's, where he worked behind the counter one or two days a week, and when Steven and I walked in, he was getting ready to paint. Prying the lids off of a few gallons of acrylic house paint, gathering up the soaked brushes to clean.

"Welcome to Babylon," Joey said when he saw us, skittishly twirling his hand in front of him, unable to hold in a nervous, high pitched laughter, tittering like a hyena. Joey had a very ambiguous look, undefined style. Not quite gothic, not quite punk. Wearing a t-shirt flecked with paint underneath, black jeans variegated in bright acrylic layers, old spattered tennis shoes worn through the cushioning. He was more of a readymade, a found object. His whole existence like the residue of a seminal acrylic splash. Punk black hair clumped into little obelisks, spearing in all directions. Pockmarked face from a childhood plagued with acne. A body with no definite shape, not fat, not skinny, just eraser marks of contour. His skin had the surface luster of amphetamines, tight and thin. When he laughed, his whole face was smiling and his thin eyelids clamped down like car hoods. Above all, Joey had a look of naive innocence, the sort of purity of intention found in asylums.

"We came to see your new paintings," Steven said. "You can keep working if you want. We won't distract you."

"Sure, man. I have a new batch," he said, gathering up a few brushes. "I'm calling it the King David series. They're up against that wall."

The back walls in the room were stacked with finished paintings. These were the ballast of the gallery. His talent went beyond the provincial and into something more universal, more ethereal. Steven may have been the ringleader of the gallery, but the artistic core was Joey. We all recognized that what he was doing was exceptional. That someday this place would no longer be big enough to house him. As a painter, he was the idiot savant. No concept of what he was doing when he was doing it. He may not have been, as Bradley kept saying, the greatest painter *alive*, but he was the greatest painter I *knew*.

Steven and I flipped through the canvases. "You're on to something Joey," I said. "There's definitely no one doing anything quite like this."

"Of course not. Who in their right mind would even wanna paint like this?"

In one corner was a CD player blaring a Sex Pistols album, paint splashes sealing up most of the perforations over the speakers. All around the room were gallons of house paint. All his color theory came from the mixing counter at the hardware store. Often times he would pick up the discounted cans that were mixed improperly or no one claimed. It was far less academic, but it was exponentially cheaper, more accessible.

The paintings were raw, undisciplined, vibrant, pyrotechnicolor explosions, a violence of action, image, emotion. Joey was raised in a thunder and lightning Christian church, where his father was the pastor. This left a toxic, unshakable fear in his brain that came out through the canvas. Born out of the nursery, the style itself not far from the cradle. Looking closer, I saw the depth, that he was going all the way back to find these images, back into the sermon of death and pestilence, fire and brimstone, into the apocalyptic destruction, the rapture and revelation. Not the work of someone who has disowned god, but from a firm believer in anything. It was more than a Christian god. It was the god in the machine, the god in the cosmos, the daily routine, the atoms and quantum particles, the collisions of stars, the microbial universe in a single drop of rainwater.

Steven and I watched in devout silence as Joey worked. He painted rapidly and deliberately as we saw the scene come alive. He directed the movement like a composer, the pitch, speed, meter, all bending from the elbow. The bottom of the canvas caught fire, tongues of flame rising out, figures falling in from above, a monster charging out of the middle ground, demon-like, the claws painted in a carmine nail polish. The monster was persecuted, crying, seeking refuge. It was everything feared, everything you fear in yourself, the monster within. Haloed angels circled overhead, diving toward the monster with bow and arrow drawn. The scene got wilder as the action of Joey became more frenzied, more paint hitting the room than the canvas.

When it came to an end, when the whole savage scene had played out and Joey was satisfied, intuitively knowing composition and when to stop, he would baptize it from above in blood-red acrylic, then sign the bottom corner in four majuscule letters, a simple: JOEY.

## Art in the Park


Installations lined the concrete sidewalk through Memorial Park, making a lap through the annual Spring outdoor art festival. Crowds came from all over the town to buy ice cream and see the works. The *Telegraph* sent me to get an interview.

 I walked around the one-mile sidewalk loop, littered with the installations commissioned by the Community Arts Coalition that organized the festival. There was a bridge made of hollow glass tubes. A metal sculpture of a large insect. Another of a rock bench, only instead of a rock, it was a cement sculpture made to look like a rock. I turned a corner to see a man covered in white, modeling the statue of David on a marble plinth, standing completely still, beads of sweat cutting small lines in the body paint.

 The sidewalk finally came back around to where it started. Under the pavilion next to the playground I found Ms. Garner, the director of the Coalition. She had connections, had her hands in everything, getting funding for workshops, landing the commission to paint the governor's portrait in the capital. She was able to raise money for anything, able to divert funds through the Coalition, giving the added incentive of a nonprofit tax write off for her big donors who wanted to move numbers around in their ledgers.

She walked around the park in an imperial blue business suit, accentuating her tall, lank figure, dark eyes, hair straight and pinned on one side, the other side curling down like a raven's wing around her sharp chin.

I got out a notebook and pen and walked up to her. "Excuse me, Ms. Garner? I'm here with the *Telegraph*."

"Just Garner will do," she said, tossing her hair out of her eye with a flick of her neck.

"I'd like to ask you a few questions."

"It's about time you get a story. The damn thing has already started. Where have you been?"

She threw me off guard. "Sorry, I just write them," I said. "Can you tell me about the festival?" I wanted to rush through this. Something about her made me uncomfortable.

"I'm trying to bring some culture to the community, even though most people don't understand or appreciate it," she said. "The people in this town don't know a goddamn thing about art. They think it's easy, or it's unnecessary, or it's a waste of money. I've heard it all, believe me. Every year I work *so* hard to put this together, and it's not cheap. We need funding, write that down in your article. People think this just *happens*, but it doesn't."

She went on like this, talking about herself, about the Coalition. I wrote down the information, knowing Gary would have to shift the article into something polite to present. Garner was a major advertiser, along with her many friends. If I didn't get something quotable, I wouldn't have much of a story.

"And how did you decide to do the festival in the first place?" I stood outside the pavilion, watching the people coming and going, dropping money into the large tin donation canister at the entrance.

"I had no choice. There would be no art in this town if I didn't provide it. I'm the only person bringing anything like this. Not the sort of investment art you find hanging in Central Bank. I'm talking about *living* art, from *living* artists."

I stopped writing for a second. "Actually, there's an art space happening downtown."

She looked sharply toward me. "What are you talking about?"

"It's a group of artists trying to open up a space," I said.

"Well, I haven't heard anything about it," she said. "And if it's unknown to me, then it's probably unknown to everyone."

"It's not unknown to the people involved," I said. "Art is being produced, even though it's not open to the public."

"Then it doesn't mean anything. You have to reach the public if you want to have any impact."

"That might happen too, someday. It's a work in progress."

"They'll never make it. Trust me, it took me years to get where I'm at in this town. It's not the sort of thing you can just cobble together."

"Maybe not," I wanted to change the subject, get on with the interview. I shouldn't have said anything about it. "Anyway, you were mentioning how the festival got started. What about you? How did you decide to start the Coalition?"

"I'm not from here, originally. But I married a farmer who wasn't about to live in New York. I never imagined I'd be living in a place like this, but here I am. I might as well make the most of it…"

When she finished, I closed my notebook. "That should do it. Thanks for your time. It should be printed in the next issue. Gary will probably call you to fact check a few things."

"I'm sure he will. Tell him I'm going to stop advertising if he continues to procrastinate like this."

"I'll let him know." I put my notebook and pen into my bag, started to leave.

"Wait a second," she said. "Where did you say this gallery was located?"

I turned back, shrugged. "What gallery?"

# Tectonic

I was at the typewriter in the office upstairs. Steven sat in a chair with a guitar, making scratch tracks on the Tascam 8-track recorder. Bradley was working on a canvas. We were all working hard into the night, intense and solitary focus in the room. Sometimes we traded places. I picked up a paintbrush, and Bradley played an instrument, and Steven sat at the desk writing. Or whatever. It didn't matter, because we had the space to be creative, to do anything, to express the effort to express. We all worked on our own projects, but the collective energy propelled us, made us want to push further, everything blending, until we had pigment oozing from the typewriter, music vibrating from the hairs of the paintbrush, a manuscript of pages spitting out the sound hole of the guitar.

    I put out my cigarette, rolled a page out of the typewriter and put it in the desk drawer. "Why don't we get more serious about opening this place? We keep talking about it and calling it a gallery." I was still mulling over my interview with Garner. "This town needs something like this. Something different."

"Be careful," Steven warned. "We don't want to fool ourselves into thinking what we're doing here is something groundbreaking."

"It's not entirely new, I realize that," I said.

"We have to presuppose that there is nothing we can do that has never been done before. None of my songs, none of these paintings, nothing you're writing."

"What's the point then?" I asked. "Why do you keep playing music if you don't feel like you can make something different?"

"That's no reason to stop doing it," he explained. "To me, the only thing that matters is whether or not you're being genuine. It's something you can hear right away in a song, or looking at a painting or a sculpture, anything. You know if the person *meant* it or not. That's all we're really trying to get at."

"Like pornography," Bradley added, somewhat sarcastically. "You can't really define it, but you know it when you see it."

"Everyone has the potential to be genuine in their work, regardless of their level of talent," Steven said.

"I doubt that," Bradley said. "If you think that art could be done by anyone, that just isn't true. It's something people say because they have trouble identifying what qualifies as art."

"Art isn't really a complex thing," Steven countered. "It's pretty simple to come by. You don't need an exceptional amount of craft. Look at Joey's paintings. They're good because they're born out of life, out of being genuine."

"But there are plenty of people doing that," I said.

"Too goddamn many," Bradley chimed in. "That's why no cream rises to the top. Everyone thinks they're an artist now. Most of it's disposable."

"I'm sure there were great artists producing at the same time as people like Picasso or Van Gogh that we've never heard of," I said. "Those are just the ones that stuck out."

"It was smaller back then," Bradley continued. "Everyone has the luxury to be an artist now. Besides, history will always pull out a select few, and it's not just because of the art. You have to have the right critic, know the right people, get the right exposure."

"But maybe it's a good thing there are so many people creating art," Steven countered. "It's democratized, makes it less elitist."

"It's an oversaturation," Bradley responded. "Too many people are trying and failing. It's clogging up the works."

"That's cause you're still hanging on to the idea of doing something special," Steven said.

"And you're too quick to accept mediocrity," Bradley said.

"Yeah, maybe. I just want the experience of writing a few good songs. It connects you with yourself, and with other people."

"Which is why I think we should open the gallery," I said. "So we can connect with even more people, not just each other."

"It's already a gallery for us," Steven said. "We have a space to be creative, and we're doing it right now. We don't need anyone else to see it in order to validate it."

"But we're right in the middle of downtown," I replied. "What's the use of being in a storefront if we're not going to open it?"

"It's not that I'm against it. But if we open a gallery we'll have a completely different set of problems. Right now I'm content solving the immediate need, which is writing music. Besides, we have an even bigger obstacle—fixing this place up."

"But we're working on it," I said. "We're getting there."

"We're chipping away at it, sure. But when it comes to actually putting this place together it's gonna take an obscene amount of money, which we have no way of coming up with."

"He's right," Bradley said. "Enjoy it while it lasts."

I opened the drawer and pulled out a fresh sheet of typing paper, squared up the page, began to type. Maybe Steven was right. The moment, all around me, that's what really mattered. Art was the thing that came after. I liked the idea of opening up a gallery, but I also liked what was happening right there, then.

Bradley opened a can of polyurethane and slowly turned it upside down, letting it run out over the painting, spreading to the edges. He was coating it with poly, layer after layer, then taking a grinder and cutting a square into the middle so you could see a cross section of all the layers down to the original drawings. Then filling the square with more urethane. Then clear coating the whole thing so you could see through the solid jelly into all the grit below.

Steven picked up the guitar again and started the reel-to-reel back up, this time he started writing a new song. Bradley and I both paused what we were doing to bear witness to the process. Shuffling through a few chords until he landed on the right one, then turning back and adding it to the rest. He played through the progression a few times until a faint hum crept in, rising slowly, slowly, tectonic plates pushing together with geologic patience. The hum continued rising in harmony with the instrument, then stepped off on its own melody, pitching and keeling, and then one single audible word broke through, and the rest of the music surrounded it. Then more words, lines, it kept going, building and adding, rising and fleshing outward, a song birthed into the room.

Of the music being pure and genuine, there was no doubt. If he ever played this song again, he would be trying to rediscover where he was right then. Bradley and I were both envious and inspired by that strange and holy place, the place where any creation comes from, and were moved to find it ourselves as we went back to work.

# Thermodynamic

Jenny was in the front office of the *Telegraph*, two hands on the keyboard of her computer, phone squeezed between shoulder and ear. I slipped through the door and closed it quietly behind me. No sign of Scott or Gary, but voices carried from the back.

I pulled an article out and laid it over a copy of *Dreamweaver Classroom in a Book* on Jenny's desk. She was alternately nodding and shaking her head into the phone. Someone disgruntled on the other end, either a misplaced ad or some unflattering copy.

"Jenny, did someone come in?" Gary yelled from the back. "Is our reporter here? I need to talk with him. A new account just broke, we need him there right away."

She looked at me, and I held my finger to my lips, motioning a thumb to the door. She set the phone down gently on the desk, a faint voice still prattling through the receiver as she flipped through the article. She dropped it in her pile of undone things and pulled out money from the drawer.

"Thank you." I mouthed the words to her, quietly making my way back to the door.

"Yeah." She nodded, waving me out.

"Jenny?" Gary repeated in vain. "Anyone?"

I left the office undetected, going to Tolson's to turn the cash into wine and cigarettes for the gallery, the energy neither created nor destroyed.

# Voice

If you could choose between having the art of someone famous or having the opportunity to meet that person, which would you choose? To have a painting by Picasso, or to actually meet Picasso?

I was sitting at the desk in the office, smoking a cigarette, working out ideas on the typewriter. Almost all my time was spent working, and I was making good headway on the novel.

Bradley came out of his studio and sat down across from me, taking a break. He asked about the new series we saw in Joey's studio a couple weeks earlier. Bradley loved to talk about Joey. He was always the first one to consecrate his work, never disputing the fact that Joey was the better painter. But his pride had him locked in constant competition with him. I told him the truth, that the paintings were incredible.

"Of course they were. You know, when I met Joey it was like tasting sugar for the first time. He has no idea how fortunate he is," Bradley said. "He's already got something great, and he still has his whole career ahead of him. I don't let it bother me. For someone to find their voice so early is a statistical rarity. I'm still a student of painting, but it doesn't matter. There are plenty of artists that had to wait half their life or more before they made it."

"Sure." I got up and walked over to the shelves full of art books in the corner. "Look at Gauguin. He didn't make it until later in life." I hooked the top of the binding and slid the book out.

"Or Grandma Moses," Bradley added. "She was in her seventies before she even started. It doesn't matter to me, as long as I can always find a way to keep painting, I'll continue learning and developing. It's not like we're athletes. We have time."

I thumbed down the pages of the Gauguin book from back to front, pausing on some. "It's the same way with writers. William Burroughs, Henry Miller, Raymond Chandler. There will always be someone older for reassurance."

"Right. For now I'm gaining experience and absorbing everything I can. That's all this gallery is for me. I'm just here to work and learn and plot the next phase of my artistic career. I know this isn't a place to stay long if I wanna develop."

I put the book back on the shelf and sat down at the desk, loaded the typewriter. This was rich, and I wanted to write it down, maybe use it in the book. At turns Bradley could be warm, gentle, full of wisdom. Other times cold and calculating, willing to cut any throat presented to him.

"Joey, on the other hand, he just does," Bradley continued. "He has no capacity to look beyond the canvas in front of him at the moment, even if he wanted to. It's infuriating sometimes. Here I am applying meticulous effort, careful study, constantly trying to explore, improve my technique. Joey just walks into his studio, puts on his painting sneakers and a punk album, and *has* it. His style is simple, his technique is rudimentary, but none of that matters because he has a *voice*. He's found his way through painting, and he found it early on and never let it go. He has no fucking craft. Pisses me off. Joey got there through inspiration, not through instruction. His only problem is that he has no audacity. He's too timid to make any demands for his art, but he's too goddamn good to fail."

Bradley paused when we heard someone downstairs. I stopped typing.

"Hello? Am I the only one here?" Footsteps on the treads. Then a head appeared in the stairwell.

"Joey, we were just talking about you," I said.

"Yeah, I was just telling Mark how you might make a decent painter one of these days, if you ever figure out how to hold a brush," Bradley said.

Joey's eyes clamped down again, teehee-ing like a pubescent.

"What have you been working on, Joey? I want to know," Bradley needled, like a predator circling and baring his teeth, trying to intimidate.

"Just painting, man. That's all." Joey responded with a dumb smile, never cowed by Bradley's viciousness. Probably through innocent misunderstanding.

"I know you're fucking painting! You're always just painting! You can't do anything else! Wait though, Joey, wait until you see what I'm working on, it's going to make you cry. You'll never want to paint again once you see this!"

"Oh yeah?" Joey walked over toward the plastic sheathed bubble of Bradley's studio to have a look.

"It's not ready yet!" Bradley stepped between Joey and the sliced entrance in the doorway. "You can't see it until it's finished. It needs more layers. I'm stacking this one up so thick it'll leap off the wall!"

"Whatever you say, man," Joey casually stepped away from his studio. "Let me see it when you're finished. I need a reason to quit painting."

"Wrong, Joey, you'll never quit painting. I won't let you. It's all you have, and I won't let you quit, because I couldn't stand to see what a decrepit specimen you would become once you had nothing left. I'll keep you going at breakneck speed, and if you slow down for anything, I'm gonna pass you by."

Joey shrugged, his drooping posture raising until his shoulders nearly touch his ears, palms supine. "Sure thing, man. I believe you."

It infuriated Bradley that he couldn't get under Joey's skin, however he approached it. Joey's ire, violence, madness, it was always depleted, poured onto the latest canvas.

Beneath all of Bradley's needling was a demented love, a desire to become Joey. To have what he had, to strip out his flesh and leave nothing but a carcass so he could crawl into it.

Putting his eyes behind Joey's eyes to be haunted by the visions that haunted Joey. His hands into Joey's to create without thinking.

Bradley cast a muttered aspersion over the entire gallery and walked out. Joey stood there, confused.

"What's he so worked up about?" Joey asked.

"I wouldn't worry about it," I said. "He respects you, Joey."

But then again, I thought, he would probably eat your heart if he thought it would make him stronger.

# Expressionism

There was a window that led out to the fire escape that we used to climb up on the roof, but only late at night when no one would notice. One night a little after midnight, Steven and I were up there splitting a bottle of wine.

He had the trumpet in his lap. I was leaning against the ledge thumbing through Selden Rodman's *Conversations With Artists*, reading in the streetlight. He held the mouthpiece and applied a little oil to the clogged pistons.

"It's my birthday today," Steven said.

"Shit, really? Happy birthday," I said.

"Thanks. You know, it's funny how you and I had never met before. The more time you spend here, the more I realize how much we have in common."

"Yeah, I agree. It's strange. Like meeting a sibling late in life."

When he finally got the instrument working, he climbed up onto the wall overlooking High Street. The night was moonless, no one around. He pulled an unlit cigarette out of his mouth, tucked it behind his ear, licked his lips. Just as he was about to blast the night with the horn, he heard another sound. A bitter wail echoed through the canyon of High Street.

"Steven!" The voice rang out.

Steven quickly climbed down off the wall.

"Who is that?" I asked.

"It's Heather's boyfriend, Casey" he replied.

"STEVEN!" Casey yelled out again.

"She has a boyfriend?" I peered over the parapet. Casey was right below us, arms covered in sleeve tattoos.

"He'll go away," Steven said. "Eventually."

"STEVEN COME OUT HERE YOU COWARD!"

I had heard stories about Steven's past, most of them from Bradley. It added up to a sort of scorched earth result with women, with everything.

"GODDAMMIT STEVEN COME OUT HERE!"

I knew he didn't do any of this intentionally. It just happened that way. I looked over the edge again. Casey didn't realize we were three stories up looking down, watching as he kicked the glass front door with the heel of his boot again and again and finally broke it open, glass showering the sidewalk around him.

"Oh fuck, he's inside," Steven said, a nervous look on his face I'd never seen before, his composure dropped, color draining from his blood vessels.

We heard Casey crashing around in the gallery below, destroying anything he could. Sounds of glass breaking, wood splitting, tables upended. The next thing we saw was Steven's guitar case flying out of the door and onto the sidewalk. Casey came out next, red-hot with madness.

"We gotta go down there," I said. "We have to stop him."

"Not a chance," he said. "He looks temporarily insane. I don't want any fucking part of that."

Casey picked up the guitar and threw it against the storefront, wanting to put it through all the paint and words and into Steven's heart. But the window held. The case bounced off and hit the sidewalk. He picked it up again and threw it harder. The glass shook but held.

"STEVEN YOU SON OF A BITCH!" he shouted, wailing the words. He snapped open the latches and pulled out the guitar, slamming it down on the concrete, then put the heel of his boot right into the belly of it, stomping repeatedly through to the other side.

"That," I said quietly to Steven, "is genuine." And it was. The beast within coming out as he became like one of Joey's monsters. Fighting the way Joey painted. Finally, he took the remains and threw them against the window. With one more unsatisfied howl, he jumped into his car and sped off down the street.

The night was moonless and quiet once again. The door was shattered. The guitar was ruined. Who knew what damage had been done in the gallery below.

Steven slowly stood up and climbed back onto the ledge. He lifted the trumpet back up to his mouth, adjusting his embouchure. He kept his eyes locked on a focal point to steady himself on the edge of the building. One leg was still palpitating nervously. Then, with a forceful burst of air, he christened the night with a blast over the rooftops, diddling the valves with his fingertips, ringing out with a scrambling arpeggio. A crash of notes, discordant as every encounter he's ever had, the last ounce of breath wheezing out of his deflated lungs.

He set the trumpet down on the ledge, breathing heavily. The night fell again into silence.

"Shouldn't we go see the damage?" I asked. It was bad. We both knew it was bad.

We climbed down the fire escape and into the nearly pitch black gallery. "Let me see your lighter," Steven said. He still had one last cigarette tucked behind his ear.

"I don't have it. It's probably on the roof."

He pulled open all the drawers of the desk trying to find one. We both paused for a moment.

"Do you hear that?" I asked. There was a faint hissing sound.

He was going through the pockets of a jacket on the back of a chair, still looking for a light. The sound continued. A low sssssssssssss.

"Forget the smoke," I said. "Let's see what happened."

We went down into the gallery. None of the shop lights were plugged in, so we had to feel our way around in the faint violet light coming through the window.

The sound was getting louder now. SSSSSSSS. We stumbled around in the dark to figure out what it was.

"I found one!" Steven announced. I heard a flint strike. "It was in my pocket the whole time." He flicked a few times, but it wasn't working.

"Wait!" I said, alarmed. "Do you smell that?" The air thickened in a roux of sulphur and oxygen, an unnatural weight settling over the space.

He sniffed audibly, feeling his way to the back of the gallery. He got closer and found one of the exposed gas pipes had been broken open in the rampage, split and leaking.

"Gas!" he yelled, violently fumbling the lighter in his hand as it dropped to the floor. "Shit shit shit!" We both turned and desperately sped out, tripping over unseen objects on the way. We got to the door and didn't need to open it. Only a frame and hole remained where the glass had been. We bumped into each other trying to get through. Fight or flight. Nothing to save but ourselves.

We leapt out onto the sidewalk, landing on the shards of broken glass, running quickly over to Mortimers, the bar across the street, to call 911.

The glass still crunched under our shoes as we rushed into the bar and quickly explained so we could use their phone.

"Slow down," the voice on the other end said to me. "We have someone on the way. Stay on the line until they get there."

As I was talking to the responder, Steven reached over the bar and grabbed a book of matches, pulled the last cigarette out from behind his ear, and finally lit it.

# Gaslight

As the sun was coming up the next morning, we examined the damages to the gallery. The firefighters were putting fans inside the front and back door to move air through the space. The gas line had been shut off.

"What's the landlord gonna think of all this?" I asked.

"I don't know," Steven replied. "Won't be good."

We called Bradley, and he showed up to see what had happened. He immediately went upstairs to his studio. Four of his paintings were slashed across the middle. A couple more kicked in and ripped off the stretchers.

The guitar was reduced to kindling and still lay on the sidewalk in front of the painted storefront. We searched through the rest of the gallery. Other than the door and broken gas line, there was no way of really knowing what physical damage was done to the building and what had been that way already. This was a difficult thing to describe to the cop after they finished shutting off the gas line and he was filling out a report.

"Let me get this straight, you're telling me this guy came in here and damaged the building?" The cop looked around the gallery, turning over a couple of pieces of plaster with his ink pen, taking stock of all the damage that had ever happened there. The gallery was a complete wreck. "And you say it was only this one guy, Casey? He did all this?" He scratched at his scalp with his pen, still trying to figure out how to delineate this in his report. How to add it all up.

"No," said Steven. "Not all this was him."

"So there were others?"

"No, I don't really know what he did inside here. It's kind of hard to tell apart, but we do know that he broke in and destroyed a few of the paintings that were in a studio upstairs. Also the guitar. He was throwing it against anything he could, trying to break it."

"He was using a guitar?" he asked, pointing his pen at the splintered wood on the sidewalk. "That's what caused all this?"

"No, I mean, he broke the guitar. The rest, I don't know."

"So, we know for sure this gas line was broken, right?" he asked, wanting to get it over with.

"Right."

"Okay, I'm going to put in my report this person came in here unlawfully, took your guitar, and used it to break this gas line. We got the gas shut off now. These fans blew all the air out to make sure it's not contaminated."

"Sure." Steven was ready to be done with it too. "That's fine."

Bradley came downstairs, his face registering no emotion.

"And what's the estimated value of the guitar that was damaged?"

"I don't know, it was given to me," Steven said.

"And the paintings?"

"Priceless," Bradley cut in.

"Uh huh…" He paused, then made a note in the report. "So do you want to press charges against this guy?"

"No," Bradley quickly said. "The paintings are ruined. His guitar is broken. If you put him in jail, it's not going to change that."

"Okay. I guess we're done here then." He closed his notebook. "Tell me," the cop added, "How is it you guys have access to a downtown building? What's this supposed to be anyway?"

"It's sort of an art gallery," Steven started to explain. "But not really."

"Hmm." The pen dove back into his scalp, scratching, scratching. "Okay, well...like I said, the building is cleared, so you can go on about your...uh...business..." his voice trailed off in confusion as he turned to leave.

# Patron

I walked down to the *Telegraph* to turn in another story. Inside the headquarters it was business as usual. Everything was behind schedule. Jenny was bearing the extra weight, picking up the slack where Scott and Gary would never make it on their own. Gary was in his office, coursing through the proofs with a red pen, checking over the ads for costly mistakes, saliva building at the corners of his mouth. He looked up and saw me in the doorway, motioned for me to have a seat across from the desk.

"Yesyes, just the person I wanted to see. I've got a few leads for you. Have you been able to drum up anything on your own? By the way how's the story going on that gallery did you get the ad yet?"

"Oh...I'm still working on that one," I said. I had forgotten all about the idea of doing an article. "It's a little bit elusive. Not really sure what angle to take on it. It's not exactly a gallery. Or at least, not yet."

"Suresuresure I understand," he nodded. "Have you mentioned the ad? Maybe you could drop a small hint to the proprietor and then I could follow up with a phone call."

I started to laugh and then caught myself. "I doubt they have the budget for that kind of thing right now, but I'll let them know."

"Well, if you're having trouble getting the story, I suppose we'll have to scrap it. I have some other things I can put you on." He shuffled through the mounds of paper. "There's something here I want you to look into." He handed me another lead.

"I'll keep after the gallery story," I offered, wanting to have the option open. "I just need to figure out how to write it."

"Well, don't get too caught up in it, you don't want to waste too much time if it's not going anywhere." He gathered up a stack of pink invoices. "Gotta go collect the rent. Keep me posted." He rushed out of the office.

I went back to the main room. All the lights were out except the lamp over the couch in the corner. Scott was sitting under it, chewing on his cigar, mumbling to himself as he scoured through the week's issue. There were a couple of stacks printed and wrapped in bundles on the floor. I popped one of the bundles open and pulled out a copy. Scott finally looked up and saw me.

"Don't waste your time reading that garbage," he said.

"I just wanted to see how this week's issue came out," I said.

"It could be better. We pulled it off, and that's all that matters I suppose." I sat down across from him. He laid the paper aside and lit the cigar he'd been chewing on. "Gary just left so you can smoke if you want. I don't give a shit."

I lit a cigarette.

Scott was kicked back on the couch and, for the first time, relaxed and forthright. "I'm a little surprised you're still with us. Most of the writers we pick up don't last more than a few issues."

"To be honest with you," I half lied, "I'm just happy to be writing anything."

"The stories you're assigned are shit, I know that. I don't like them either. I've become a pushover, letting Gary convince me this is the only way to keep the paper running. If I took it in the direction I wanted, I suppose we'd already be through. I guess he deserves some credit."

"I understand. It's a business." Surprised he was telling me all this.

He leaned back in his chair and puffed perfect rings into the stagnant air, staring wistfully at the ceiling for a minute before continuing.

"I remember that article on the new chaplain. I saw the copy Gary cut before we laid it out, the stuff about the Barnett Newman paintings. That's the kind thing I'm talking about. If it were me editing the story, I would have left that in."

"He does that with all of them," I said. "I'm used to it."

"I'm the goddamn editor, I shouldn't be letting…" he grumbled to himself, clamping down on his cigar.

After a minute of silent brooding he continued. "I heard you talking about the art gallery to Gary. There's never going to be an ad, is there?"

"Not a chance," I said. "We're just a collective of people trying to make something."

"We? So you're involved with it too? That's why we haven't been seeing you as much lately," Scott said. "Well, do you want to write an article about it?"

"I'd like to. It would be good to get it out there, if we ever open."

"Then do it. Forget about selling the ad. When you have it, don't give it to Gary. Bring it straight to me. I'll make sure it runs."

"Thanks. That's good to know."

"Now get outta here, let me enjoy having this place to myself."

I got up, left quietly without saying another word. I had a newfound respect for Scott and was charged about the possibility of doing an article on something I cared about. I hurried over to over to Tolson's to buy some booze to take to the gallery. I needed to talk to Steven about the article, and I was anxious to see what was happening there, what I might be missing.

# Darkroom

The gallery was empty when I arrived. There was plywood stuck in the door where the glass had been. The dust had settled since that night the gas line broke, and Steven somehow convinced the landlord to let us keep the building. Only now we had been given an ultimatum. If we wanted to continue using the space, we needed to start showing real progress.

I walked upstairs, but there was no one there either. Then I heard a noise down in the basement. A hammer driving nails. Someone was down there working. I skipped back down the stairs to the gallery and down the next flight into the basement below.

"Steven?"

A woman's voice came from inside the room in the corner of the basement. "Hello? Who are you looking for?" It was a dirty, unfinished bathroom we'd been using during late nights at the gallery. It was different now, though. All changed around. The door was closed off. Everything covered. A woman stepped out with a 16-penny nail hanging from her lips like a cigarette. A hammer in her hand. A gorgeous woman, small frame, dark, sinuous hair curling around her shoulders. Small glimmer of metal in her left nostril. Thin legs wrapped in dark jeans. A warm, liquid smile and fire burning above the waterline in her onyx eyes.

"Steven isn't here, if that's who you're after," she said. "He gave me a key and said I could go ahead and start setting up here in the basement. I'm Meredith, by the way."

She gave me her hand. All her beauty ended at the wrist bone, and the hand I shook was hard, calloused, deliberate. Chemical stains at the ends of her fingers.

"What are you setting up here?" I asked.

"This'll be a darkroom." She tossed the hammer onto the floor. There were battered cardboard boxes lined against the wall that hadn't been there before. She opened one of them and took out some equipment. A changing bag. Bottle opener. Scissors. Film canisters. Then she opened her shoulder bag and pulled out three rolls of black and white film. She sat down on one of the crates and loaded the equipment and film into the black changing bag, zipped the top shut, and slid her arms into the sleeved openings on either side.

"You mind cinching these a little tighter for me?" she asked. "I wanna get some of these negatives developed."

I tightened the elastic cord on the sleeves, pinching them around the flesh of her arms. Her hands moved inside the bag, shuffling, feeling their way around, seeing the contents, popping open the film with the bottle opener and carefully pulling the celluloid reel out, winding it into the canister, all by touch.

I sat down opposite her, mesmerized. "I've never messed with film. You mind if I stick around and see how it works?" I lit a cigarette.

"You mind if I get one of those from you?" she asked. "You might have to help me with it though."

I pulled out another cigarette and placed it in her lips and lit it. She took a drag and held it in her mouth. She was still moving her hands, still working inside the bag on her lap.

"So are you one of the people involved with the gallery?" she asked. "I ran into Steven the other night and heard all about it. He's the one in charge of this, right?"

I shrugged. "Sort of. There isn't really anyone in charge, or anything to be in charge of."

"Well, anyway, he was at Pat's Place the other night. We kind of hit it off over photography. We talked for hours about it. I told him about this photo essay I'm working on, doing all film photography. I have everything to put together a darkroom but nowhere to do it. That's when he told me about this place. He gave me a key and told me to come over whenever and set it up. That's okay, right?"

"Fine with me. Like I said, no one's really in charge. You have the same access as anyone else now."

"Great. I'm almost finished. Right now I'm just sealing it up, shutting out all the light. Actually, could you give me a hand with something? I need to nail one more thing up."

"Of course." Her hands were stuck inside the bag so I went over to help her out of it. Before I got there she flicked the cigarette out with her tongue, leaned down, and unzipped the bag with her teeth, pulling three skillfully loaded canisters out and setting them aside.

I followed her into the darkroom, and she had me hold up a board across the door while she hammered it in, my fingers inches away from the nail, but she didn't miss. I watched her face as it twisted in concentration, distorting all her beauty into determination. I wondered if Steven was already sleeping with her.

She drove the last nail. "There, that should do it. You can't have any light leaking into the room or it will fuck up the negatives. Even the smallest amount can ruin everything. Move over," she instructed. "Let's close this door and see if it worked."

She pulled the door shut, closing the two of us into the room. Everything went out, a blinding darkness.

"You have to wait a second to let your eyes adjust," she said.

I couldn't see her anymore, but I knew she was standing next to me. The image of her burned into my brain. In the dark, I transposed the image into the place where I knew she was standing. I lifted up my arm, wanting to see how close I could reach for her.

The room became intoxicating, the darkness, the sound of her breath. I put my hand out a little closer, uncertain if I'd miscalculated where she stood, if the image of her was closer to me, or the reality. I reached farther, my hand must have been just above her right hip. I could feel the body heat radiating into my palm.

"Do you see anything?" she asked. "Have your eyes adjusted?"

"No, I don't see anything."

"Me neither. I think I finally got it." She pushed open the door, and I was blinded again. My hand slipped furtively back to my side. She walked out, unaffected by the change in light. When my eyes adjusted, she was gone.

I found her outside the darkroom. She walked over to the boxes and threw off all of the lids. She started pulling out equipment and bringing it into the darkroom. I wanted to learn about film, about her.

"Can I help?"

"Sure, I don't care."

I helped her bring everything in and set it up. She popped the lids off three plastic bottles. Developer. Stop bath. Fixer. She poured them into shallow trays on the vanity. The sweet chemical smell permeated the room. She moved through all of this with the grace of experience.

"Check this out," she opened a bottle and took my hand, dabbing liquid on my finger. I instantly got a familiar taste coming through the roots in my teeth.

"I taste...licorice."

"Yeah, it's called pyro. It's pretty powerful stuff. Goes right into the nervous system."

She capped the bottle and tossed it into a box. She kept setting up while she told me about film processes and photographers she loved. Cartier Bresson, Walker Evans, Edward Weston, Diane Arbus. There was passion in her voice, talking about the beauty in filth, the decisive moment, the love of street photography.

She had the darkroom ready to go in no time. She brought in some of her developed negatives and took me through the process.

Under the crimson safe light, she bent to the enlarger, dodging and burning, the latent silver emulsion coming through. Then she tossed the 5x7 print into the developer, then the stop bath, and finally the fixer.

"To rinse the negatives you have to keep them in running water," she explained. "You don't need anything fancy." She went over to the grimy toilet and pulled the lid off the back tank like a seasoned jack, reached in and modified the plumbing to keep a pool of water constantly running.

When she bent over, something like a glass monocle hanging from the end of a necklace fell from her shirt. She caught me staring.

"It's a neutral density filter, something you can hold up to your eye to neutralize all the tones. When you look through this, everything becomes black and white."

She pulled the print out of the fixer and tossed it into the tank behind the filthy toilet. It floated around, bouncing off the sidewalls, the image becoming permanent.

I helped her develop more as she walked me through the process. We did this for the rest of the night. She told me more about photography, and I told her more about the gallery. Prints went in one side, came out the other, and fell into the tank. This went on and on. She had limitless energy, talking, dodging, burning, as my initial attraction to her slowly emulsified into genuine admiration.

# Disassociation

Every day that I went to the gallery after meeting her, I would go straight down to the darkroom to see if Meredith was there. After several nights together, she taught me everything I needed to know to develop film on my own.

"We should go take some pictures," I suggested one day. "I still don't know much about that side of it."

"Sure." She sounded a little reluctant. "It's usually something I do alone, but I can get you set up."

She loaned me one of her cameras, and we went out walking around the town, talking, laughing. She pulled out a small device and pointed it at a few different things.

"You need to meter the light first." She adjusted the dials. "I'm metering to the shadows, so you'll be good as long as you stay on the dark side of the street."

She handed the camera back, shutter speed and aperture set. We kept walking. Her camera stayed strapped behind her arm.

I stopped at the corner to take a photograph. I didn't really know what I was shooting, just wanted to get more familiar with using the camera. I took my time to adjust the focus, finally released the shutter. When I pulled the camera away from my eye, Meredith was gone, off to take photos on her own.

I hustled through some of the back alleys, shooting more, hoping to run into her. I only had one roll of film, and when that ran out, I walked back to the gallery.

Meredith wasn't there yet. I walked upstairs and found Steven sitting in front of the desk. Behind the desk was Garner, dark hair and wiry limbs, affected smile, two serrated front teeth pointing inward in a V shape. She acknowledged my presence with a glance but didn't pause her conversation. In front of her was a laptop turned toward Steven with a PowerPoint presentation opened.

"As I was saying, I've been in this business for twenty years already. I've had art history. I've studied this stuff, so I know what works and what doesn't. I just wish people would trust me more."

She stood up and opened a faux leather briefcase. "Here, let me show you some of my latest work." She pulled out some pamphlets. "This is what I want to talk to you guys about. I'm trying to sell the town on this idea of culture zones. Are you familiar with this concept?"

Steven shook his head. "Nope." His hands were clasped behind his neck, putrid pheromones soaking through the armpits of his t-shirt.

"You promote young entrepreneurs to revitalize an otherwise blighted area. Art attracts business, which spurs economic growth. Simple as that. This is a model that's been proven in cities all over the country. Culture *sells*."

"What happens to the artists?" I cut in.

"What do you mean?"

"After you revitalize an area and it becomes too expensive?"

"That's the least of our worries right now. Who is this anyway?" I realized she was talking about me, though still looking at Steven.

"I interviewed you for the *Telegraph*, remember?"

"Oh yeah, that's right. What article are you working on now? You want to write a profile about me? *Maverick Artist: One Woman's Struggle to Overcome*." She laughed sardonically as she swept the headline through the air. "I could give you an interview if you had awhile. Someone needs to understand what I go through every day. I have to figure out how to make money. That's the tough part. Sure, I'd love to be an artist who just sits around creating all day long, but I don't have time anymore. I have a gallery space too, you know. And it truly is *contemporary* art."

"Right. You mean the space that rents out for catered events and weddings, things like that?" Steven asked.

"Get over it. This is how it works. You have to come up with a revenue if you want to survive. Right now I'm working on this thing called *Bigwig Art*. I'm getting a group of wealthy people together at the Coalition, the bankers and politicians, people with money, and I'm gonna load them up with wine and teach them how to be artists. They'll all have an easel and paints, and I'll help them create something. Then we'll have a fundraising dinner, and we'll frame all of the art and sell it back to them. They'll love it."

"Sounds pretty brutal," I said. She looked at me with exhausted condescension.

"Don't think too hard about it. This is business. Have a seat. Let me give you all a hard lesson."

I sat in a chair next to Steven opposite the desk, like we were in her office.

"The biggest obstacle with running a gallery is money. You have to know where to find it and how to get it. I'm connected to every person in this town. Except for Samuel Cole, the owner of Central Bank. He's the whale, a *billionaire*. I've asked him for money several times, and he always turns me down. And now I can't even get in there to see his collection. Can you believe that! Won't give *me* a tour! They have no idea what I do for art in this town. He sinks millions into his private collection but not a dime into the community, into the things I'm trying to do. Not once has he donated to the Coalition. That's what's wrong with this system. Believe me, I understand your struggle. We may not be able to keep going. We can't continue if they're going to make us suffer so much. You have to be able to survive, first and foremost."

While she was talking she stood up and walked across the office, staring out the window over High Street with a look like she wanted to spit on the whole town.

"What does any of this have to do with us?" Steven asked. "Where do we fit in this picture?"

"Well..." She put on a fake smile, sat back down behind the desk, softened her voice. "I like you guys, and I think even though what you're doing may be, how should I say it, a little rudimentary, as far as *real* art is concerned, I still want to see you succeed. And I can tell you right now the only way you're going to make it is if you let me help you. We'll make this place part of the Coalition. It can be a branch of my larger projects. I have connections, and I could pull the right strings for you. I could get you the funding you need to fix this place up and open it as a real gallery. Plus, I could use the extra space for events and fundraisers. There are plenty of opportunities with a building like this—"

Steven cut in. "No thanks," he said. "We don't want to be connected."

"Connections are your only friend in this business. If we can work together, I think you'll see that it can benefit both of us."

"We're pretty happy with the way things are going," he said.

"What things? Going where? You don't have anything here, and no one even knows this place exists. If you want to make art, you have to make money. Which means you need to spend money to fix this place up to make it look respectable. Then you'll be able to attract the sort of people that can buy art. I know how to do that, which is why you need me."

"We're not interested. We want to figure this out on our own."

"But you'll never make it on your own," she insisted.

"Then we'll fail on our own, too," he said calmly.

"So that's it? You're not even going to hear me out?"

"No. We don't want any part of it."

She shook her head, both hands flat on the desk, pushed back her chair. "I had hoped you would be a little more pragmatic." She stood, brusquely packing her things back into her bag. "It's too bad, for you." She slung the bag over her shoulder and walked out the door.

# Bodhisattva

Steven and I coursed through the aisles at Tolson's. We went to the back, and Steven pulled the largest styrofoam cup they had off the stack and started filling it with Dr. Pepper, no ice. We were talking about Garner coming into the gallery.

"Maybe we were too quick to dismiss her," I said. "We'll never be able to afford the renovations on our own."

Steven didn't respond. He clicked the release on the fountain machine a couple of times, topping off the cup.

"You said the landlord is gave us an ultimatum, right? That we have to start improving the building if we want to keep it? Would it be so bad if we got hooked up with her? She could provide a lot of help in the one area where we're all pretty helpless."

He put a lid on the cup, stabbed through it with an extra long straw. "Come on, let's go see Michael."

"Who's Michael? Has he been around the gallery?"

"No, he doesn't get out. You have to go to him. He hasn't left the house in two years." Steven put the soda on the counter and asked the clerk for a pack of Winstons, then turned to me.

"Do you have any cash on you?"

I paid the clerk, and we walked out. It was five o'clock, and traffic was clotting downtown as we walked several blocks to where Michael lived. We stopped in front of an old house with a sign out front for P&T Tax and Accounting. I followed Steven inside. The front room was a labyrinth of file cabinets and white cardboard boxes with dates written on the lids in thick black marker, all centered around a large oak desk. Behind it sat a corpulent woman in a Hawaiian-print shirt.

"Hey Terry," said Steven. "How's our Michael today?"

"Hello!" she said, a warm, hearty smile across her plump cheeks. "I think I just heard him coming out of hibernation. Go on back."

We went to the tiny room in the back of the house and knocked on the closed door. We heard a hacking black lung cough on the other side before he finally replied, "Come in."

We opened the door and found him inside a dark den surrounded by books, six foot four inches stretched out on a ratty five foot something couch, giant feet hanging off the end, sweatpants down around his ankles exposing ashen thighs, red right hand clenched in a fist around his hypertrophic cock. He didn't make any move to cover himself. The hypnotic voice from an Eckhart Tolle lecture came from the CD player in the corner.

"Hey Michael," Steven said. "How's the self actualizing going?"

"There is no self," said Michael, hand still wrapped tight. "I was just getting a grip on reality."

Steven wasn't taken back by this at all, as if this was how he always found Michael.

"Don't be alarmed," Michael said to me, noticing my discomfort. "Nothing you can see with your eyes actually exists. The mind is only a tool." Then he turned to Steven. "Who's your friend?"

"This is Mark. He's part of the gallery," Steven explained.

"Ah, how are things going at the gallery? One of these days I'll have to come see it," said Michael.

"Kind of a lost cause at this point," Steven admitted.

"Love is the only cause," Michael said.

Behind us we heard the accountant gather up her purse, then she came over and poked her head into the room. "I'm going home my son. Enjoy your world."

"I love you with the universe of love, mother. I will see you tomorrow." She disappeared through the columns of tax documents, and we heard the front door open and close.

"We brought offerings," Steven said. He threw the pack of cigarettes out, and Michael let go of himself to catch it. Steven put the fountain soda in his other hand.

"Manna," Michael said. "Let's retire to the porch."

Michael pulled on his sweatpants, and we all went outside. He sat down and after a little effort managed to tug his legs under and cross them. He opened the pack and lit a cigarette. It was dusk on the horizon, and Michael stared wide-eyed into the almond setting sun..

"The ancients believed you could get all the sustenance you need by eating the sun with your eyes." He took a drag from his Winston and sat silently for a minute without blinking.

"Tell me about it," Michael said finally, looking toward us now. "What's the problem?"

"The head of the Arts Coalition came in to try and co-opt the gallery," said Steven. "She wants to throw money at it and fix the place up, but only so she can use it as one of her event spaces."

"But we would have an open gallery," I interjected. "Right now all we have is a dilapidated building. And even that's gonna be taken away if we don't do something."

Michael pursed his lips around the teat of his fountain soda straw and took a long, disinterested pull. He was staring off across the street, watching the groundhogs digging into the hillside below the Simenson Middle School, not saying anything.

"I don't see why we need to have the gallery open," Steven said.

"So we can open it to the public. Not just to make money like Garner wants to do, but to share what we're doing and figure out a way to make it sustainable. It's great to have the space to work out ideas, but we need to figure out how to keep it. I think we all have a desire to do that, even you."

Steven was anxiously running his hands through his hair, shaking his head. "I just...I don't know."

"Why not? What are you so worried about?"

"What if we fail? If we open the gallery we'll have to run a gallery. What if we can't do it? We could end up losing the space and everything we have now."

"But this would bring it outside, make it less amateur."

Michael loudly slurped out the last bit of soda through the straw before finally speaking up. "Amateur. That's interesting. Root word: Amatorem. Meaning lover." He set the soda down gently next to him.

"I'm sorry," I said. "I don't follow."

"Never mind that. Failure is a false perception. There's no such thing as truly failing, no matter what you do."

"Just out of curiosity, what is it you do?" I asked. "Steven didn't give me any back story, so I'm a little confused."

"I am a human being, not a human doing," Michael replied. "Failure doesn't really exist. Some people might look at my life and call it a failure, and that's okay. I'm thirty-four, living in the back room of my mother's office. No job. No money. These things are all true, but if someone considers that failure, then that's their reality, not mine."

"How's that working out for you? No offense, but I can't imagine being cooped up here all day. What do you do with your time?"

"I'm still trying to figure out what *time* really is. Take a look over there." He pointed to the hillside where the groundhogs were digging their little holes. "Every evening I sit out here and watch these loving animals. To the custodians who try and maintain this lawn they are little pests. But for them, they spend all day digging and playing, doing only what comes natural. When you observe nature at work, you start to see the least effort is expended. As for me, I have everything I could ever want right here. I am living in the moment of now..."

I sat back, truly listening as he kept talking. Something very soothing about being there. His life seemed a complete contradiction, but the longer he talked, the more I realized he was fully aware of his own hypocrisies and made no apologies for them. He was a sort of adulterated bodhisattva, smoking Winston's in sukhasana pose, third eye open. Bald head reflecting a sheen of natural light. Belly round and full. He was like clarified butter.

We spent the rest of the evening listening to him and learning from those groundhogs, and I knew I was wrong. There had to be a better way than Garner.

# Artist Statement

Steven was sitting at the table in the gallery when I walked in. Joey was across from him shaking his head. Bradley was standing back from the table pacing, hands on his hips. Steven had a pen to an open notebook, half full of illegible scrawls. Meredith was standing behind Steven, one hand on his shoulder, watching him write.

"Joey, you need to be doing this yourself," said Bradley.

"I don't know man, I'm just not good at this sort of shit," said Joey. "I'm a painter, man, not a fucking…you know," his fingers purling through the air, "whatever this is. I don't like talking about my art or having to explain anything."

"You're an artist, Joey," Bradley insisted. "You have to be able to write your own goddamn artist statement. It's not just about writing *this* statement—which, who fucking knows why you think Steven is competent enough to do this for you—it's more about taking responsibility as an artist. You need to know how to do these things if you're going to make it on your own. Besides, Steven can't even spell his own name."

"Spelling is obsolete," declared Steven.

Joey didn''t say anything, but he also didn't look concerned. An apparently meaningless hurdle.

Steven saw me at the door. "You're just in time. We're trying to write Joey's artist statement."

"I don't know the first thing about it," I admitted.

"Doesn't matter," said Steven. "We'll just make something up. It never has anything to do with the art anyway."

"What's it for?" I asked.

"I'm getting a show for Joey," Bradley said. "I've called a few galleries in Chicago that are definitely interested. These are established art galleries that can actually help further Joey's career."

I thought of the artist statements I'd seen elsewhere. No real pattern emerged, other than maybe the excessive syllables, the effort to confound something into importance. I poured myself a drink from the bottle next to Steven, pulled a pack of cigarettes from my pocket, took one out, and threw the pack into the middle of the table.

"What do you have so far?" I asked.

"Never mind. You're all incompetent," said Bradley. "Here, write this down."

*Joey Wagner (pronounced Vagner, like the German composer)...*

"Vagner?" asked Joey. "What's wrong with Wagner?"

"It sounds better," said Bradley. "The more foreign you can become the more important the art will seem."

*Joey approaches art with a keen but primitive eye, systematically deconstructing the technicolor American Dream...*

Brad spewed out lines like this, and Steven wrote them down. Each one more absurd than the last.

*Exploring the dialectic between the nature of morphogenesis and obsolescence of acculturation...*

"What does that even mean?" asked Joey.

*The alchemical wonder is implicit in the corporeal essence, the juxtaposition of emotions, the manifestation of form...*

Steven was shaking his head as he wrote it all down. "Where are you coming up with this horse shit," he laughed.

*The accumulation of ultimate knowledge, the content of consciousness, the hellish dream made real...*

"This is absurd," said Steven. "You can't actually use any of this."

I looked over what had been written so far. "I'm with Steven," I said. "This would sound horrible to anyone taking it seriously. There's no rule saying you have to do it this way."

"Most of them are, though," said Bradley. "There are some serious artists out there whose statements read like a paragraph in a thesaurus. This is just how it's done, because some people have trouble forming their own opinion. If you wanna get a show, Joey, you'll have to play along."

"Whatever you think, man," Joey shrugged.

"The art should speak for itself," said Steven. "You don't need any of this. Just show them your work and that's it."

"Don't be naive," said Bradley.

"What do you think?" I asked Meredith. "You're being quiet over there."

"Looks like you guys have this all figured out," she said, laughing slightly. "It sounds ridiculous, but it might be what they're looking for. I'd just write something down and go back to working on the paintings." She stood up straight, her hand sliding gently off Steven's shoulder. "I'll be down in the darkroom getting some work done," she said. I turned in my chair as she walked to the stairwell and disappeared below.

"Trust me on this one," said Bradley, going back to the statement. "Keep writing this down."

He spouted off more lines of obscure pomp as Steven wrote it all down and tried to lash them together. I wanted to stay and help out, be a part of it, but more than that I wanted to spend time with Meredith. I pushed my chair back and went down to the darkroom.

# Nude

Several cotton strings were festooned overhead in the darkroom, 5x7 prints hanging wet like dew-covered fruit. The room was full of them. The floor was now tiled in the overexposed stillbirths of working prints. Meredith was sitting outside the darkroom, smoking a cigarette and thumbing through *The Daybooks of Edward Weston*, her feet kicked up on an inverted mixing tub.

"I can't believe how much you've done already," I said, examining a few of the prints clothes-pinned to the lines. "These are incredible."

"Thanks," she said, exhaling smoke, turning another page. "It's not as much as I hoped to have done, but it takes quite awhile doing it this way."

"Why do you still use a darkroom, anyway?" I asked. "Everything is digital now. Why go through such a labor intensive process?"

"I don't know. Why do you still use a typewriter? Don't you have a computer?"

"I don't know either," I replied. "I guess there's a desire to keep one foot in analog, no matter what medium it is. Partly because I feel more connected with what I'm writing. Partly because there's no easy delete button. Plus, I like the mechanics of it, I like the sound. But in the end it's all the same, just words on paper." I looked through some of the prints lying on the floor, some of them looked perfectly good. Wondered what little flaw might have made her throw them out and start over.

"It's not like that with photography. The difference between silver and digital is huge." She put down the book, voice welling with passion to talk about photography. "You have to work harder for it and be more selective when you're shooting, but it's worth it. When I look at a film print, I immediately have a certain level of respect. Take someone like Cartier Bresson, or any street photographer, you appreciate it more because of what it took to get that image, having to be present and ready in that exact moment. Add that on top of all the hours of work it takes to then develop the print and get it right. The end product is something that represents the process, and if you look closely, you can tell it's authentic."

Footsteps shuffled around the floorboards overhead as everyone else left the gallery, leaving the two of us.

"I know film is already on the way out, but there are still people using it," she continued. "Most people just see it as something romantic at this point, and some people will cling to it no matter what. I do it because I think it's a more natural process. Something about digital seems so impersonal, but that's just me. It's too easy, sterile, too perfect. I don't want things to be perfect. I'm more drawn to the corruptions in an image."

As she was talking I reached into the back of the toilet tank and pulled out a couple of wet prints. A nude of a beautiful woman lying in the sun on an asphalt roof. I looked closer. "Is this...?"

"Yeah, it's me."

"Oh, sorry." I put the photograph back into the tank.

"It's okay. It doesn't bother me. Just don't get any ideas."

I picked it back up, admired the natural posture, perfect structure. Then I recognized the rooftop of the gallery. The same place Steven and I were the night Casey broke in. She was lying just below the brick ledge that overlooked High Street, naked, gorgeous, nonplussed.

"You look pretty comfortable for having to set a timer and get into the frame."

"I didn't use a timer. Steven took them." She took another drag from her cigarette. "I was surprised. He's a damned good photographer."

I could feel the blood warming in my forehead. "Really? I didn't know that. So you and Steven have a thing going then?"

"It's not like that. He just took some photographs, there's nothing going on between us. Besides, I don't date creative types. I have enough of my own problems to deal with."

I didn't know what to say. I looked through some more of the hanging prints. Wanted to change the subject. "What are your plans for these, once you get this series finished?"

"I don't know. It would be nice to show them somewhere, but I haven't had any luck with that yet." She tucked her calloused thumb in the fold of the book and set it on her knee. "Maybe when this place opens up, I can do a show here."

"Yeah, we've been trying to figure that out. It's not looking good at this point."

"What do you mean? You have a gallery, what's the problem?"

"We're severely lacking in resources. There's no telling how long it'll last."

Meredith shifted in her chair. "Resources? What resources?" Her eyebrows scrunching on her opalescent forehead. "You have the space, what more do you need?"

"You've seen the space, it's a disaster. We need everything. And as of right now we don't have anything."

Meredith laughed. "You're kidding, right? You have no imagination at all."

"We've been imagining it, believe me. Imagination is the one thing we have no shortage of."

She kicked her feet down onto the floor and put out her cigarette. She glided up the stairs into the gallery. I followed after her.

She was pacing around the space, sizing it up. "You're trying to finish this entire space. Maybe you should stop thinking about finishing it and just open it like it is."

"What about the mess? You can barely walk through here."

She looked down the length of the building. "Cut it in half," she declared. "You could put a partition right across the middle of the gallery. Push all of this stuff to the back and we'll clean the front as best we can. And don't worry about the floors or walls being fucked up. If you really wanna have a gallery, this would do it."

I imagined the long narrow room halved. It would solve the major problem. The worst of the building was in the back. All the major overhaul would be there, where the pipes were exposed and the walls were half torn down. The front of the building wasn't that bad at all. Just a little raw.

"That's a great idea," I said. "We hadn't even thought of that. We would have an open gallery. And we could worry about the back half later. Meredith, that's fucking brilliant!"

"Thanks," she said, smiling.

# Company Van

I managed to pull myself out of bed early in the morning, an increasingly rare occurrence. Without a real job I grew accustomed to the luxury of time. Time to write, time to be idle, time to stay out late and sleep late, time to waste.

But we were all meeting at Coffee Zone, and Bradley insisted we get there before dawn. We were going on a road trip.

I walked to the coffee shop. No one else was there yet. Taisir was behind the counter as usual.

"Hala hala! You want coffee, my friend?" he asked.

"Rocket fuel," I said. I was finally starting to acquire a taste for the fossil fuel.

"How are things going next door? You guys ever going to open your gallery? I would like to see it become a success."

"No doubt about it." I pulled a couple dollars from my pocket.

Taisir waved it away. "No need, my friend. You are part of the block now. Rocket Fuel is on the house."

I thanked him and walked out the front, took a seat at the wrought iron table and lit a cigarette, wondering how long until the others showed. If this was even going to happen. Chicago. Where Joey had a chance to get a foothold with his art. Bradley set the whole thing up for him. He wanted Joey to succeed, to make a name for himself. Joey couldn't figure out getting a show on his own, so Bradley played the agent for him.

"You the only one here?" Bradley walked up in a heavy clip, like we were already running late.

"I just got here. Have you been over to the gallery yet?" I asked. "I'm guessing Steven's probably passed out there."

"Come on, let's go wake him up." He was already halfway to the gallery door when I stood up. "We have to stop by Joey's on the way out to get the paintings."

"How we getting there, anyway?"

"Got a van. Pederson. Don't ask me how," he called back to me from down the block. "Come on, we need to hurry."

No sign of Steven in the gallery. Just more empty bottles, cigarette butts, material waste. The usual. We went upstairs to the office, where we found him passed out on the floor behind the desk, laying on a rough pallet of drop cloths over some tattered foam. On the other side of him I saw a woman, sleeping head down in the crook of his arm, smooth white skin of an uncovered thigh gleaming in an otherwise silt-swaddled room. I looked closer. The hair. It was Meredith's. Long dark curls swirling around the naked shoulder. I couldn't believe it. What the fuck was she doing there? Jealousy, anger, a gauntlet of emotions. Smell of copulance filling my nostrils.

"Hate to break in on you," Bradley said impatiently. "But we need to go. Where's Pederson?"

Steven picked his head up off a rolled up jacket and saw us standing in the doorway. He nodded and waved us out, indicating that he's right behind, go ahead.

We went back downstairs. I let Bradley go first so he wouldn't see my flushed face.

A dirty white Econoline van pulled up to the front of the gallery, orange caution light over the cab, oil-smoke coughing out the tailpipe, Pederson at the wheel. There was a faded logo plastered on the side from Vanguard, a now defunct airline, failing to keep up in the corporate accretion.

"What? We have a van now?" I said.

"Help me unload it," Bradley said as he opened the back door.

The interior of the van was like a scale model of the gallery itself. Full of refuse, garbage, lumber, chunks of concrete, a smell. There was a bench seat up front but the rest of them were removed. In the cab were two blue cloth-covered seats on either side of the plastic motor cover.

I grabbed a handful of boards and started unloading it. *Don't think about Meredith*, I told myself. I brought the boards into the gallery and threw them on the floor, letting them crash loudly. *Don't think about Meredith.* I couldn't help it. Like a contaminant that gets into your mental tap water. She was still upstairs. Directly above me. I went back outside, tried to stay distracted.

We jettisoned everything from the back, hauling it into the gallery and throwing it onto the piles. We were in a hurry, and there was nowhere else to put it.

Steven came outside as the last of it was removed, walking a little slow, blinded in the morning sun. He walked around, inspecting the new old van, nodding.

"That's fuckin awesome," he said, voice still hoarse.

"Is Meredith not coming along?" I asked sharply.

"Of course I'm coming." I turned as she came from around the corner. She was sipping a cup of coffee, freshly showered. Meaning there was no way it could have been her upstairs. I was overwhelmed with relief, and at the same time burdened. For the first time aware of how much I really wanted her, and of how impossible that would be.

"What are we waiting for?" Meredith asked. "Let's go."

"Toss me the keys," Steven said.

Pederson threw him the ring with one key for the ignition, one for the doors, and one flat rubber keychain with the words "LOW COST LOW FARE" fading away.

We piled inside, Steven behind the wheel of the gallery's new de facto company van.

We pulled out onto High Street, and Pederson reached up to the dash and flipped a switch, turning on the spinning yellow caution light on the roof as we made our way to Joey's house.

# Art Heist

Joey's wife Carly threw open the door as soon as we stepped onto the porch. Black hair, eyes narrow, piercing us each in turn.

"I'm going with you," she said. "Joey said I could come along. He won't go unless I come too. He knows how hard you are on everything, and he doesn't trust you with his paintings. He wants me there to make sure none of you scamps fuck them up." Carly showed her passionate distaste for every one of us.

"He said all that? Doesn't sound like our Joey," Bradley said mockingly.

Her jade-colored eyes plunged into Bradley like a shiv. He was the one she despised most of all. She said nothing.

Steven spoke up because no one else would. We were afraid of her. "Where is Joey?" he asked. "I need to talk to him."

"He's in the nursery." We carefully slid past her and through the door. "It won't matter what you say!" Her words dogging us down the hall. "Don't even think about trying to change his mind!"

We got to the room at the end of the hall, found Joey inside clapping the lids onto a few gallons of house paint, tamping them down with the heel of his paint-mottled sneaker. He waved us into the room. Carly came down the hall after us but stopped at the threshold. She controlled every aspect of Joey's life, feeding him, buying his clothes, telling him when and where he could go, everything. But they had an agreement: She never went into his studio, and he never went into hers.

Joey walked over and gently shut the door as she stared him down. He looked at the floor anxiously, never made eye contact.

He grabbed Steven's elbow and brought him over to the opposite corner of the room where Bradley and I were standing.

"You gotta help me. She's crazy, man. I didn't tell her she could go. But I don't know what to say. You gotta talk to her for me. Please. You're the only one she'll listen to," he whispered.

"I don't know, Joey. She's seems pretty serious," Steven said.

"You can't let her go, man. Trust me, it won't be good." Joey, eyes wide and desperate, pleading in whispers, helpless.

"I'll try. First let's load up the van. Which of these paintings are going?"

Joey flipped through the canvases against one of the walls. They were five, six, seven deep in places and stacked around every perimeter foot. There were upwards of fifty in this room alone. Bradley and I went across the room, looked through some of the others.

"Fuck," I heard Bradley mutter to himself as he stared at one of them. "This makes me want to quit painting."

"How many do they want?" Joey asked.

"Uh...well." Bradley hesitated. "They didn't really say, exactly. We'll just bring them a stack and let them choose. The rest we can bring back."

Joey flipped and flipped through the different paintings, going front to back several times.

"I don't know, man. I can't decide." He turned to us. "What do you guys think?"

Bradley, Meredith and I chose a few paintings and pulled them aside.

"These are the best ones," Meredith said.

"Let's get them in the van so we can go," said Steven. "I'll go talk to Carly."

"We need to be careful," Joey said as Bradley and I hoisted up a canvas. "We should put these inside of something, right? To protect them?"

"They're six foot canvases Joey. The only thing we can put them inside of is the van," I said. "Grab some blankets if you want and we'll wrap them up."

Bradley, Meredith, and I took the first three paintings, and Steven opened the door for us. Carly was still standing in the doorjamb, cheeks red with wrath, fresh pink lines scratched into the flesh of her forearms. We went past after Steven took her aside, started talking her off the ledge. We got the paintings out to the van where Pederson was still sitting, looking out the window.

I heard parts of the conversation happening inside as we came and went from the nursery with more paintings.

"You're taking a fucking airport shuttle, and you're going to tell me there's no room?" I heard her say.

"Unfortunately, no," Steven said. "With these oversized canvases and six giant egos, we're full up."

She wasn't buying it, but he kept trying. We made another trip out to the van, back to the nursery.

"Are these your paintings too, Joey?" Meredith called from the room down at the other end of the hall.

"Those are mine!" Carly ran down the hall, where she had her own studio. The walls were covered in sketches and canvases. She was also a talented artist, doing mostly a sort of anime or manga illustration style. Her studio was off limits, but Meredith had waltzed in on her own.

"These are really good," Meredith said just before Carly laid into her. She was flipping through one of the sketchbooks.

"Thanks," Carly softened up at the compliment.

"These are great illustrations. Do you know Dark Horse Comics?"

"Of course," she said, surprised. Meredith's interest had taken some of the edge off Carly.

"You should submit something to them. I bet you would have a good chance at getting these published."

"I don't know," Carly said. "They're pretty big. You really think they'd go for it?"

"Time to go!" Bradley called. Everything was loaded.

"Sorry, gotta go," Meredith said, handing the sketch book to Carly. "Seriously, these are right on. I'd love to see more of your work sometime." She turned and hurried out to the van and was the last one in.

Carly put the sketch book down and came out onto the porch as we were pulling away. "Wait, you fuckers!" She picked up something off the porch and hurled it toward the van. Bradley waved to her from the passenger seat. She gave a feline arch of her upper lip, curling her claw at him, then flipped us all off, her middle fingernail painted in a deep carmine polish.

## Counter Movement

Steven turned onto Interstate 70 toward St. Louis, pushing the van as hard is it would go to make up for lost time. The windows were down, road noise filled the interior, dirt swirled around in eddies throughout the van for the first several miles. I sat behind the driver's seat, next to Meredith, squeezed in close by Bradley and Pederson on the other side.

"So you said you talked to this person?" asked Joey from the passenger seat. "And she said she wanted to show the paintings?"

"I talked to her on the phone," said Bradley. "I told her everything about you, about your art. Of course, she can't wait to see it."

"Wow, man, this is going to be the first big show. You tryin to make me famous, Bradley?" Joey laughed. "Hey Steven, pull off at the next truck stop, I need to get something."

We pulled off the highway, and he leapt from the van and ran inside. He was going to feed his addiction, an insatiable love for over-the-counter speed pills. When the rest of us got inside the truck stop, he was already standing in front of the register, scanning the little spinning kiosk of cellophane wrappers. Bradley went through the racks, filling his pockets with food. Meredith went to the bathroom. Steven was outside gassing up the van.

"Umm...can I get three packs of the Trucker's Luv," said Joey. "And six of the Black Ice." The hare-lipped man behind the counter gave him a questioning look, but it didn't override his implicit faith in America's various freedoms. He rang Joey up. Steven came inside and pulled out some bills and paid for the gas and a coffee and a pack of smokes.

"How did we get the gas money?" I asked.

"Amy, back at the gallery. Last night she offered to lend us some for the trip," he said. I nodded. Somehow people were always offering whatever they had to Steven.

We all loaded into the van and got back on the highway. Joey tore away at the pill packages. The one called Black Ice was a dark purple packaging with a picture of a wolf howling at the full moon.

"You used to be able to get ephedra over the counter," he explained. "But then all the junkies ruined it. When I heard they were taking it off the shelves, I ran out of the house like it was Black Friday. They're these big blue pills, man. The best ones. I still have half a jar at home, but I save those for when I'm painting. Here, you guys want some of these?" He passed them around and we all popped a couple.

Steven reached into his pocket and pulled out few small white pills. "I have some muscle relaxers too. Anyone?"

"Sure," I said, taking one from his palm. Joey declined, too devoted to the speed. Bradley and Meredith both took one. Steven popped the remaining pills and washed them down with his coffee. I also saw him eat at least four of the uppers. No one, not even Joey, could eat pills like Steven.

By the time we crossed through St. Louis, we were all strung tight like strings on a guitar. Everyone talking loud over the road noise, over each other. Joey put in an old Nirvana CD, one of only two that came with the van, and turned up the volume. Everything accelerated, moving fast as we headed east, passing backward through the Gateway to the West. The Arch was pinned in the air off the highway. The interstate riding on bridges above the city. I looked out over the scene of St. Louis, the menagerie, the wasteland, the junkies.

"That Arch is crazy, man," Joey said. "How do you think they made that?"

"It's a catenary arch—" Meredith started to explain.

"An oversized paperclip," Bradley interrupted. "You want to know how they made it, Joey? They lifted it with a Brunelleschi hoist. They had to have a team of oxen pull it up. They used to ride their covered wagons through the arch when they were pioneering the West."

"No way, man. Really?" Joey said.

"Yeah, it was a law, made by the Hoover administration. If you wanted to go West, you had to first pass through this arch."

"Why would they do that?" Joey asked.

"It was part of the Census Act, so they could count people as they went through."

"Wow, man." Joey said, his forehead against the windshield as the arch passed overhead. "That's government control. That shit's all in the Bible, man. They'll ask you to put chips in your hand pretty soon. That's when I'll know it's time to get the hell outta here."

Joey, a firm believer in the faith, the fire, the brimstone, anything you told him. For the next several miles he told us all about how he had heard the electric synthesizer is really the devil with a thousand tongues. No doubt planted by Bradley, blotting his subconscious like a watercolor and watching the dyes bleed together.

# Rejection

When we got to Chicago, we went straight to a place called Modish Gallery. The building was new, clean. All glass front. Everything crisp and white. Sans serif fonts in the crystal clear window. We parked along the street and got out. Bradley opened the back door of the van and pulled out one of the paintings.

"Shouldn't we go in first?" asked Joey.

"She's gonna need to see the paintings if she wants to make any kind of judgement," said Bradley. "Everybody grab one. We'll come back for the rest."

We walked through the front door, each of us shouldering a canvas, six by five, making 180 total square feet of Joey's madness entering the space. There were a couple of customers walking along the perimeter. The owner of the gallery intercepted us in the middle, a tall woman, bangled wrists, business smile.

"Excuse me. Can I help you?" she said, stopping us.

"Hello Robin, my name is Bradley." He spoke to her in his most affected Patrick Bateman voice, choking with artificial sweetener. "I believe I talked to you on the phone a few days ago about an artist I'm representing, Joey Vagner."

"Joey?...oh, yes. I remember. Didn't I ask you to send me slides of the work?"

"You did say that. But we had *such* a good conversation that I thought maybe you would rather just see them in person. And having worked closely as his agent, I can say the only way to really judge Joey's work is to be standing in front of it." He gave a small, fake laugh.

She rubbed the back of her neck with her hand. "Well, you see...that's not really how it works. Normally you send slides first and then—" She was distressed. One of the customers walked around to the front side of the canvas I was holding. The other peered around to get a look. "Can't you just—" She was irked. "Fine. Follow me, we'll bring those to the back and have a look."

We followed her to the back of the gallery. She didn't hide her animosity.

"It doesn't work this way, you know," she said in her office. "Normally I would have to tell you to leave. I have customers here, and every piece of art that goes through this gallery has to *represent* the gallery. You can't just walk in. Now, set those down over there against the wall."

She dropped her irritation to give the work a serious look, ever-professional. She walked down the line of the six canvases, stopping at each one, thumb and finger poised on her chin, nodding her head occasionally.

"I like these. I like what I'm seeing here. There's a certain rawness, a sort of rusticated quality to them. Yet—" She walked up close to one of the paintings, inspecting every detail, then backed away again. Turned. "Are you the painter?" Joey nodded. "Tell me, where did you study?"

"He started out at Lincoln University," Bradley answered for him. "But Joey realized in order to further develop as an artist, he would have to complete his study on his own."

"I'm afraid I've never heard of Lincoln University. What about other galleries? Where else have you shown your work?" she asked.

Joey looked to Bradley with a shrug.

"I see," said Robin. "Well, there was a time when I would have shown these. They do have an undeniable vibrancy. But I prefer something a little more...refined."

And just like that, the promise of a show was off. Joey stood there, dumbfounded.

Robin led us to the back of the gallery and opened a door to the alley. "If you go to the end of this and take a left, you'll be back on the main street. Thank you for coming. Keep at it Joey, and...who knows."

We carried the canvases around the block and back to the van.

"I'm sorry, Joey," Bradley apologized. "I didn't expect that. I thought for sure if she could see the paintings she would give them a chance."

"That's okay, man. Don't worry about it."

"We'll try a few more," Bradley said. "Maybe the trip won't be a total loss."

We drove around the gallery districts, stopping in at every one we saw. We didn't bother bringing the canvases inside. Bradley went in first and talked to the curator, and sometimes he came out alone, sometimes the curator came out to the van and thumbed through the paintings. We got the same response everywhere. They all wanted to know where Joey went to school. Which other galleries had shown his work. What he had already established. Whether or not this was something other people were paying attention to, to gauge whether or not they should pay attention to it. But they all said they liked the paintings, it just wasn't right for them, for their gallery.

Only one place showed any real interest. A gallery called Swank. A man named Jerry with a white vest and white-rimmed sunglasses walked out to the van with Bradley.

"Ooh, love the ride boys," Jerry said. "Now let's see these paintings you can't stop gushing about, Bradley."

We opened the back of the van and pulled the canvases out one at a time as he examined them.

"Are these paintings finished yet? You know I'm kidding!" He lightly patted Bradley's arm. Bradley glared at him with disbelief. "Seriously though, these are everything! These are doing the most! You know what I mean? A little bit juvenile with all the primary colors, but this might actually be working for me. This could be good for like a guest room or a hotel. I'm kidding!"

"Look, do you want to show them or not?" Bradley said impatiently. "We have appointments with several other galleries so we don't have much time."

"Well, let me see. *Hating* your use of color, *loving* the anti-religious theme. In fact, I'm putting together a show of different iconoclastic artists, you know, to expose the absolute *horrors* in the Church. Believe me, I know all about it." He rolled his eyes.

"But that's not what these paintings are about," Bradley said.

"Who cares what they're about. To me they *scream* atheism, and that's what I'm looking for in this show."

"Well, it sounds like you're a big fan of Joey's work," Bradley said with heavy sarcasm. "Now if you'll excuse us, we need to get to our next appointment."

"Okay, rush rush. The show will be in September. How do I reach you Joey?"

Joey pulled out one of the business cards he had printed at Kinko's in his down time. It was plain white, and he had forgotten to put his number, just these words:

```
┌─────────────────────────────┐
│                             │
│                             │
│                             │
│           JOEY              │
│          Painter            │
│                             │
│                             │
│                             │
└─────────────────────────────┘
```

"Here you go, man." Joey said. "I'm really glad you like the paintings."

Jerry took the card and turned it over a couple of times as we got back in the van and drove off. That was the last gallery.

# Untitled #37

The van sputtered and smoked into the parking lot of the Chicago Art Institute. The one pilgrimage that would keep this trip from being a complete bust.

Before the van even came to a stop, Pederson slid open the side door and hopped out. The rest of us parked and walked up to the wide front steps, where Pederson had planted himself in front of the south lion sculpture, transfixed, gazing at the big bronze animal as it gazed off into the distance, wind occasionally blowing his blond hair across his eyes.

We left him there and went into the museum, joining the bottleneck crowd as it filtered through the door, charged through the turnstile like pigs through a chute.

"This is real church for you, Joey," Bradley said, when we got inside. "This is where you'll find the holy spirit."

In the main hall there were people herding together to be led around by one of the docents. Touring through the history and meaning of Modern art. Bradley and Joey wandered off together on some kind of mission. Steven, Meredith, and I decided to stick with the tour for a bit, see what the docent had to say. We stood on the fringe and listened as he explained the art.

"...you'll notice there is an heroic style, a stoic quaintness that is inherent with this piece. The metaphor has been removed, it's been denuded of context." As he talked he kept reaching behind him, pulling his red weaved ponytail through his hand. "The artist acknowledged that each color choice had representative meaning but doesn't come right out and say what that meaning is..."

Everyone's attention was directed at a simple wooden box on the floor painted different shades of blue.

"It's a byproduct of human activity rather than a war story of the human experience. People are already drowning in metaphor—"

Then he broke out of academic character for an aside. "By the way, my mother, oddly enough, only likes the European abstract expressionists. She's very particular about that."

He went on to the next piece. We trailed along behind the group, and he stopped in front of a work by Dan Flavin. Three tubes of fluorescent light set up in the corner.

"Ah yes, one of my favorites. Notice these lights are deliberately arranged like a steeplechase, just imagine a horse leaping over them! You see there was an effort at this time to learn how to be one step ahead in the strategy of art."

The people in the crowd nodded agreeably when he made eye contact with them.

"Of course light is a strange material to work with because it needs something else to make it apparent. You can't see the photons until they hit the wall behind the light source. There is no tangible material other than the surface that happens to reflect the light back to you. It both highlights the corner and also dissolves it, obliterating the wall around the work, while at the same time making it a part of the art."

Everyone was staring pensively into the lights. A man raised his hand with a question. The docent looked at him.

"Yes, what is it?" he asked.

"How did he assemble this one? Does he ship it this way, or is this an installation?"

"Well, he didn't actually assemble it *himself*. He sent a diagram to the museum, and they had the pleasure of putting it together according to his instructions."

The guy started to ask more about it, but before he could he was cut off.

"Moving on, you'll notice that sometimes Mr. Flavin uses different colored bulbs. Sometimes this bar of light is at the bottom. Sometimes it's at the top. It's wonderful the way he could change the meaning with these subtle variations. I think he loved to invite a radical sort of interpretation."

Steven and I were at the far back of the crowd listening.

"Four shop lights with colored bulbs," I muttered to Steven.

"At the right place and the right time," he muttered back.

"A really good work is very much of its time and also changes meaning with time," the docent continued. "Flavin's work, for instance, is now a lightning rod for environmental discussions due to the bad fluorescent bulbs. You can't even get the red ones anymore…"

"Okay, everyone, this way." He clapped his hands together rapidly above his head. "This way everyone, follow me." The crowd shuffled along after him to the next room.

"You'll be quite interested to know the next piece on our tour was done around the same time by a female artist. Rumor has it the two of them were actually sleeping together. You can imagine how they might have influenced one another's art, among other things…" He trailed off, chuckling to himself.

I glanced over at Meredith.

"It's always about the biography," she said to no one in particular. "Who gives a shit. It's not the work, it's the artist everyone talks about."

The docent led us into the next room. "I've never seen this one before." He walked to the middle of the room. One tile was carefully removed from the floor and laid aside. Next to it laid a monkey wrench, a silver spool of solder, and a blowtorch.

"This is a *very* fascinating installation. It seems to show the naked interior, removing the edifice and reminding us of the soul of the museum."

He walked over to the nearest wall, looking for the exhibit label to discover who did this. He was still searching the perimeter and didn't notice when the facility worker came into the room, walked over to the removed tile and strapped on a pair of kneepads. The tour group was gathered around watching as he knelt down, picked up the solder and torch, and fixed the leaking water main on the "installation."

The three of us looked at each other, all giving the nod that we were ready to go. We left the group, and walked off down the halls by ourselves. We stopped in front of Picasso's Red Armchair.

"Picasso said that every good work of art has to be a destruction as well," I said. "I guess in some ways that's what was happening back there."

"Imagine when Picasso made one of these paintings," Steven said. "It might have been tossed around his studio, or maybe it was almost thrown away or painted over, or it could have been whipped out in a day just so he could pay his rent. Who the hell knows. And now it's worth millions and requires all this care and climate control and guarding. It's like a study in inconvenience."

"I think Bradley was right. This is exactly like church," Meredith said. "The docents are like the vicars in the religion of Modern art, turning these painters into martyrs, their paintings into relics. Even this museum itself is a sort of holy temple."

"Yeah, and here you can have eternal life," I added. "Salvation is granted through the church. We should just sneak one of Joey's paintings in and hang it on the wall."

"Already been done," said Steven.

We were walking through the different rooms and turned a corner just in time to find Joey and Bradley in front of an untitled Jackson Pollock painting. Bradley had his back turned and was on the lookout for the museum guard. He gave the all clear, and Joey dropped to his knees right in front of the enormous canvas, his arms cruciform, as he leaned forward with his tongue hanging out and licked the painting. Something he had always wanted to do.

# Decisive Moment

On the way out of the museum, we found Pederson in the same place we left him, in front of the bronze south lion. He was down on all fours in front of the sculpture, smacking kisses at an ugly, mangy dog. The dog stood facing him a few feet away, covered in scars, fur splotched and dirty, an obvious city stray. He whistled, smacked more kisses. The dog inched closer, head hanging, approaching cautiously. Strange, honest scene, seeing the three animals on all fours. Proud, wayward, beaten. The dog got closer, finally sniffed at Pederson's outstretched hand.

Meredith pulled out her camera and quickly set the aperture, braced the strap against her shoulder like a rifle stock, adjusted focus, hunting the image. Released the shutter. Snap.

Pederson started petting the dog, then rolled it over and scratched at its asphalt-black belly. He pulled some food he had stashed in his pocket and fed it to the hungry mutt.

Pederson saw us heading to the van and came along. The stray rolled back over and followed after him. No one said anything when we loaded into the van, Pederson last, and the dog jumped in after him. We pulled onto the wide interstate, headed home, sun going down, a combination of speed and rejection leaving an empty void in the conversation the first hour or so as we drove back toward the vanishing point of the Middle West.

"It's bullshit, all of it," Bradley finally said.

"I don't know anything about it, man," said Joey. "They have all the power, I know that."

"Bradley's right," said Steven. "It sucks that you have to go through all that shit that ultimately doesn't matter. Who cares where Joey went to school." Steven the autodidact, not having finished high school, had a sour taste for anything academic.

"Joey's a great artist, and he's doing something original, and I wish people could see that," said Bradley.

"It's genuine," said Steven.

"Maybe this is why we have the gallery," I said. "It's a way around all this traditional shit. It doesn't matter where you went to school or what other galleries you're connected with or who you know in the art world. Maybe it's time we open it up."

"We can't afford it," said Steven. "Not without Garner's help, and we decided that'd be a bad idea."

"Meredith had a great solution the other day," I turned to her. "Tell them your idea."

"That's okay," she said. "You tell them. It's not much of a solution, just something that might work for now."

I gave everyone the rundown on what Meredith and I had talked about the other night. Partitioning the space, finishing the front, leaving the back as it was. Focusing on what was actually possible.

"I can't believe none of us ever thought of that," Steven said. "That could work."

"I don't see why not, man," Joey said. "Doesn't have to look perfect, as long as we can hang some paintings up."

"It won't have any merit," said Bradley. "No one will give a shit if you have a show at a gallery you opened up on your own. You might as well hang them in your grandmother's living room."

"Yeah, but who cares," I said. "You saw where merit gets you. What's ultimately important?"

"You'll never pull it off," said Bradley.

"Don't be so defeated," said Meredith. "It seems to me you're spending so much time down in the mouth when you could just buck up and do it. Quit being such a pussy."

Bradley fell silent.

"We have to at least give it a shot," I said.

"Count me in," Joey said.

"You're right," Steven said. "Let's do it."

Throughout the ride home, we hashed it all out, belief systems were solidified, new meaning was found, a vindication in the space of defeat. By the time we rolled into town, we were all convinced that we could open the gallery and make it work.

# Sculpture

By the time we pulled the van up to the front of the gallery, it was around 4 in the morning. The speed had dropped off, but we still had plenty of energy. Invigorated by the new idea, the new plan.

We piled out of the van and onto the sidewalk. Steven unlocked the door to the gallery. The street was quiet and empty. I looked at the painted-over window that masked the gallery and wondered how different it would look from the outside once it was cleared and you could see in.

We went inside and pulled out extension cords and all the shop lights we could find. Every corner was lit up. We looked around the enormity of what lay ahead. Mounds and mounds of dirt and scrap. Wine bottles and trash and cigarette butts. Every bit of the place cluttered with something.

The mutt came into the gallery with Pederson, circled a few times but never laid down. Pederson grabbed some scrap lumber and built a raised bed, an oversized plinth made out of gallery refuse. He laid a paint-stained dropcloth over the top, a couple of feet above the floor. The dog jumped up onto it, circled a couple of times, and settled in, keeping watch as the rest of us went to work.

We all pitched in, even Bradley. Pederson took up a shovel and scooped into one of the mounds, lifting out a heap of rubble and tossing it as far back into the gallery as he could. It cascaded down the top of another pile, sending a cloud of dirt into the air. The subtraction of medium began.

We divided the good from the bad, pushing everything back as far as possible and claiming the front half. Steven finished breaking the plaster off the old brick. Meredith and I started hauling the rubble back, sweating, working hard. She was invested in the idea the same way I became invested, wanting to see it happen. We were certain that we would have an opening, and this was the way to do it. Pederson was still picking up one shovelful at a time and hurling it toward the back wall. The shop lights gave off a diffused, ambient glow through the cloud of dust filling the back half of the gallery as we worked into the morning.

We stepped outside just before dawn to take a break, get out of the gallery for a minute. We had already made a lot of progress. It was starting to take shape in our minds.

"Once we get this front half cleared, we'll have to fix it up," Steven said, lighting a cigarette. "We need wood, drywall, paint, fixtures, everything. We need money."

I was burning to get this thing started, to somehow make the space decent enough to call it a gallery.

"I can get the materials," I said.

"Is there another job site we could pilfer?" Steven asked.

"Sort of. I'll take the van and pick up a few things."

"I'll go with you," Meredith said. Steven tossed me the keys to the company van, and the two of us left while the others went back inside to keep chipping away at the gallery.

# Golden Hour

Meredith and I took the van as the sun was coming up and the hardware stores were opening. First, I had to make one stop. I pulled up to the front of my apartment building.

"What are we doing here?" she asked.

"I have to grab something at my place real quick," I said. "You wanna come in?"

"Sure." She followed me inside.

I went over to the box in the corner and pulled out the copy of *Ulysses*. Meredith walked around, taking in the state of my apartment.

"This is where you live? There's hardly anything in here." She tried flipping the light switch, but nothing came on. "I think your power is out."

"Yeah, I forgot to pay it. I don't spend much time here." I pulled a few bills out of the middle of the book, the money I had saved. The stack had gotten smaller over the last six months, dissipated through rent and booze and cigarettes. All out, no in.

Meredith walked over to the window, pulled up the blinds, letting in more light. "I can see why. This place is desolate. You're not moving, are you?" she asked, noticing that most everything was in boxes. I hadn't bothered to unpack anything I didn't need.

I stuffed the bills into the pocket of my Carhartts. "I was thinking about it, but—"

"No, you can't move," she said.

Surprised at how quickly she said it, I put the book back into the box and walked over to Meredith. "Why not?" I asked. I wanted her to show more of her hand. I was standing in front of her, silhouette outlined by the golden-hour light coming through the window.

"Because—" she started to say. I waited for her to finish, admiring the rim of light around her, picking up the loose strands in her thick, brown hair. She was the most incredible woman imaginable, and the most unattainable.

"Because...?" I moved close enough to smell the mixture of soap and sweat.

"Because...I don't want you to."

I reached out and put my hand on her side. Pulled her closer. She didn't kiss back at first, her hands between us in fists. Then she let herself go, her mouth softened along with her hands on my chest, the weight of what was happening almost toppling me.

It was only a moment, brief and everlasting as a snapshot, when it could have escalated, before she grabbed hold of my shirt, pulled back.

"No, I can't," she said.

"What's wrong?" I asked.

"I don't get involved, remember?" She pushed me away and swung open the apartment door to the hallway.

"Come on," She looked back. She was smiling. "Let's pick this stuff up so we can get back to work."

# Artless

I carried a round of whiskey to the back corner of Pat's Place, where everyone was sitting around the table. We hadn't slept much and were exhausted after working on the gallery all day. We'd been at it for over a week, and it was coming along, but there was still a lot to be done.

"The *Telegraph* article will help get the word out for the opening," I said. "I'm turning it in tomorrow, so it should run in the next issue."

"You've done it now," said Bradley. "Before you only had to be failures in each other's eyes. Now you're gonna let the public watch it burn down."

"This is a good idea Bradley," I said. "We spend all this time sitting around the gallery drinking and talking about all these possibilities and not doing anything about it. Now we're doing something."

"Who's gonna hang for the opening?" asked Bradley. "I'm sure as fuck not putting any of my paintings up there."

"Joey's art is chaotic and destructive," Meredith said. "It seems like this gallery is the perfect backdrop for his work."

We all looked to Joey, sitting at the end of the table.

"What's everyone looking at, man?" asked Joey. "You guys want me to put some painting in there? I can do that. Just make sure no one fucks with them."

"We're actually pulling it off," Steven said, surprised, even getting a little excited. "I never thought this day would come."

"It's happening," I said. "When this article goes to print, there will be an opening date set. That should give us a few more days to finish up. There's one last thing I need for the article: a name for the place."

Everyone thought about that for a second. Until now it was just "the gallery." It hadn't occurred to any of us to give it a real title. I pulled out a pen and small notebook.

"Any ideas?" I asked. "We have to come up with something to put in the paper."

We all started pitching out ideas, but no one could agree on any of them. There was always something wrong. Too cliche, too pretentious, too whatever.

Meredith was sitting quietly the whole time, not giving any ideas and not shooting any down. The rest of us kept going back and forth, deliberating, getting nowhere. Every time I wrote a name down, it was immediately scribbled out.

"Come on, we're not naming a child here," I said, slightly frustrated. "It's an art gallery. Every name we come up with is gonna sound pretentious to someone."

"Maybe we shouldn't name it at all," Joey suggested. "Let it be nothing. I don't know."

The table was quiet. I tapped my pen against the page, now full of ink scratches.

"Hey, wait a minute," Meredith finally spoke up. "I think Joey's onto something."

"What do you mean?" I asked. "You want to call it nothing?"

"No, but what about Artless?"

Bradley immediately started laughing at her. "That's rich, I love it. It captures the fact that the gallery doesn't produce a damn bit of art."

Meredith got up and walked over to Arvin's dusty bookshelves, pulled a fat dictionary down and strolled confidently back. She opened it up and flipped through the A's, then let the book drop heavily onto Bradley's lap. He looked down and read the definition aloud.

> **art·less** |ärt-lis| *adjective* **1**: without guile, cunning, or deception; genuine **2**: without artifice or pretension; natural; simple **3**: without knowledge or craft **4**: without art

"We've always said the only thing that mattered was being genuine, right?" Meredith reminded us.

"It does say *without art*," Bradley said.

"Well, that's also part of the gallery," Steven said. "That's something we've been struggling with, so it makes sense to let it exist as part of the name. What do you guys think?"

"Sounds cool to me, man," Joey shrugged. "I don't have any real knowledge or craft anyway. None of us do. We're just figuring it out as we go."

"I like it," I said. "Here are things that don't get accepted as art, so call it Artless."

Steven raised his glass. "Okay then, we'll call it Artless." Everyone raised their glass in agreement. Meredith didn't make eye contact as we tapped our drinks together. I leaned back in my chair and watched as she tilted her head, fluid and confident, draining the last of her whiskey.

Artless. Being genuine, simple, straightforward. And besides, there were some days we spent so much time drinking and playing music and having long bouts of conversation and just existing in that moment, that we didn't always produce anything tangible. We all agreed, the gallery had a name, and we could go home and get some sleep.

# Above the Fold

I went down to the office of the *Telegraph*, carrying the mess of pages I had written about the gallery. I walked in the door and knew right away something was off. The drafting tables were missing. The main room was now open and empty. In one corner there were three tall, skinny computer towers, rows of lights blinking at random, a low, steady fan motor humming quietly. Scott was sitting in the easy chair, chewing on a cigar, reading the *Post*. I walked over to him, buzzing, excited.

"I have the story! I finished it!" I held it out to him.

"You can give that to Peter now," he said languidly. " He's our new layout man. He's in the back. We cleared out an office for him."

I walked down the hall. In the new office was a younger guy wearing a loosened tie, dark-rimmed glasses, staring at a new Mac computer screen. I took the crumpled pages and tried to smooth them out on my leg, then handed them to him.

"Here you go," I said, still confused. He took the pages, pinched and held them in the air like a dirty dishtowel. "Scott told me to give this to you. It's for the next issue."

"Got it," he nodded dismissively and laid them aside, turned back to the computer, hitting a rapid succession of keyboard shortcuts, toggling the screen from one program to the next.

I went back to the main room. Scott was still sitting there, squinting at the *Post* and fellating his cigar.

"What's going on?" I asked. "Where's Gary?"

"Times are changing around here. Peter back there is the new order. He's a web developer. We're shifting the whole paper online."

"Really? I thought this paper was insulated from the change?"

"Yeah, I thought we'd be able to hold out, too. But we've been having a hard time getting new advertisers, and the old ones are dropping off steadily. We're cutting all the overhead of printing and distribution and going digital."

"What about the revenue? Gary was saying how small the price of online advertising was compared to print. How are they gonna pay your salaries? Along with this new guy, Peter?"

"We're not paying my salary anymore, I'm stepping back. That'll go to Pete. And with the drop in print revenue comes the drop in print costs. Now we just have to make rent and keep those boxes over there in the corner purring." We both looked over to the towers of bits and bytes, thrumming and blinking in little patterns of green dots. A random, clustering illusion.

"But you started this paper. How could they let you go?"

"Relax, it was my idea. I'm ready to be finished with this business. I've been doing it for 38 years, and I've enjoyed it. But I've outlived my usefulness. The future is online. I am the past, and I'm tired."

I sat down with Scott and lit a cigarette, still taking it all in. "So no more tangible, smellable copy of the *Telegraph*. That's hard to imagine. I really like having the hard copy every week. It gives me some sense of accomplishment."

"Well, you've got one more print issue, then everything goes online, and I am officially retired." Scott said. "I'll make sure your gallery article is included. I'll even put it on the front page, above the fold."

# Copy

**HED:** COUNTDOWN TO ARTLESS GALLERY
**DEK:** New creative space opening on High Street
**BYLINE:** Story by Mark Bernard Steck

**LEDE:** On a walk through the downtown area you may not have noticed an obscure window on High Street, opaque with black paint and poetry. Behind that window is a skeleton of rough framework upon which an art gallery is being built.

**BODY:** A small group of locals have banded together to create Artless, a space for showcasing original work. "It's taken a long time," said Steven Carrel, "but there is no funding, and all the work is being done out of passion, by the people involved, doing the grunt labor to make it happen." Carrel originally acquired the space after it had been left abandoned for years, and the electricity of people drawing together has convinced them that the gallery will come to fruition.

When asked how this came about, Carrel said the initial goal was to have a studio space to work on projects. Over time, they decided to open to the public. "It all goes back to the people involved and what they want to express," says Carrel. "There's an undercurrent of talent in this town, and there's no connection to any established institutions, so you're free to do anything you want."

When the doors open you will find several mediums in one place. "There's a lot of different skills represented," says Carrel, "not just painting, but also music, photography, writing, anything." There are plans to build a stage for music and spoken word and to install a projector for viewing independent films. There are also plans to explore other things, such as culinary work. The idea, according to Carrel, is to set up long tables and host harvest-style meals that are open to the public. "Food is something simple we create everyday," says Carrel. "It's one of the great reasons to bring people together."

One prominent idea behind Artless is that it's more than displaying something tangible. It's about people connecting and celebrating the dialogue of questioning. In that sense the gallery is already happening as more people have come together. "The only thing we ask of anyone and of ourselves is to be genuine in whatever we're trying to do," says Carrel.

More and more of these individuals are coming out of the woodwork every day, reaffirming the nucleus of art. The actual space is merely a backdrop to the community of inspiration.

The building is still being renovated, but will be opened as a work-in-progress. A canvas will be stretched over a floor to ceiling partition and painted by Joey Wagner, part of his first show, *Monsters and Angels.*

This Fourth of July weekend the doors will be open to expose the efforts within: a group of people trying to create something aesthetic, something genuine, and share it with the public.

# Primed

The day the article went to print, I walked into the gallery with a dozen copies of the paper and spread them out on the table. The opening was set. It was official.

"What you have in your hands is the last printed issue of the *Telegraph*," I said.

Everyone took one and started reading through the article.

"Front page, nice work," Meredith said.

"What's this about me painting a partition wall?" Joey asked, reading the article.

"Oh yeah, forgot to tell you," Steven said. We're gonna partition this with a giant canvas, wall to wall, floor to ceiling. That makes it about 15 feet tall and 30 feet wide. We'll build the stretcher in place."

"Holy shit. You want me to paint it in here?"

"Think you can do it?"

"Sure, I'll try. That's gonna take a lot."

"Pick out the colors and we can get you some paint," I said. "We'll all help do the underpainting, and you can finish it."

"Joey's the painter, he doesn't need our help," Bradley said.

"It's cool, man," Joey said. "I never collaborated on a painting before."

We jumped in the van and went to the hardware store to get 50 yards of drop cloth, ten gallons of paint, a few light fixtures, an OPEN sign and a few bottles of wine to get us through the night.

Steven walked up to the cart with a pack of expensive carbon drill bits to anchor the wall into the brick. He carefully wrapped them up inside the drop cloth and put it in the cart.

"Gift sale," he said, grinning at me.

"Too bad the drop cloth isn't included," I said.

"Guess you have to spend money to make money."

"I think that's everything," I said. "Where's Joey?"

"He's in the paint section."

We found him standing in front of the paint counter, hypnotized by the machine as it mixed the different colors.

"Look at this, man!" Joey said when he saw us. "They have a new color." He held up a sample. "Look at this red!"

"Yeah Joey, let's go," Steven said.

I paid for the supplies, and we went back to the gallery.

We built a simple framed wall across the middle and stretched the drop cloth over it. We all helped prime the canvas, put some fans on to dry it quickly. Then everyone started painting, going off in their own direction on the portion of canvas in front of them. Everyone but Bradley, who sat at the table watching.

Joey approached it timidly at first, his every movement expressing a native terror. He had never painted out in the open before. Only in the biosphere at his house, with all the windows covered and the door closed.

Bradley got up from the table, walked over and turned the CD player on, putting in a Violent Femmes album and turning the volume to full blast. Then went and sat back down. Joey slowly came out of the stupor that he had been put in by the sheer volume of the canvas. Now he started to move a little faster. Still just methodically covering area with paint. The music seeped into him, and he started moving even faster, more erratically. He popped open the lids on every can of paint and shoved a brush inside. Before long, he was channeling something supernatural.

The rest of us stepped back and let Joey take over. He dove into one paint can and removed the brush, color pouring down his hand, attacking the canvas. This was the difference between taking paint out of a gallon versus the bottle or tube, having all that mass. He climbed to the top of the ladder, painted, climbed down, moved the ladder. Doing ancient pictographs in primitive reds, yellows, blues. Working the giant canvas with the blind precision of a skywriter. Angels, demons, monsters, all swirling in a parable of color. Joey kept going, going, without pause, the electricity streaming out from an underground store of crude energy. The motor of war.

Finally, he baptized the painting from a ladder with crimson paint, letting it flow down until it dried in place. A superfluous stream of extra color, a thing he liked to call "Excessivism." Like putting sugar on fruit.

He climbed down off the ladder and walked over to the corner to sign the painting in his simple signature: JOEY. It was finished.

"Wait," said Meredith. "Now how do we get through? We just cut off our only access to the back of the building." We all stared at the maddening image on the canvas.

"I guess we'll have to walk around to the alley to get in through the back door," I said.

Steven walked up to the canvas, pulled out a pocket knife.

"What the fuck are you doing?" Bradley jumped up quickly. "Don't—"

Before he could finish, Steven made two vertical slits in the lower left corner and one slit across the bottom.

"Sorry, Joey," Steven said. "It was necessary." Joey shrugged.

Now there was a door-sized flap that we could pass through to the other side, a nexus between the public eye and the private reality that still lay beyond.

# Opening

On the day of the opening, the partition wall was completed. Lights were rigged up. Meredith, Bradley, Pederson, and I were cleaning up the last of the mess. The walls and floor were unfinished but clean. It almost looked intentional.

"There's only one thing left to do," Meredith said. "The window."

The layers of painted words still covered the glass, shrouding the gallery from the street. We all grabbed knives and razor scrapers and together we peeled back the paint, giving a clear view into the viscera of the space. We were finished. Behind the giant canvas partition there were still cairns of raw material. But you couldn't tell, walking in the door.

"We need booze and snacks," said Bradley. "You have to have something for the reception. Does anyone have cash?"

I opened my wallet and pulled out the remaining bills. I had been buying supplies over the last couple of weeks as we fixed up the space, spending the rest of my savings without thinking about it. It was gone, all of it.

I tossed what was left onto the table. Around 40 dollars. "That's what I have," I said.

"I have a few bucks," Meredith said, tossing more on the table.

Bradley added a little of his own. "That might be enough."

The three of us walked to Tolson's. Bradley picked out some food while Meredith and I went to the coolers and pulled out every type of cheap twelve pack they had, filling the cart with a rainbow of slug beer.

When we got back to the gallery, there was a car parked on the curb outside. Joey was standing on the sidewalk, wearing a bright red tracksuit. Carly was sitting in the passenger seat of the car. When we walked up we could feel the tension, both of them silently staring at each other.

"What's going on, Joey?" I asked.

"Joey doesn't want me to hang my paintings with his!" she yelled out the window. "We're supposed to be a team! A pair!"

"I just told her it wasn't up to me, man. You said you wanted me to hang my paintings so I'm hanging them."

Carly glared hawkishly at us. I could see her digging her nails into her arms inside the car. Clawing at some invisible sore, breaking the skin in places, exposing blood. Joey lit a cigarette.

"Give me one of those," she snarled. "We both have to smoke at the same time so we can die with each other, you coward."

He pulled another cigarette out and handed it to her.

"I'll go in there and cut every one of your paintings into ribbons, Joey." She lit her cigarette and took three nervous drags in a row, puffing the smoke out the window.

"You're not gonna do that," Bradley said. "You don't have the sand."

"Oh no? You don't think I will! Fuck you Bradley!" She went for the door handle, then hesitated, let go of it. "Ahh!" She clawed at her arm again. "Fuck all of you!" She slid over to the drivers seat and fired up the engine, peeling out into the street.

"Would she really do that?" Meredith asked.

"I don't think so. She's always saying that, but she never does it. She'll hold a knife to one of my canvases and threaten to cut it, but she always ends up running into her own studio and slashing at one of her paintings instead. That's probably what she's gonna do right now. I don't know what to do, man." Joey was rubbing the back of his neck, hanging his head in sadness.

"Come on Joey, let's get inside," Bradley said. He put his arm around Joey's and they headed for the door.

"What's with the outfit, anyway?" Bradley asked.

"I figured I should wear a suit, man. For the big opening."

We brought Joey into the gallery and tried to distract him, had him hang his work as we set up the last of it. I looked over at one point and Joey was standing in front of the brick wall holding one of his canvases, medicated stare, unsure what to do. He looked at the painting, then picked up a hammer and tried swinging it ineffectually. Like nailing jelly to the wall.

Pederson walked over and gently moved Joey aside, taking up the hammer. Joey stood by while Pederson hung the painting on the wall for him. They went around hanging the rest of them in the spots where Joey pointed.

I dumped the beers into a big concrete mixing tub and covered it over with ice. Bradley was carefully cutting up hot dogs into thin slices and topping them with a single crumble of bleu cheese, skewering them together with a toothpick.

"That's disgusting," Meredith said as she watched him slide the toothpicks in.

"No one cares about the food anyway." Bradley thought it was hilarious, cracking himself up every time he jammed in another toothpick.

The plinth Pederson had made was set in the front window, chair on top, to be a stage for Steven to play music. No one had seen or heard from him, but it was still early.

We all cracked open a can of Stag from the mixing tub.

"We may have actually pulled it off," Bradley said. "I'm a little surprised."

"I thought there was gonna be music," Joey said.

"Yeah, where's Steven?" Meredith asked.

"I doubt he shows up," Bradley said, putting the last hors d'oeuvres together.

"He's still coming," I said. "I'm sure he'll be here."

It was quiet inside. We were all shuffling around. Waiting for something to happen. Pederson went over to the table, ate a hot dog off the toothpick, then set it back down with the crumble of cheese still speared.

"Now where are all the people?" Joey asked.

The paintings were all up, everything was finally finished. The article was out there. On top of that Joey had printed off a stack of flyers at Kinko's that we'd plastered all over town. So where was everyone?

# Monsters and Angels

All around the gallery were cans of beer cracking, music loud, cigarette smoke rising in the room, the whole place alive. The opening was happening. Once the first few people had come through the door, it didn't take long before others followed. The crowd drawn by the crowd. Now the divided front half of the gallery was barely big enough to hold everyone.

    I stood in the back, below the enormous canvas, taking it all in. People talking, laughing, telling Joey how they loved his paintings, his style. Joey looked a little anxious in the limelight, but Bradley was there by his side, taking the edge off, filling in the conversation when Joey became uncomfortable. His bright red tracksuit contradicting his desire for anonymity. Meredith was by the door, welcoming people as they came in. The monsters and angels on every canvas loomed over the room, the entire back wall covered in bright acrylics. Steven hadn't shown, so we rotated through a few of the CDs we had lying around.

I lit a cigarette, enjoyed being outside the conversation for a bit, observing the scene. Relishing that we actually did it. After all this time, we opened the gallery.

A couple more new people came up, asking questions. I showed them around, telling them about the gallery, talking about all the things we planned to do. Brought them to the studio upstairs, the darkroom below.

"I can't believe it," one of them said. "This space is incredible."

"So how you guys running it?" the other asked. "Are you gonna let other people show here?"

"Of course," I said. "It's always been kind of an open source project, and now we're officially open to the public."

"Cool, I'll bring in my slides, you can see if my paintings work for this gallery."

"Just come by next week and hang out," I said. "And bring a few of the actual paintings with you."

When he walked off his face was lit up with thrill and confusion and expectation, and I could feel it too, remembering what it was like when I first found the building.

I saw Garner come through the door, passing by Meredith without acknowledging her. She walked around, looking at Joey's work. Taisir came in too, bringing in a carafe of Rocket Fuel and the remaining baked goods from Coffee Zone. Even John, the landlord, showed up. I had rarely seen him over the last few months. He took a quick lap, glancing at the art.

"Hey John," I said to him. "What do you think of the place? We've put a lot into it lately."

"It's looking a little better in here," he said to me. "At least you got rid of the piles of shit everywhere. What's going on with this wall, though? How are you supposed to get through now?"

"Uh, right here," I said, reluctantly pushing the door flap open in the canvas. "We're still working on the back half."

He poked his head through and saw the displacement of material waste on the other side.

"What a mess," he said. "Listen, the deal was, you work on the space, you don't have to pay rent. But you need to work on the space, not just tear shit out and push it around."

"We will," I promised. "Now that we're open, we'll be doing all kinds of work."

Bradley walked up, handed me a Stag. "Hey John. You made it for the opening. Check it out, we've got a packed house."

"Hmm." He looked around at the gathering, mostly young blades, alternative styles, the sort of crowd he probably never expected to take over there. By this point in the night, cigarette butts littered the floor again. Empty beer cans accumulating on every surface.

"What the hell is wrong with that guy?" John asked. "Is he alright?" He was looking over at Pederson, passed out in the corner at the base of Joey's enormous painting.

"Stendhal syndrome," Bradley said. John glared at him, sensing the sarcasm. "Don't worry," he added. "It's not contagious."

"And why the fuck is there a dog in here?" The mutt was over by the table, lapping up a pool of spilled beer.

I changed the subject, tried to talk to him about our plans, ease him a little. Bradley walked away, leaving me hanging. "…and we've got a working darkroom in the basement, and we'll build a stage in the front for live music—"

"Yeah, that's all well and good. But what about the building? Steven and I talked about what needed to be done here. Where's he at, anyway?"

"He's…uh…" I looked around as if I would spot him.

Garner came up and interrupted our conversation.

"Wonderful show. Really, I'm very impressed," she said warmly. "You've managed to get it open after all. It's nice to have more art in the downtown."

"Thanks," I said.

"I was worried about you guys being able to pull it off, but here you are." She looked around the room. "I like the look of the place. Very…primal."

"It's getting there," I said.

"Of course it is." She turned to John. "I'm sorry, we haven't been introduced. I'm Garner, head of the Arts Coalition."

"John," he said, shaking her bony hand. "I own the building."

"Really? You don't say."

A guy came stumbling up, eyes looking sickly. "Bathroom," he said with alarm. "Need a bathroom."

"That way," I said, pointing to the basement stairs. He stumbled off.

"Interesting crowd you've got here," Garner said.

I looked over, the drunk veered the wrong way, went to the flap cut in the canvas and pushed his way through.

"Is he supposed to be going back there?" John asked. A crashing thud, body falling into one the piles in the back. John looked at me with liable eyes.

"Hold on," I said. "I'll take care of it." I rushed over and through the flap.

"What the fuck are you doing?" I hissed. "Bathroom's downstairs."

"Ugggg. Feel sick," he groaned.

"Get up! You can't be back here."

I tried pulling him up. Dead weight. I could still barely hear Garner and the landlord talking on the other side of the scrim.

"So you're the landlord, huh…venture capitalist, more like it, taking a risk on a group like this—" Garner was saying.

"Well," I heard John say. "It's not exactly…we had this arrangement—"

"Eeeeee," the drunk moaned. "Something poking my spine…can't move." Somehow he'd fallen over the back of one of the piles of debris, feet up top, torso jammed between some old boards.

"Goddammit, get your shit together. This is not the time!"

"Mmmm…great time, having a great time. This place…uggggg…place is awesome."

"Shut the fuck up!" I hissed through clenched teeth. "Come on. Up!" I planted a foot on something solid, put a hand under his shoulder to hoist him. Still trying to make out Garner and John's voices from the crowd, hear what they were saying, overwhelmed on all sides by the cocktail problem.

"Owwww."

"Shhh! Quiet!" I paused, straining. I could barely overhear Garner.

"…very philanthropic…just giving it away like that…letting them do whatever they want…even had the fire department called on them, so I hear…"

I looked over at the canvas, the light coming through to the back, casting a large silhouette negative of monsters and angels.

"...that's right..." John said. "...just a kind of oral agreement...no...:nothing binding..."

I had to get back in there, before everything fell apart. But I was trapped in the back, dealing with the drunk, piles all around, how the gallery had always been.

"Uhhhhoooohh." I looked down just in time to see it happen, gut heaving, vomit popping out of him, adding to the pile, a little splattering onto my shoe.

"Goddammit," I said, watching the vomit soak into his shirt.

"Mmmmm sorry, man. Fuck, sorry."

This time I yanked him up, grabbed his collar to steady him, trying not to touch the saturated circle on his chest. "Come on, let's go."

I led him out through the back door and into the alley, roughly tugging him back up every time he was about to trip.

When we got outside I leaned him against the brick wall.

"Chill man...shit...thought you guys were cool..." he said, eyes still half closed.

"Listen, I'm sorry," I said. "You alright? How you feeling?"

"Just need...need to rest a minute."

"Here." I opened the side door of the gallery van, helping him in, where he immediately collapsed onto the bench seat. "Just lay down, you'll be fine."

"Don't leave me out here," he pleaded, cheek pressed against the seat.

"I'll be back in a minute, I promise. I'll give you a ride later if you need. Just stay here."

"Cool, thanks."

"You sure you're alright?"

He didn't answer, just passed out. I pushed his feet clear of the door and gently slid it shut. Then hurried back into the gallery, through all the scree piles, through the flap.

As I walked up, Garner turned, gave me a slight, conquering smile, then looked back to John.

"Come by my office in the morning." She handed him a thick, monogrammed card. "We'll draw up the paperwork." She walked away.

"What just happened there? What did she want?"

"Sorry kid, I got bills to pay."

"What does that mean?"

"Look, I get it, I'm not against art, but this just isn't what I had in mind. I know you guys are trying, but really, how long do you think this could last?"

"I don't understand. We're working on it. We're getting there."

"Sorry, I'm not a philanthropist, I'm a businessman." He turned and walked out of the gallery.

# Implosion

A big, deep explosion boomed over the gallery, an unexpected blow you could feel in your solar plexus. It cracked open with a shower of sparks as the street was lit up in a cloudburst of multicolored light.

"Fireworks!" someone shouted. "They're starting!"

"Let's head up to the roof!" Meredith shouted. "We can watch from there!" She led the charge upstairs.

Everyone rushed up and out onto the fire escape that led to the roof. Pederson woke up, saw the commotion, immediately hoisted the tub full of beer and shouldered it up the stairs.

As people were filtering out, Steven finally showed up, walking through the front door with a borrowed guitar. He set it down in the front, grabbed a Stag, and lit a smoke.

"Holy shit," he said. "Where'd all these people come from?"

"Where have you been?" I asked.

"It's fine, I got hung up. Looks like I made it in time for the fireworks though," he said nonchalantly. "How was the opening?" Another explosion. You couldn't see the sky, just the afterglow as it cracked into little clusters of reds, blues, oranges.

"Listen, I need to talk to you," I said to Steven. "Some shit just went down." More people were rushing past us and up the stairs.

"Tell me on the roof," he said, then grabbed his guitar and followed everyone up.

"Hey, Bradley," I said as he hurried past.

"Yeah, come on!" he called back as he and Joey both disappeared with the rest of the crowd. They were the last ones up the stairs, trailing the whole circus to the rooftop, and I was left standing alone in the empty gallery.

I went over to the front door, put my key in and locked it. Then went upstairs and out onto the fire escape. When I climbed over the ledge onto the roof Meredith was there and she instantly grabbed my hand. "There you are!"

"Hey, we need to talk, I think we have a problem—" Explosions of fire interrupting, building into a crescendo, but they were blocked by the much taller bank building across the street, leaving a corona of color around the skyline, giving it an eerie effect, like the whole town was being firebombed.

"What did you say?" she asked, leaning in close.

"We need to talk," I said. "I don't know what just happened, but—"

"We pulled it off! Can you believe it? It couldn't have gone any better."

"I know, but there's something—"

"And now we have this." She took my hand, looked to the sky, smile illuminated in fire, unadulterated happiness. "It's perfect. Everything about it. Tonight is perfect."

She was right. There was nothing I could say to ruin that. I didn't even know what happened, but I knew it was bad and that it was coming. But not tonight, tonight would remain perfect.

I erased everything from my mind. No point in bringing it up now. We were all irrigated with the drink and feeling good, and I wanted to keep it that way as long as possible. Fireworks continued to explode above, punctuating the night.

Steven pulled his guitar out, playing the set he was supposed to perform at the opening. All of his songs were finished now. This was the first time I had heard them together, realizing that he now had a whole career of music in the ready.

Regardless of how the opening went, we were all together. Bradley standing on the ledge of the building leaning out over the street as far as he could without falling. Pederson stomping on the asphalt to the music, making the whole building a percussive instrument, trying to bring it to ground level under his shaking blond hair. Joey laying back with his arms stretched out, waving snow angels in the gravely roof, watching the harlequins of fire burst out from around the buildings with every explosion. Meredith and I spinning each other around to the music, the sun's stored heat in the asphalt radiating up between us, intoxicating, spinning around and around as the rest of the world imploded into the two of us. Energy becoming matter. Synchronous rotation of the moon. Planets wheeling in the sky. The fireworks popping and fizzling into thin air above us.

# Fogged

When I woke up, the sun was just breaking. I sat up, looked around, not recognizing my surroundings at first, a drunken haze still hovering in my brain. The end of last night a sort of rolling blackout.

I looked over. She was lying next to me, tangled up like blankets in the morning. Sheets in angles across her navel. Thigh exposed. Legs bent. Fingers curled between her breasts. Eyes closed. I put my arm over her and drifted back into sleep.

The next time I woke up I was alone, the sun now higher and beating through the window. I lifted my heavy head off the pillow.

"You're awake," Meredith said. "Coffee?"

"Sure."

Meredith was on the other side of the half-wall in her small studio apartment. She had on a t-shirt, hair pulled back. She filled a kettle and put it on the stove.

The apartment was clean and well lit from the tall windows lining one wall. The wall opposite was filled with books, lots of books, shelves reaching the top of the high-ceilinged room. I threw my feet over the edge of the bed and looked around for my clothes. I found my pants by the door and pulled them on. My shirt was on the other side of the apartment near the bathroom.

I walked up to the shelves. There were several unframed 5x7 prints leaning against the books. Some were hers. Others were reprints of the photographers she always talked about. The one directly in front of me was neither. A family photo. What looked like a vacation somewhere on the East Coast, rocky surf in the background. Meredith never spoke much about her family, and I was beginning to think she didn't really have one.

"Cape Cod," Meredith said, watching me from the kitchen. "That's where my parents live. The one next to it is the house where I grew up."

The house in the next picture was enormous, old, the money that bought it must have been just as old. A wealthy family stood in front, a younger Meredith among them.

"I didn't know you were from there. How did you end up here, anyway? Usually people move out of the Midwest, not into it." I walked into the kitchen and sat down in one of the two bent plywood chairs at the small table, watching her fill a little two-cup French press with hot water and coffee grounds, her t-shirt not quite long enough to hide the smiling creases above her thighs.

"Journalism school. My parents wanted me to go to Columbia University, because that's where they went. I wanted to do something different, so I went to the University of Missouri instead."

She set the French press on the table, went back, and opened her cabinet to a sparse collection of dishes. Pulled out the only two coffee cups and brought them over, sat down across from me. "So my parents basically cut me off from any kind of support. Which is fine, I prefer it that way. After I got my degree, I decided to stick around for a while. It's cheaper to live here, so I can spend more time focusing on photography. It doesn't really matter to me where I am. At least, not for now."

"What do you mean, for now?" I asked. "You're not sticking around?" I took a deep inhale, holding in the clean smell of citrus and vinegar of the apartment.

"Not forever, no. What about you? I thought you weren't staying either."

"I don't know, at one point my mind was made up and I had everything ready to go. But things have changed recently."

"Yeah, we have a good thing going here." She slowly pushed the plunger down on the press. Filled the two cups. Slid one over to me.

"Thanks," I said.

"Listen, about last night—" She started, but hesitated.

"Yeah?" I took a sip of my coffee, waiting.

"It's just…you're the first person—"

Her phone started vibrating on the kitchen counter.

"Hold on, let me get this." She stood up, answered the call, listening for a minute. "What the fuck. Are you serious?" she spoke into the phone, then put it to her shoulder. "It's Steven," she said. "There's something wrong. He thinks we might have just lost the gallery. We need to meet them down there right now."

Everything halted as the events of the opening night came flooding back to me, the conversation I'd forgotten with Garner and John leaked in, corrupted the morning, the image of Meredith and I together, fogged before it had a chance to develop.

# Requiem

It was a long, heart-sinking walk to the gallery. Streets still littered in the red, white, and blue holiday aftermath. Meredith kept speculating out loud, trying to figure out what was going on. I didn't say much. She didn't know what was coming, but I knew.

When we walked in there was a pall hanging over the gallery. Everyone downcast, circling toes on the floor. Joey's monsters and angels still girding the barren, stale-smelling room.

Steven brought us up to speed.

"So did he say why?" Meredith asked. "Why now, after all this time, does the landlord decide he's gonna start charging rent?"

"He said there was someone else interested in fixing the place up," Steven said.

"Too bad," Meredith said. "This is ours. We put all the work into it."

"Someone told him they would pay rent *and* do the renovations, and we aren't paying him anything. It's simple math, for him."

"How much are they paying?" asked Joey. "Maybe we could come up with it."

"I could sell some of my equipment," Meredith said. "I have some old cameras that are worth quite a bit."

"And last night went pretty good," Joey said. "Soon we'll be selling paintings, right? We can pay rent with that."

"The new tenant already signed a lease and paid three months in advance," Steven said.

"But don't we have an agreement?" Bradley asked.

"Not really," Steven said. "Just something we talked about."

"He can't do this. There has to be some legal reason he can't do this," said Bradley. "It isn't right that he can just kick us out. There has to be something we can do."

"Funny that you should be so concerned," Meredith said. "I thought you were the one that didn't want anything to do with it?"

"Yeah, well, I just don't know what you animals are gonna do if they open the zoo, that's all." Bradley said.

"Let's think, what can we do?" Meredith asked.

"How about we stage a sit-in until they have to forcibly remove us," Bradley said. "Squatters rights. As long as one of us is here all the time, they can't do anything." He went over to the tub of remaining beer from the opening, pulled a Stag out of the lukewarm pool of water, cracked it open, and sat down in the front window. "I'm not fucking leaving."

Steven cracked open a beer and sat at the table next to him. "Sure, squatting might buy us a little time, at least."

"That's your solution? To sit here and drink until they come drag you out?" Meredith asked.

"You got any better ideas?" Joey asked, then cracked open a beer and sat down too.

"Fuck this. Fuck John, and whoever this person is. They have no idea what we have here, what they're doing to us." Meredith said.

"Who is it, anyway?" Joey asked.

"I don't know," Steven said. "John wouldn't say. I guess they didn't want it to be known."

"Garner." I finally spoke up. Everyone looked at me.

"How do you know?" Steven asked.

"I overheard her last night," I said. "She was talking to John about it."

"What the fuck?" Meredith snapped. "You mean you knew about this? Why didn't you say anything?"

"I tried to, but—"

"Why didn't you try and stop it?" Bradley asked.

"I didn't know what—" Heavy silence. Pressure change in the room. "I wasn't sure what was happening...there was so much going on...I had a lot to deal with, you don't understand—"

"Yeah, man. Maybe we could have reasoned with him, tried to work something out," Joey said. "*Before* the lease was signed."

Everyone's eyes aimed at me. I didn't know how to explain. Everything tensed up, choking with accusation. I needed air. "I have to go...I need to do something...I'll be right back—"

"What? You're gonna leave? Right now?" Meredith asked.

"We can figure this out," I said. "I'll be right back."

I hurried out the front door. I didn't know where I was going, just that I had to leave. I walked down to Tolson's, counted out some change, and bought cigarettes. Spent half a pack walking around downtown trying to clear my head.

I thought back to that first interview with Garner, realizing that I was the one that told her about the gallery in the first place, the butterfly effect that led to this. It was all my fault. I'd never felt more defeated.

I circled around the capital building, wanting to go into the House Lounge and sit with the Benton mural, but it was closed, the doors locked. I kept walking, walking.

It was a devastating blow. Everything we had worked so hard for was now being ripped apart, and after just one opening. I thought about the money I had saved, how all of it had been sunk into the gallery. And now it was gone. There had to be some way around this. I ran through everything in my head, but came up with nothing. We had no contract. No leg to stand on.

Eventually I walked back into the gallery. Quiet. Steven sat at the table, strumming the guitar lightly. Pederson was in the back, digging the staples out of Joey's big canvas wall, one at a time.

"Where's everyone at? Where's Meredith?" I asked.

"She's gone. She didn't have much to say after you left. She just packed up the darkroom and took off." Steven said.

"What about Bradley and Joey?"

"They loaded their stuff into the van to take back to the nursery."

"I thought we were squatting. We can buy some time, right?"

"We've gone over it, there's nothing we can do. Best that we just get our shit out before they change the locks on us."

"Goddammit, I didn't know—"

"It's alright," Steven said, handing me a Stag. "There's nothing you could have done."

"There was, though," I said.

"No. Garner has money to invest. We have nothing to fight that," Steven said.

"What? So it's over?"

"No choice. Time to let it go."

So that was it. There was nothing we could do. It was over. I wanted to tear down all the work we'd done, take everything back. Looking around, there wasn't that much. We had removed so much of the old, but had only started building it back up again. I walked over to one of the walls and kicked it, shaking the frame, punching a hole through the new drywall. I picked up one of the empty bottles and threw it against the brick wall, sending shards of glass flying. What could I do? Spread the rubble back out? Put the plaster back on the walls? Everything that happened there was in the name of deconstruction. There was nothing to take back. Steven was right, all we could do was let go, walk away. But where could we go? This was the place, we wanted no other.

I had another empty bottle in my hand ready to throw, but let it slide out, fall to the floor. There was no point, just needed to get it over with. I started combing through the gallery for my things. I locked the typewriter back into its case. Pulled the books off the shelf and packed them away. Loaded up my construction tools.

Steven was still at the table, playing a somber, funereal song on the guitar. I helped Pederson remove the last staples from the canvas wall. Together we folded it in thirds, rolled it up with pallbearer reverence.

That was the last of it. We removed any trace of ourselves from the space, leaving it barren, empty as a pocket, full of possibilities to become anything. Anything for someone else.

"Of course," he shrugged. "How else?"

*Ambition is the last refuge of the failure*
　　　—Oscar Wilde

# PART 3

# Fallow

The gallery was the core. The physical nucleus that brought us all together. Without it, we didn't know what to do with ourselves. At least, that's how I felt. I didn't know about everyone else, because I didn't see much of anyone. Occasionally I went downtown, passing by the gallery. No one was there. My key no longer opened the door. The windows were veiled by brown masking paper.

I lay around my apartment for days. Running it over in my mind, how I could have stepped in when she was talking to the landlord, how I could have stopped that conversation from happening. All the things I might have done differently.

I walked over to the corner of my apartment and picked up the copy of *Ulysses*. It was empty, some of the pages bent where I had thrown it across the room and left it lie there half open. I couldn't go anywhere now, and I couldn't do anything here. I was stuck, full of dread, out of options.

I went to try and find Meredith at her place for the fourth time. I really needed to see her. She was the only thing left that offered any semblance of hope.

I walked down the hall of her apartment building, knocked on her door.

No answer.

I knocked again, listening, remembering that clean citrus smell on the other side. I hadn't even talked to her since that morning together. She was nowhere to be found.

I left and walked to High Street. I thought about calling her cell phone but realized she never gave me her number. I always just went to the gallery and knew that's where I'd find her.

As I approached the gallery, I could see the sheets of brown masking paper. The door opened, and a construction worker walked out, the motor hum of power tools sounding out behind him. He went to a clean blue work truck parked on the street, unloaded and packed in more tools, more new building materials, more of all the things we never had. He disappeared inside, the door pulling itself shut behind him. The plywood we patched in had been removed and the door was repaired. A "Coming Soon" sign with the logo for the Arts Coalition hanging behind the brand new glass.

Two other workers were up on ladders, painting the exterior above the storefront window.

"Did you hear what that lady says to me earlier?" One of them griped. "She had the nerve to be critical of the way I was doin my job. Says I wasn't paintin right. Tellin me about *even brush strokes*."

"Well, figures she'd have a complaint. What I hear is she's one of them interior designers."

"Exactly. An *interior* designer. This here's *exterior*, so the way I see it, she's outta her jurisdiction…"

As they were talking, I tried to slip by them to get a peek inside, see what was becoming of the space.

"Hey," one of them said, stopping me at the door. "Not supposed to let anyone inside."

"Really? Can't I just have a look? This used to be our space, you know." I could tell I still had a bitter tinge in my voice.

"Don't know anything about that. Just know we cain't let anyone in before the grand opening."

"The grand opening of what? What are they turning this into?"

"No idea, buddy." He sounded impatient now. "I just work here. Got nothin to do with me."

"Fine." I left, walked on to Coffee Zone, where Steven was sitting at the little cafe table outside, smoking a cigarette. He looked worn down, sleep deprived, unwashed.

"Hey," I said.

"Hey." He was picking the label off his coffee cup with his thumbnail.

"Be right back." I needed some coffee first.

"Sure." He was still staring at the half torn label.

Inside, Taisir was standing behind the counter, smiling. He started pouring a cup of Rocket Fuel as soon as he saw me.

"My friend, hala hala! I'm very sorry to hear about your gallery. I was pulling for you all. I had my hopes high. It would have been good for the block, you know."

"Thanks Taisir. We had our hopes high too."

"Don't sound so down my friend. Other things will come along. It was good while it lasted, no? How about that opening? I haven't had fun like that in a long time."

"Yeah. It was great. Really great." I reached into my pocket for money, even though I had nothing.

Taisir waved it away. "That's okay. Still on the house my friend." I thanked him and went back outside, pulled out the wrought-iron chair across from Steven and sat down.

"So what've you been doing?" I asked.

"Me? I don't know. I've been trying to find a better place to sleep. I'm homeless now without the gallery, literally."

"I'm right behind you. I still owe July rent and it's almost August now."

"You're still writing for the *Telegraph*, right?"

I shrugged. "I haven't done an article since it went online. It wouldn't matter anyway, it's not even enough to buy cigarettes."

He pulled out another one of his cigarettes and handed it to me.

"Where is everyone else?" I asked. "You're the first person I've seen in awhile."

"Joey and Carly are packing up their things to move to L.A. and try and make an honest run with their paintings. They're leaving in a couple days. I don't know about Bradley. He said he needed a break. A fallow period, he called it. I haven't seen him lately. Pederson's around here somewhere." He turned and looked down both ends of the street like he might see him anywhere.

"Have you seen Meredith? I went by her place again, but I still can't find her."

"Oh yeah, she already left."

"What do you mean she left?"

"She hit the road. Said she was gonna do some traveling to work on a new photo essay."

"What? How do you know this?"

"She told me. She was pretty down about the gallery ending. She put a lot of energy into it." Steven pulled out another cigarette and lit it. "Anyway, she said she needed to get out of town. She wanted to put a little distance between her and everything that happened and keep working on her photography. I guess now that the gallery is over there isn't much left to keep her here."

"So that's it." I leaned back in my chair, staring pensively into the bank clock on the corner.

"No, she also said to tell you she was sorry. She didn't say why though. Did something happen between you two?"

She was gone. Without a word, she was gone. I was still coming to grips, trying not to let on. "No, nothing." I wanted to change the subject. "Have you seen the gallery?"

"Fuck no, I don't need to see it."

I took a long drag, leaned back, looked down the block at the old building. Workers were still coming and going, hauling the old stuff out, new stuff in.

Then the door opened, and I recognized one of the workers. It was Travis, walking out with a bucket of mud in one hand and a pan and knife in the other.

"Travis!" I yelled. I hadn't seen him since the day I had quit.

"Holy shit." He dropped the bucket and tools in the middle of the sidewalk and walked over. "What the fuck are you doing here? Thought you were leaving?"

I felt a little shame, seeing him. I had made a promise that I was going and once again I hadn't followed through.

"I don't know, it didn't work out, exactly." Travis took a seat at the table. "This is Steven," I introduced them.

"Well, what the hell are you waiting for?" Travis said to me. "You're supposed to be my inspiration."

"I can't now," I said. "I'm broke."

"Ha! Broke? All of it?"

"Yeah, all of it."

"Well, don't even think about coming back to do drywall. Riley was pretty miffed about the way you left. He actually accused you of stealing drywall from him, believe it or not. Like you would actually want that shit. He's been a fucker lately. At least I get to work downtown now instead of those shitty burbs. You should see this place over here, it's pretty impressive."

"We know all about it," Steven mumbled, still picking at his label forlornly.

I groaned to myself as it occurred to me. What if I hadn't quit? I would be in there right now, working for someone else's space, with no clue.

"I need some kind of work," I said to Travis. "Just need to make a few bucks and get back on track. You know of anything?"

"Hmm…maybe. You still wanna get outta town?"

"More than anything, now."

"I talked to a guy at the bar the other day that has some out-of-town work. It sounds horrible, but it pays. I thought about it myself, but I couldn't do it. Probation officer won't let me leave the state."

"How many people do they need?" Steven asked.

"Sounds like they could use a few dumb laborers. You could probably both get on. I got the guy's number, all you'd have to do is call him."

"What kind of work is it? And where at?" Steven asked. "You know what, it doesn't even matter. I'll do it."

"I don't know," I said, reluctant to go back to the trades, even though I knew I had to. "I guess if we both went, it wouldn't be so bad. Yeah, count me in."

"Okay," Travis said, laughing. "But you're not gonna like this."

# Grind

No matter what you do, how long you step off the moving train, the work will always go on. People getting up in the morning, putting on their boots or ties, setting aside their desires, and going out into the world to become a part of the progress.

The dry Texas desert rolled by out the open window of a loaded down one-ton work truck. On the flatbed in the back were gang boxes full of welders, iron, and tools I'd never used or even heard of before, with names like chain spreaders and sheet dogs. We were doing construction, only this was ironwork, a world to me both familiar and completely foreign.

Steven and I were riding in the back seat. Corby, the foreman, was driving. He was a large man, all gut and gristle, fingers like threaded bolts on the big steering wheel, hair crew cut, dark eyebrows tracing the arc over a pair of shaded safety glasses that came to a point at the sides. In the seat next to him was a copy of *The Man Nobody Knows* by Bruce Barton. In the passenger seat was Kessler, a younger guy, wiry frame, probably around our age. He had a mustache, longer hair tucked under a ubiquitous arabesque bandana, veins like twisted licorice wrapping his forearms.

After a long, silent ride into Texas, Corby finally spoke. "Tell me something. What are your occupations, when you're not doing ironwork?" he asked in a polite but brusque tone.

"I play music," Steven said. Corby peered at him, then over at me through the reflection in the rear view mirror.

"Uh…I'm a writer," I said, more reluctant.

"Hmm." He grunted under his breath. "Well, this should be good for you then, to do some real work."

"Yeah," Kessler chortled, none of the politeness of Corby. "Maybe you can write about this in your fuckin mem-wars."

Corby turned and silenced Kessler with a look. Then looked back at us in the mirror. "Listen, when we get there we'll have no time to waste. We have a job to do and eight weeks to do it. The rest of the crew is coming down tomorrow, and I'll be busy managing the project. You two will report to Kessler, who will line you out with work."

"Damn right," said Kessler. "There's a peckin order here. Far as you two go, I'm the pecker, and you're the pecked."

"Quiet, you," Corby said to him. "Anyway, the most important thing is to stay busy. You're on company time now, so if you run out of work, then tell Kessler and he'll find something for you to do."

That was the last time Corby spoke until we rolled into Temple, Texas. It was a small factory town in the middle of the state, littered with strip malls. We pulled into the parking lot of a cheap highway motel and got out of the truck. The dry desert air had the smell of chlorine from the small swimming pool in the middle of the asphalt parking lot.

We checked in and dropped our stuff off in the room. It was clean, but everything was old. Walls sheathed in thin wood paneling. Threadbare carpet. A small Thomas Kinkade print in a gold-colored frame screwed to the wall. I put the case that contained my typewriter on the desk in the corner. Steven propped the loaned guitar against the desk. We had no time to settle in because we had to go straight to the factory where we would be working.

The place was called Texas Hydraulics, an enormous cube of metal and concrete where they had an assembly line that churned out some ten thousand hydraulic cylinders a day. Our job was not to make the cylinders, but to make the factory. They were adding on a new automated production line, and the company we were working for specialized in installing the monorail and equipment that ran those lines. A series of stations performing a different task, each of them manned by a single technician at a computer, eliminating all human error.

Corby took us into the plant office where we got our temporary contractor badges. We walked past rows and rows of stainless tubes of metal being carried around the factory, dangling from the I-beam monorail as they were formed and polished. Then they were crated and shipped to other factories where they were assembled into larger machinery that used hydraulic equipment. Everything streamlined. Machines made by machines. Like Russian nesting dolls, behind every machine is an even smaller one that put it together, until you break it all down and the last one is nothing more than a lever, a pulley, an inclined plane, one Big Screw.

After we got our badges, Corby led us into the new addition, a vast open room, metal roof, concrete floor. This is where they would put the new line.

Kessler pulled the work truck in through one of the open bay doors, and we unloaded the tools off the back.

"First thing you must know about welding," said Corby as he took us over to a large stack of I-beams on the floor. "A weld is intolerable of polymers, so we must expunge all weld surfaces."

Kessler cut in, assuming we couldn't understand, "What he means is you cain't weld them fuckers with the paint on it, so we gotta grind that shit off."

"Thank you, Kessler," Corby rolled his eyes. "This entire stack must be completed. It will take you awhile and it's going to be monotonous work."

"But that's why we hired you two wingnuts," Kessler said. "So us union guys can do more important shit."

"Go ahead and get started, and finish out the day on the grinder. Tomorrow we'll pick back up at 5:30 a.m. We work twelve-hour days, including weekends, until the job is complete. It will get pretty grueling by the end, but you'll be compensated for it."

"Damn right, that's why we do it!" Kessler said. "Time-and-a-half, woot woot!"

Corby shook his head, turned and walked off, with Kessler following him obediently.

Steven and I each plugged in a grinder, turned them on and put them to the metal, shooting acrylic dust into the air. A slow, methodical process of removal.

After about half an hour, I turned off my grinder and pulled the handkerchief out of my pocket. I looked at Steven, still bearing down on the metal. We were both already dripping with sweat in the Texas heat. He shut his grinder off, blowing the remaining dust off the end of the beam.

"You know, it kinda feels good to be working like this," Steven said. "Like we're doing something, we're part of this big industry that makes everything."

"For what though?" I thought about all the countless hours doing drywall and what I had to show for it. "I'd rather be back at the gallery, working on the book, or doing anything else but this."

"At least with this kind of work there's nothing to think about. There's nothing to figure out. All we'll have to do is show up, do the job, then leave it all behind at the end of the day."

"Yeah, what little day we have left. We're working 12 hours, remember?"

"We'll get a bottle later and go back to the motel and work on whatever we want."

Kessler walked by, checking on us. We flipped the grinders back on and finished out the day, until the bones in our hands were vibrating.

The sun was setting as we loaded into the truck. On the way back to the motel, we stopped off for a bottle of whiskey and a big can of loose rolling tobacco, dragging our boots all the way back to our drab motel room. Steven immediately fell onto the bed. We were both exhausted. I set the bottle of whiskey on the desk next to the typewriter case.

"I need to take a shower, you mind if I go first?" I asked.

Steven waved his hand in the air, eyes closed.

I climbed into the shower and turned the water on as hot as it would go, scrubbing away all the work sweat and metal dust that had penetrated every exposed pore. Grinding it out with a little washcloth, another methodical process of removal. When I finally got out and dried off, Steven was asleep on top of the covers in the motel bed, fully dressed, his boots hanging off the end.

# Factory

All we could do was knuckle under, join the ranks of Industry, put our heads down, and begin the interminable march forward. We worked seven days a week, twelve hours a day. Before, we seemed to have all the time in the world. Now, it was all eaten up in the machine. Same shit, different day.

Our job was to do all the menial tasks. Grind metal. Run welding lead for the ironworkers. Haul tools and metal around the factory. If nothing else, sweep floors. We worked all day, went back to the motel and passed out, then got up at 5:00 a.m. to do it all over, ad nauseum. It rolled by in a confused whirl as we started to dull down, lose our identity, becoming cotter pins in the very machines we were supposed to be operating. Material commodities in a high-speed work world. There was no feeling, no color. Everything was cold, gray metal. I looked around the factory and what we were building and thought of Henry Ford, machinery as the new messiah, architect of this whole process. Somehow I figured he was to blame for all of it.

One day Corby was sliding on his long, leather welding gloves, getting ready to tack up some metal beams. The more I got to know him, the more I liked him. He told me about how he got into this, how he planned to go to college, how his SAT scores would have earned him a full ride, before he got his girlfriend pregnant. He was here, he said, to do the right thing.

"Is that hard to do?" I asked, squatting down next to where he was working, handing him a welding rod.

"What, welding?"

"Yeah, I've never done it before."

"You want to give it a try? Here, I'll show you." Corby expounded on the beauty of a good weld. For him it was more than just function; it was an aesthetic, something he was very proud of, even passionate about. He did one himself to show me, and it really was a beautiful thing, the bright arc light, calibrated eye, smooth bond that was formed.

He pulled the helmet up and looked at the weld with pride, his eyes glowing like iron fires in a scrap heap city.

"You want a clean, smooth bead," he said. "If done properly, a weld will be stronger than the metal around it. Here, you try."

He handed me his flat black welding hood. I put it on, got everything ready as he instructed, but I started the weld too soon, before dropping the hood over my face, the explosive light blinding me, roughing up my retinas like sandpaper.

"Try again," he said calmly. "You won't be able to see it until the welder is already going. You just have to feel it, remember where it is."

I held the rod carefully in place and nodded the hood down over my eyes, then gently touched it to the metal, that arc light of release as the metal started to pool. It was a powerful feeling, something larger, and I was in control of it. I understood why Corby felt the way he did. A machine that could make men from boys. That could hold marriages together. That could weld dreams.

I lay down a long, thick bead and pulled the hood back up to admire it. What I saw was a large ball of slag.

"It is what it is," Corby said.

Kessler walked up and looked at the slag caked around the beam. "Ha! Looks like hammered shit," he said.

"That's okay," Corby said to me. "You'll figure it out, it takes time. Go ahead and finish what you were doing."

I went back to the other end of the factory. I was by myself, putting together the chain that would slide onto the monorail. Assembling the assembly line. Connecting four links, a set of wheels, and a hook, four links, set of wheels, hook, four links—

I pulled out a marker, found an empty spot on one of the I-beams, and wrote:

*I am nature—Jackson Pollack*

The factory was filled with the sound of engines running, industrial exhaust fans blasting overhead, machines whirring all around. We wore ear plugs, these little foam bullets you had to twist and slide into your ear canal, slowly drowning out the sound as they expanded, like slipping underwater. I spent every day inside my own head, performing simple tasks. I couldn't stop thinking about Meredith. I went back over everything a hundred times, that night together, the next morning, wondering if there would have been some way to keep her from leaving. If I had only had the chance to catch her beforehand. I had no idea where she was or if I would ever see her again.

I found another spot on the side of the of a big acid-wash booth and wrote:

*I want to be a machine—Andy Warhol*

Kessler came over to let me know it was time for lunch. Because of the noise, we made hand signals to communicate. He held two fists together at the thumbs, moving them apart and down, like breaking a stick. I walked over to the plastic folding table set up in the corner of the factory.

Steven had been given the job of going to the store. He was setting down plastic grocery bags full of food for the crew. He handed the credit card back to Corby as the rest of the crew circled around for the feed.

The company paid for lunch because it was cheaper, Corby explained to us one day. When you had an entire crew leave the job and they only had thirty minutes to order and eat, most of them were never back on time. So, if $X$ amount of men were $Y$ amount of minutes late every day, it would cost the company $Z$ amount of dollars in Man Hours. With prevailing union wages this was far less than the cost of groceries for $X$ amount of men. Bottom dollar.

"What the hell is this?" Kessler pulled an avocado out of the grocery bag.

"You serious?" Steven asked. "It's an avocado."

"How do you eat it?"

"You're a grown man and you've never seen an avocado?"

"Hell no. We're workin men, we need meat and potatoes. None of this rabbit food. Where's the baloney?"

"I ain't sposed to have baloney no more," said Rat. He was one of the journeyman welders. A scraggly little guy with thick glasses, sitting there scratching his back with a framing square. He'd been on this crew for over twenty years.

"Doctor says I got too many nitrates," he explained.

"Not my problem," said Kessler. He pulled a baguette out and looked at it, shaking his head. "Corby, you cain't let that one do the groceries no more."

Steven and I took our lunch break outside. We usually spent our thirty minutes of freedom reading a book or sleeping under the blower tube of the huge exhaust system, pulling off our Brahma boots, now scuffed down to the steel in the toes, and using them for a pillow, draping sweat-soaked socks over the iron handrail, drying them out as much as possible before we had to put them back on again.

"I can't believe it's September already," I said to Steven.

"No kidding," he said, his voice tired. "An entire month, gone."

"We can never get August back, and now they're taking September. I won't give them any more than that."

"My back is killing me," he mumbled.

"Same here. I think my spine is two inches shorter than it was a month ago." I rolled back and forth a little, trying to get comfortable. I could feel every bone in my back, bending the way metal fatigues over time. "At least you got to leave the factory and go to the grocery store."

"Yeah, that'll be the best thing that happens all day. I sat in the truck in the parking lot for a long time smoking cigarettes, listening to the radio, trying to feel something again."

"I can't believe these guys exist like this. This is no kind of life."

"Nah, they're just built differently. We all do something, whether it's this or writing or whatever. There's nothing wrong with this, it's just not fulfilling for you or me."

I thought of the other workers on the crew. The way they patronized us, the "sub-cubs," for our lack of skill. As if they were born melding metal to metal, their birth just another construction, and they took up the torch, the welding rod, and burned it into the night.

"I want to go back to living life again. It's so hard to come by here." Steven didn't respond. He had drifted off to sleep under the shade of the exhaust motor. I closed my eyes, and just as I started to drift off too, Kessler came outside. "Break's over ladies. Back to work."

We got up, put on our damp socks, and went inside the factory, put in our earplugs, went back underwater, retreating within, building links of chain on the assembly line, one at a time, becoming the pattern makers, workers of the world. Slave, save, and retire.

After work Steven and I were in the motel room, feeling filthy, living like a couple of sweathogs. I took off my boots, the horrible smell of work sweat saturating the little room, the feet starting to deteriorate. Steven was grinding his rashy toes into the carpet for solace. I looked over at the little desk in the corner, the typewriter still in its case. Hard to write anything when only three hours of the day really belonged to me. And those three hours tempered by aching body, weak back, sore feet. Steven hadn't touched his guitar. We were both empty. No energy. No ambition. To build factories you have to hollow out mountains.

I stripped down to my Carhartts and lay in bed. Steven was flipping through channels on the cable television, while I hand rolled cigarettes on my bare stomach. It wasn't the hard work I minded so much; it was that it had no real purpose for me. I kept rolling more cigarettes, faster than I could smoke them, setting them on the nightstand. It was something to do, something basic that didn't require much thought, rolling cigarettes like a factory before it was time to go to sleep again.

# Still Life

We woke up at 5:00 a.m. for the last time. Two months now chewed up in the machine. No distinct memory, just a general feeling of exhaustion, ache. But it was over. Today we were going home.

We packed up our things to leave the motel room. I went to the desk in the corner, looked at the telling composition of the last two months. Typewriter still locked in its case, guitar still in case, ashtray full of butts, single-serving wrappers of BC aspirin powder, slag mound of loose, unkept coins, all scattered on the formica surface.

We left the mess and the laundry for the maid to clean up after we were gone, all of us trading away our labors. We threw our things in the back of the truck and went to work. The new production line was built. Hydraulic cylinders were carried around the factory through the paint booths, wash booths, drying ovens, and came out slick and clean on the other side. American industry. No one had to touch them.

We put in a full day cleaning up the last of the mess and packing the tools to leave. After work, the boss paid for all of us to go out to a steak dinner. We went to Texas Roadhouse, where the cold beef cuts were on display in a franchised box. We all ordered a stiff drink on the boss. Even this was just another ploy to keep the workers productive, wanting to come back.

"I like my steak kinda well done," said Rat, looking over the menu.

"Oh you don't wanna order that at a fancy restaurant," said Kessler. "They take offense to that sorta thing, cause they think cookin is some kinda art form. Might upset the chef and you get it back charred up like a briquette."

"Well, from what I hear it don't take much to upset them kinda fellas," Rat muttered.

"Here comes our gal. You guys ready to order?" Corby asked the table.

"Yeah, uh, gimme one a those chopped steaks," Rat said to the server. "And tell him cook it however he sees fit. And bring me another one of these tasty whisker drinks." The server wrote down everyone's order and left, the same dark lines under her eyes that were under ours.

Kessler turned to Steven and I. "I'll be goddamn, y'all actually made it through. You gonna be on the next job with us?"

"Not a chance," Steven said. "You couldn't pay me enough to do this again."

"You oughtta join the union like me. In five years I'll be makin good money, and I can buy a decent-sized house. I'll have a big enough bathroom I can wipe my ass with either hand without scrapin my knuckles on the wall. Then maybe pay off my truck, and after that I can buy me a spankin new boat. Then I'll kick back and enjoy life."

"Shit, if you still got any life left in you," Rat muttered into his whisker drink. "And you'll be wiping your ass in porty-john's til then."

"I don't get it, Kessler," I said. "Your life is happening right *now*. Why would you wanna wait that long to enjoy it?"

"Yeah, yeah, I know what you're gettin at. I've been through that wild stage, and it was damn good times, but I gotta settle down now, pay my dues. I'm gettin too old for that shit."

"But we're the same age," I said.

"Exactly," Kessler said, raising his glass. "My point is made, thank you." He took a gulp of his whiskey.

"You should be proud of the work you did," Corby cut in. "We built something here, and you two did good work. Kessler's right, you should think about joining the union."

Steven and I gave each other the same look. A weary protraction of the last eight weeks into an entire life. The server came back and stepped between us to plunk down the plates of food on the table. After she walked off, Rat stared down at his. A patty of ground beef with mushrooms and onions spread over the top.

"This ain't no goddamn steak," he said.

"Hell no it ain't," Kessler agreed. "That there's a burger without no bun."

When the server came back, Rat ordered a bun. And another tasty whisker drink. She didn't say anything, her patience reaching the service ceiling.

No one spoke once the food was in front of them. Heads occasionally coming up, like deer drinking from a pond. Steven and I ate ours hungrily, ripping into the steak, oozing thin red blood, the first real color we'd seen in this metal-gray world, our appetites returned now that the notion of leaving was real. As soon as we finished, we both pushed back our chairs and walked over to the bar before the conversation could start back up where it left off.

We sat down and ordered a couple of drinks. I still had a ferric residue in my mouth, skin off the tongue, metallic aftertaste from the job that wouldn't go away. Even the whiskey couldn't cut through it.

"It's finally over," I said. "No more ironwork."

"At least we have money in our pockets," Steven said. "I guess now you can go anywhere you want."

I thought about the idea of actually leaving. All of my reasons before had changed. The gallery had shifted my whole perspective. I didn't know what to do, where to go.

"What about you? Do you know where you're gonna go?"

"Not really."

"I like what we had going before. It'd be nice to find it again."

"Yeah, I miss that."

"I was writing more than ever. The past couple of months have been a vacuum. Not a single page. I'm ready to start creating something again."

We both took a sip of our whiskey quietly. I knew it had to be right there on the surface, because I was thinking it too. It was an infection. A sort of malady in remission you can never rid.

"We could make another run at it," I finally said, bringing the idea out onto the table.

"I knew you were gonna say that," he said. "Yeah, why not?"

"We have a little money now. We could find a space and rent it."

"Yes, a finished space this time," Steven said, getting more enthralled with the idea.

"Right! One that's ready to go, we don't have to put any work into it."

"And we sign a lease so we can't get kicked out. At least, not without a reason."

"We'll get everyone back together," I said. "It'll be great."

We talked excitedly about doing it again, starting Artless back up. All the reasons why this was something we *had* to do. We hashed it out. We would go back and find a finished space and rent it. We had all this money from the ironwork, and now we could fund anything.

Steven took another sip of his whiskey. "We have to go for it, even if we do fail."

"What do you mean?" I asked.

"I mean, we'll be on the hook for rent every month. Not like the last time. It makes me a little uneasy, that's all. This is gonna be a big commitment…and…I don't know…for some reason I'm just no fucking good at that. I try to be, but look at my track record. I've had a pretty consistent history of failure."

"What are you talking about? This is not going to fail." I said, a little irritated that he would even consider it.

"Maybe not," he said. "Fuck it, right? What else we gonna do?"

"It's not gonna fail," I reassured myself. "I won't let it."

## Immoveable Beast

There were few people downtown the day we got back. High Street seemed desolate. I walked by the old gallery, my stomach dropped, bile rising into my throat just to come near it. Remembering things past. The window was still shrouded by sheet rolls of paper taped to the inside. I didn't even want to see it. I didn't want to know.

I went on to Coffee Zone, and Taisir was there, smiling, always full of optimism and high-octane coffee.

"Hala hala! Long time no see!" He immediately started pouring me a cup of Rocket Fuel.

"Hey Taisir, how have things been around here? Have you seen anybody from the gallery?"

"No, my friend. The block has been quiet the last couple months. Where have you been?"

"Kind of a long story. I gotta run right now, though, but I'll be back." I pulled out a wad of cash, purse proud from the ironwork, paid for the two Rocket Fuels and stuffed more bills into the tip jar. "Thanks, Taisir."

I walked several blocks until I got to 704 West Main, the address where we were supposed to meet. It just happened that this was right next door to Pat's Place. There was a storefront space for lease in an old brick two-story. It was divided in half, with an operating business on one side and an empty window on the other.

I looked at my watch, wondering where Steven was. The landlord would be showing up any minute. I peered into the building. It was long and narrow, shotgun style like the last one. Only this wasn't like the last gallery at all. It was a clean, finished space. No garbage, no rotting lumber, no walls piled on the floor. There was something seductive about an empty space, that fertile feeling of possibilities. Every cubic foot of volume a blank canvas in itself.

I stepped back and looked at the big red, white, and blue placard from a local realtor, the bar across the top reading FOR LEASE. How many squirrels in the course of evolution jumped to their death before one finally flew, I wondered.

The landlord pulled up to the curb, stepped out of his car. He looked at me, then looked around. Looked at me again.

"You're not my three o'clock, are you?"

"Yeah, that's right," I said.

He walked up, an enormous ring of keys clanging at his side like a jailor. Color-coded keys. Keys to lands and rents and wealth.

"Weren't there supposed to be two of you?" he asked.

"Yeah, he's on his way." I looked at my watch again. Dammit, where the hell was Steven. He's probably not going to show, I thought. He's already bailing on me.

But then the old reliable airport van came around the corner, pulled up and bounced over the curb where I was standing, forcing me to jump out of the way as the transmission was prematurely slammed into park, wrenching it to a halt in front of me.

"Here he is," I said.

Steven hopped out, leaving the van door wide open as he walked over. His eyes had more life in them than they had in the last two months, maybe more than I'd ever seen.

The landlord sized us both up for a second, the look on his face written with distrust and future regret. He spun through his ring of keys and found the one he needed, then pulled out a handkerchief and used it to turn the knob, not wanting to touch it with his hand.

"I have to let you know right away that I'll need to see some references," he said, trying to discourage us before we even got through the door. "And I'll have to do a credit and background check. No offense. I've been burned before, so I have to be selective."

The landlord stayed by the door, still holding his keys, ready to lock it back up.

Steven and I walked through the space. The building was shaped like an L with an office in the back around the corner.

The walls were painted in an ugly, jaundiced eggshell. Finished hardwood floors ran down the length. Mostly-intact acoustic ceiling tiles overhead, symmetrically interrupted by paneled fluorescent lighting. It had none of the character of the older buildings on High Street. But it was turnkey, and this was cheaper than any of the others we had called about.

"Damn, not quite what I was expecting," I said. "It looked better from outside the window."

"A fresh coat of paint on the walls will do a lot," Steven said. "And some better lights. That's a pretty easy fix."

In the back was a big wooden door, a pane of translucent glass in the top half. I pushed it open. "Wow, it's got a great office," I said. "It's huge. We could find another big desk like we had before to put in here."

Steven came back to the big, open room in the back, one window looking right out to the patio behind Pat's Place. "So what do you think?" Steven asked.

"It's not nearly as good as what we had on High Street."

"True, but do you see trash? Do you see an enclosed landfill? This is a thousand times better, for that reason alone. We might even be able to let people walk through here like a normal gallery without getting piss on their shoes."

We turned and went back to talk to the landlord. As soon as we were outside, he grabbed the doorknob with his handkerchief, pulled it shut, and locked it.

"Also I have other people looking at this space, so it might not even be available," he picked up where he had left off.

"We really like it," Steven said.

"Okay, well if you want I can take your contact information and let you know."

I reached into my pocket and pulled out the wad of cash, the product of eight weeks labor. Steven did the same.

"What if we paid you in advance?" I asked, sifting off bill after bill.

The landlord stared hungrily at the cash being counted out by the two of us.

"Here's the first month," Steven said, pulling off crisp hundreds. "And the last month."

"And here's the deposit," I added. "And another month."

The landlord put his handkerchief back in his pocket and took the money, pathologically thumbing through the sweaty, iron-stained bills like it was soap. Like there was something in it's composition that made it immune.

"Well, there's always exceptions," he said. "You seem to be good for the rent. What did you say you do for a living?"

"Construction, of sorts," I said.

"Oh, that's great. It'll be nice to have tenants who know how to take care of things." He pulled the keys to building off the larger ring and handed them over. "There you go. My receipt book is in the car," he said, still clutching the money. "I'll go write you one out for this cash."

"Don't worry about it," I said. "We trust you."

## The Quest for Beauty

We put out a call to let everyone know we were back and had a space for a gallery again. Soon enough there would be a gathering of clouds, all of us connecting like pearling opals of water, forming puddles in the rain.

Steven and I moved boxes into the office. Books, instruments, power tools. All the things from the last gallery that had been stored away before going to Texas, along with everything I had packed up from my last apartment, which had lapsed while I was gone. We didn't bother looking for an apartment or any kind of place to live. Instead we went to a thrift store and picked up some cheap furniture for the office. We put an old, green tweed couch on one side of the room where Steven slept. I rolled out a sleeping bag on top of a long folding table on the other side. We also found a big, oak desk, which we put in the middle of the room.

A couple of days into the new space, Steven and I were unpacking a box full of books and arranging them on the shelves we had put in the corner. I heard the front door open and close, then footsteps on the hardwood floors, walking through the empty gallery.

"The worm turns again," Bradley was standing in the doorway.

"Bradley!" I shouted. "Check it out. What do you think of the new space?"

"Fine, we'll talk about it later. Right now we have to go," he said urgently. "Joey's not doing well. We have to go get him. Now."

"What's wrong?" Steven asked.

"I'll tell you about it on the way. But we have to go."

We put the books down and followed Bradley out of the gallery. We didn't know why Joey was in trouble, but we knew Bradley well, and we knew that he meant it.

I was the last one out, locking the door behind us. "Where are we going, anyway?" I asked as the three of us climbed into the van.

"L.A." Bradley said.

"You want to drive to L.A.? Right now?" Steven asked. "You fucking kidding me?"

"No," Bradley responded. "I'm not kidding. I wouldn't be saying this if it weren't absolutely serious. Come on, I'm really worried. Joey needs our help."

We didn't argue. We drove the Artless van through the night and all the next day without stopping. Along the way Bradley filled us in on what was happening. Joey and Carly had been at each other's throats, fighting constantly and intensely. And not like they normally fought. Something was different. And Joey hadn't been painting, which was the only thing that kept him sane. Now they were on a collision course, and Bradley was afraid someone was going to get hurt.

We kept driving, driving. Stopping every couple hundred miles for more gas and coffee, taking turns behind the wheel, catching small naps, until we finally pulled the dusty white van into the slums of North Hollywood, where Joey was living in the back half of a low-rent duplex. We found him in the garage, standing on top of a gallon paint can, pontificating and twirling a palsied finger through the air.

When Joey saw us at the door he gave us a nod, waved us in, but didn't stop his dissertation. As if we had driven across town to get there instead of across the country.

The garage was a mess. Trash everywhere. Open paint cans, brushes sticking out of the top peel of dried acrylic. Cigarette butts overflowing out of several ashtrays. Only one canvas had been stretched, leaning against the far wall. It was thick and textured from several layers of underpainting, now buried under fresh gesso, bright white in the filthy room.

In a chair in the middle of the garage sat a guy with dark-rimmed glasses, short sideburns shaped into a fine point. He was nodding his head, swallowing constantly, hanging on Joey's every word.

"It's part of a series called Sympathy for the Devil. Because he always takes the blame. Don't just stand there, man. Come on in," Joey said to us. "Shut the door behind you. You need to meet this guy. Daniel, right? This is Daniel. He's the producer for the Ellen Degeneres show. He's gonna help me with my paintings. He *knows* people."

"Production assistant, actually. Nice to meet you. Um..." He got up nervously, looked around. "I think I need to go." He paced toward an old deep freezer in the corner of the garage. Then turned back to the door. Then back to the freezer. "Uh...yeah. Yeah, I have to go." He headed for the door. "See you later Joey...I'll...uh...talk to some people for you...see what I can do."

"Welcome to Babylon!" Joey said after Daniel left, twirling his finger in the air. "How'd you guys get here, anyway? This place is crazy, huh?"

"How's everything, Joey?" Bradley looked around the garage, at the one unfinished painting. "Looks like you're in a rut."

"That one's not finished yet. It's not even a painting, man. It's more like a painting *painting* a painting." I could see his jaw twisting slightly. His eyes looked sunk back and sallow. He wobbled around on top of the paint can, holding a tattered paperback in one hand throwing off his balance. "I'm trying to paint the devil for the first time. Because if I can see him, I can defeat him. It's the hardest painting I've ever done, because I'm trying to make the devil beautiful."

"What's that book Joey?" I asked.

"This book?" He looked at it for a second, confused. Then realized what he was holding. "Oh. This is my whole philosophy. It's called *The Quest for Beauty*. That's why I'm here. I'm on a quest to find beauty. That's what L.A.'s about, man. It's fucked up. But they have it all wrong. There is no perfect face, perfect body, anything. Perfect is wrong. Or we're all perfect, everything is beauty and the truth. I made a pact with God, a painting pact, that all my art would represent truth. And that's where you find beauty. My paintings are beauty out of chaos." He couldn't stop talking, jaw popping to the side, rapping the book with a stiff finger every time he made a point. "I haven't even read this thing yet. I don't need to, I've already figured it out. Art that makes me want to scream and puts me in a place by myself, that's great art. The quest for beauty will make you crazy." Out of the corner of my eye I saw Carly pass by the window of the garage. Then pass by going the other way, her fists clenched, head shaking. Joey saw me notice this and dismissed it with a wave of his hand.

"Don't worry about her, man. She's insane. She threatened to kill me. She won't do it though."

"Joey, do we need to get you outta here?" Steven asked.

"You just got here, man. You're my guests. Have some cocaine, it's over there." He pointed to the deep freezer. On top of the rusted lid were laid out windrows of powder. "You're in Babylon now, man. I'm not going anywhere. I'm a warrior here. I dreamt of being a warrior my whole life and always believed there was a battle going on. And now I've found it, right here in the city of angels. I'm trying to bring down Babylon. That's why I paint monsters, because that's what we fear. People say they're too violent. Maybe so, but violence is the language of animals. I want to excite the beast within, man. Within us *all*." He signed a J in the air and tipped forward on the paint can. "I found out how to control the thoughts in my head. I know what it all means now. I paint to get a reaction from people. I'll laugh till I'm crazy, whatever. But you have to have an image to sell paintings here. That's my other quest for beauty, finding my image. How do I get people to look at my paintings like they look at a book." He flicked the cover with his finger. "Pick it up, put it down. Like *The Quest for Beauty*."

"Seriously Joey," Bradley said. "You should come with us."

"I want to paint like Norman Rockwell, man," Joey continued. "Because he painted *life*, he showed the *imperfections*. There are no imperfections here. The people in L.A. are plastic, and when the ozone opens up, they'll all melt on the sidewalks and beaches.

Carly passed by the window again, and this time she came to the door, flinging it open, slamming it against the wall.

"What the fuck are they doing here?" she demanded. Her jaw twisting like Joey's, skin paled.

"Who? Them?" Joey asked, playing dumb. "They just showed up."

"Yeah, right. You called them didn't you?" she shouted.

"No, I didn't call them," he said.

"Yes, you did, I know you did. You called them. You're gonna try and sneak out of here."

"No, I'm not."

"Yes you are. I know you. You're a *sneak*. Always hiding from everything, aren't you? Including yourself."

"Would you please stop it." Joey said calmly.

"Stop what? Huh? Stop what!" she shouted.

"Just stop it! Stop it!" Joey started shouting back, huddling now, hands over his ears.

"What, baby." She switched to a soft, mocking voice. "Are you finally getting mad?"

"Stop it!" he shouted, his voice cracking with desperation.

"Are you mad? Huh? Go ahead. Get mad." Her jaw stretching out the speed tension.

"Stop, please." He was quiet again, sobbing.

"You're mad! You're crazy! What, you want to leave? You think you're actually gonna leave me? Go ahead. Be mad! Be a lunatic! You're not leaving me! You think they'll take care of you? Ha!" She grabbed the door and slammed it shut, shattering the glass pane, and stormed passed the window back into the house.

Joey was slumped over now, head down. "It's been like this ever since we got here, man. I think she's been doing drugs." The three of us looked at each other, wondering if he was being ironic. "I don't know why we need to fight so much. That's just how we show affection. It gives us a reason to think about each other. Maybe we're not good together. How do I know? I've never been with anyone else. I lost my virginity to her when I was sixteen. The church told me I had to marry her, to make it a *sacred union*. Now she hates me. She hates me because she's unhappy with her art. That's why she's trying to kill me. She's the one who got me started on this." He pointed over to the freezer. "She's like my Eve, man. This is my Last Supper. Marrying her was my sacrifice."

"Fuck that, Joey," I said. "You don't have to stay here."

"I don't know, man. Did you guys really come here to get me? I don't know if I can. Yeah, fuck it. You're right. I have to get out of here." He pointed over to the deep freezer. "First we have to do all this coke. We can't leave it here, not with her."

"Forget it, Joey," Bradley said. "Leave it."

He jumped off the paint can and went over to freezer and snarfed up a long line. "No way, man. Either you help me or I'll do it myself."

I walked over to the freezer, the windrows of crystalline powder. I picked up the rolled dollar bill. "This is my quest, man." Joey said, his arm on my shoulder. "You're the bohemian. You'll have to find your own quest for beauty someday." I drug one of the lines, picking up flakes of rust along with it. An instant chlorinated burn as it shot straight up, like taking in water in a pool.

"Joey, this isn't cocaine," I said. Feeling the nerves tighten in my brain, like pulling weeds from the dirt.

"It's fine," Joey said dismissively. Steven and Bradley both did a long line, clearing the last of the powder and rust flakes off the freezer.

Joey got back up on the paint can. "In 3rd grade I tied two desks together with my shoestrings, and when the teacher came up to me, you know what I said to her? I said, 'The witch overloaded and exploded!' That's how I feel about it all now, man, the witch that overloaded and exploded."

"Fine, Joey, let's go now," Bradley said. He grabbed the unfinished canvas.

"The witch overloaded and exploded!" Joey shouted toward the house.

"Come on Joey," I said. I gathered up a few of his supplies.

"The witch overloaded and exploded!" Joey kept shouting, shouting to L.A., to the heavens, and started cackling in his high-pitched, anxious laugh. Laughing out everything he had until his eyes filled with sugar water, all polluted and caramelized, running down his cheeks. Steven walked over and put his arms around him, and Joey folded forward off the paint can, onto his shoulder.

"The witch..." he was quiet now, weeping the words "...overloaded...and exploded."

Joey passed out before we even got him to the van. We laid him across the seat, pointed the van back to the Middle West.

## Artless 2.0

I carried a fresh, new box back to the office of the gallery and set it on the desk, pulled out a pocket knife, and cut the packing tape around the edges.

"What's this?" Steven asked. "Not using the typewriter anymore?"

I slid a brand new Mac computer out of the box and set it on the desk. "Applied science," I said, "Finally getting with the times, making the move from paper to pixel."

He ran his hand along the top of the sleek, aluminum body of the desktop computer. "Damn, it is a well-designed machine, I have to admit."

"This is far more practical. Plus, I just wanted to indulge in something with the money we made from the ironwork, before it's all gone."

"I still like your typewriter better."

"There's recording software on here," I suggested. "You can start putting together an album."

"Really?" he thought about it for a second. "Not so sure I'm ready for that, yet."

"I got a cell phone, too." I opened a smaller box and took out the new phone. After I got it powered on, I put it into the desk drawer. "It can be the official gallery line."

"I did a little splurging of my own. Check this out," Steven said. Snapping open the case to a new used guitar. He pulled it out of the plush, red lining. It was small-bodied but deep, wide neck, the back and sides made of rosewood, sitka spruce top fading toward the center. "It's a Gibson Nic Lucas Special," he said excitedly. "It's pre-war, from the golden age of guitar making, before industrialization when things started being mass produced. I found it in a pawn shop. They had no idea what they were sitting on. They just thought it was some old guitar."

"That's awesome," I said. "How much is it worth?"

"I don't know," Steven said, sitting in a chair in the corner with the guitar, tuning the strings. "But it's a lot more than what I paid. To me it's priceless."

I finished setting up the computer, plugging everything in. Then I dug out the scribbles and pages for the novel I had packed up and dumped them on the desk to sort through, try and make sense of it all. Turn the insides back out.

I powered up the new computer, opened up a blank document, hands poised, electric current pulsing through the smooth, conductive keys, negative and positive, completing the circuit. The feeling of being alive drummed back into my nervous system as I started typing. Steven was tuned and plucking strings on the new guitar, playing for the first time in a couple of months.

Bradley and Joey showed up, carrying their canvas bags full of paint supplies. Joey had been crashing at Bradley's since we got back from L.A. a few days earlier, getting over the addiction and back to what, for him, was considered normal.

"Look at you," Bradley said, eyeing the new computer. "Joining the rest of civilization."

"Cool guitar, man," Joey said to Steven.

"We're gonna set up outside here and get to work painting," Bradley announced as they put their bags down outside of the office.

"Go for it," I said. "We should probably put some drop cloths down, though. The landlord seemed a little edgy."

"Sure, man. We can do that," Joey said.

They brought in more supplies, drop cloths, cans of paint, turning the back half of the gallery into their studio. Then they went to work. Joey and Bradley painting side by side for the first time.

Over the next few days, Joey fell back into painting frenetically, turning out canvas after canvas. Bradley followed suit, infected by the store of energy Joey had from being dormant so long. All of us did.

We were all back together, being creative, working on projects, as it was before. Even Pederson showed up out of nowhere one day, riding laps in the big, open space on a random pink bicycle, the mutt jogging along behind him.

This was our own private Florence, our Paris, our New York. All of us producing, talking, consumed by what we were doing, inspired by one another. The sum of artistic energy greater than all the parts. Inspiration all around. More than that. There were possibilities. An open space where anything could happen, and that was something you could feel. Now we had it back.

That is, all of us except for Meredith. No one had heard from her over the last two months. I wanted her to see the new gallery, to be a part of it. But the more time passed, the more I figured she was gone, and I would never hear from her again.

# Stage

We made a sign with an arrow pointing to the right, the way to the bar two doors down, put it in the gallery window, and went to Pat's Place to hear Steven play. This was the first time we would see him play a real gig, outside of the late-night hours of the gallery. This time he would be getting paid.

The bar was packed with people. We went to our usual table in the back, while Steven went to talk to Arvin about setting up. Bradley sat down, started practicing his signature on a bar napkin. Joey tore open a sugar packet and was licking his pinkie and sticking it inside, over and over. Pederson carved off the ends of his long, brittle fingernails with a Buck knife, stacking the clippings on the corner of the table.

Steven started a tab and came over and dropped off a round of drinks for everyone, then went to the front of the bar where they had cleared out a couple of tables for him to play. He was shuffling around in his ragged black boots, cigarette burning down in one hand, adjusting the microphones, getting out his guitar, moving around with that begrudging air of having to actually perform his music, put himself out there for strangers.

"It's good to be back here," Joey said. "I don't know how to thank you guys. I don't know what I was doing. Things were getting bad."

"Fuck that," Bradley said. "We needed you back here. This is where you belong, Joey. There's no way we could let these guys start another gallery without you on board."

I lit a cigarette, pulled out a small notebook, and started writing in it.

"You guys need another?" Bradley asked, holding up his empty glass, shaking the ice cubes.

"Sure," I said. He got up and went to the bar. Steven finally started to play. Pederson got up and went to the front, sat in a chair right in front of the stage.

"You doing okay?" I asked Joey when we were alone. "Everything cool with you and Carly? I know you guys were together a long time."

"I'm okay, man." He stuck his pinkie in another packet of sugar, then set it down. "I…I want you to know something—" He leaned in close, confiding. "I was with other women. I just said I was only with her to keep my tracks clean. I don't want anyone to think…you know…that I'm weak…in that area."

"I understand." I pulled out my pocket notebook and scribbled in it.

"What are you guys talkin about?" Bradley asked, setting the drinks down on the table.

"Nothin, man," Joey said. "Just talkin."

As Steven started singing, the whole place fell silent. We had all heard him play before, but it was something entirely different to see him up on a stage. He was sitting in a chair, torso leaning heavily to one side, feet pulled underneath, head dropped behind the fretboard, eyes rolled back and closed.

After a couple of songs, his voice changed, his whole demeanor. He came out from behind the guitar, sang louder, more confidently. All meat and metal, wood and wire. He found his presence on the stage. He commanded the entire place, a voice and style both harsh and melodious. What he lacked in musical craft, he made up in genuine timbre, a juxtaposition of painful celebration, joyful melancholy. The emotive yield of three whiskeys and half a pack of smokes.

He played through his set while we all watched reverently. The whole bar hushed and listening. I could see why he was so passionate about the old Gibson guitar. It had a rich, beautiful tone. A tone that was in the grain of the wood, seasoned with years of use. The sound it produced was felt by your entire body, resonating as if you were part of it. A sound that owned the room the way Tom Waits' voice could own a room.

When he finished everyone was clapping and cheering. He climbed off the stage, by this time whiskey drunk, a look of post-coital disillusionment hanging in his eyes. He hurried to the back, uncomfortably passing by the people who were congratulating him, telling him how much they loved his music. He quickly slipped passed them all and got out of the crowd.

He snapped the guitar back in its case and joined us at the back table, all of us now getting soaked, having a good time, trying to sort the first opening of the new gallery.

"Joey should do the first show," said Bradley.

"It's okay, you do it, man," Joey said. "I did the last one."

"No, I'm not ready yet," Bradley said. "I don't have enough canvases that I'm happy with to do an entire show."

"Why don't we all do this one," Steven said. "We've all got a little bit of work we can contribute. We could do a salon hanging, cover all the walls floor to ceiling. Everyone from the original gallery will be represented."

"Not everyone," I said. "Meredith won't be there."

"Oh yeah. Still no word from her, huh?" Bradley asked.

"I tried to call her several times," Steven said. "She never answered. I left her a couple messages but no response. I don't think she's coming back."

"We can't do it without Meredith's photography," Bradley said. "If it's gonna be a group show, then she should be part of it."

"I have some," I suggested. "She gave me a few of her prints. I could put those up."

"That's better than nothing," Steven said. "She'll be there in spirit, at least."

"Now all we have to do is paint the walls and set it up," I said. "We can start tomorrow."

Arvin yelled for last call. He came back to our table and hovered over Steven, counting off money for him. "You have a good time tonight? The crowd seemed to really like it," he grumbled, handing him the cash.

"Yeah, thanks." Steven looked at the money. "Is this all of it? I thought you said—"

"That's after subtracting your tab. You and your friends drank it up."

"Oh. I thought with most places that was part of the gig."

"Not here, and especially not for the lot of you."

Steven laughed and threw the cash on the table. "Here, then give us one more round of your well water."

Arvin glared at him, sorted the bills back into a neat pile, turned, and walked away to get the drinks.

We closed down the bar that night. The first opening was sorted out. We all wanted to go to the gallery where we could keep the momentum alive, play music, and talk until dawn. We left out the back door, carrying our drinks with us, the glasses etched with the Pat's Place logo. We did the Drunkard's Walk through the alley, arm in arm, back to the gallery, feeling like the talentgangs of American literature.

# Salon

Joey got his old job back at Kinkos, working one or two days a week. When we went in to print off fliers for the opening, Joey was standing behind the counter shaping paperclips into monsters and angels.

We waited as one of the paying customers described at length the printing job they needed.

"I'm sorry, man. I'm not authorized to do that," Joey finally said to the customer, setting aside the little paperclip sculpture. "You'll have to talk to that guy over there." He pointed them toward the line at the other register. The customer looked down to the other end of the counter, angrily took his printing needs and his irritation and went and stood at the back of the line, four deep with people, looking at his watch and shaking his head.

Steven and I walked up to the empty counter in front of Joey.

"Looks like you pissed that guy off," Steven said.

"I really don't know how to do that," Joey said to us. "I don't even know what they were talking about."

"What do you mean?" I asked. "You've worked here for a couple years, haven't you?"

"Yeah, man. But I've never been trained to operate most of this equipment. Anytime they show me how to do something, I just play dumb. Eventually they stopped trying."

"I'm surprised they don't fire you," I said.

"So am I," Joey said. "But I guess I'm technically not violating anything in the corporate manual, so they can't fire me."

The main reason Joey went back to the job was because he had access to these huge printers, machines that looked like they could crush cars. He was working on something new, where he made three-dimensional arrangements of his monsters and angels using shadow boxes, then scanned them through the printers when no one was paying attention, running off enormous full-color prints. The cost of these was even more than his hourly wage. Bradley was starting to rub off on him.

"How about some fliers for the opening this weekend?" Steven asked.

"Oh yeah, I can do that. How many do we want?"

Joey printed off a stack of fliers, and we plastered them all over the town. Then we stopped by the hardware store and picked up five gallons of paint. The only thing we had to do to get the gallery ready was paint the walls a flat white instead of the jaundiced yellow.

Bradley, Steven, Pederson, and I got out some rollers and went to work. This time we masked everything off so none of the paint spattered onto the other surfaces. We made quick work of it, each of us starting in one corner and meeting in the middle, not worrying much about the runs or uneven areas. We stepped back to a fresh coat, the whole gallery now clean and neutral.

"It's like a blank canvas," I said, looking at the pure, white wall.

"Yeah, I kinda like it how it is," Steven said. "What if we just leave it like this for the opening. It's Artless. We'll fill the place up and this can be the backdrop, and the people that come through are the foreground."

"Great idea," Bradley said, putting on his Patrick Bateman voice. "You can see the tormented soul of the artists that made this piece. Notice the subtle shading through deliberate variation of medium and the rich, drip-like texture. They were clearly petrified with metaphysical anguish..."

As the walls dried, Steven and I took the van out and found some old pallets. We broke them apart and used the gray-weathered wood to build a small stage in the front of the gallery. When Joey got off work, he came and painted Artless prominently on the storefront window in his primitive, blocky handwriting. I made an "Open" sign for the door, even posting regular hours. Instead of 9-5, it was 5-9 at night, when it was most likely to find someone around and awake.

On the day of the opening, we covered the walls salon-style, floor to ceiling. Digging up all the old paintings and photographs we could. Steven and I put up some of our old paintings. I hung the prints I had from Meredith. Joey and Bradley hung most of their new work, some still wet with paint.

Arvin walked in, and we all quickly grabbed the glasses scattered around that had Pat's Place etched into the side and hid them in the office. No one expected to see him. I didn't think he ever left his bar.

"Brought you some ice," he said.

"Thanks," I said. "What do you think of the gallery?"

He looked around at the hodgepodge of art on the walls. "Gallery? This isn't a gallery. This is a drinking club for a bunch of river city bums. But we're neighbors, so don't say I never did anything for you."

"You've always been a keen observer of humanity, Arvin," Bradley said politely. "Thanks for the frozen tap water, I really can't tell you how valuable that is."

"Y'all are just trying to make heroes out of hobos. You either feed each other or feed off each other. That's the way of everything, don't forget that." He turned and walked out without saying anything else.

That was it. Everything was ready. We opened the doors. Steven pulled out his guitar and set up on the new stage.

As soon as the music started playing, people filtered into the gallery. Within the hour the space was full, a constant flow of people rotating in and out. Everything we had lost in the first gallery was here again. A space to work, a space to open up and bring people in, a space to have fun.

Having the doors open cast the net back out into the town, pulling more creative people in. We met other painters, musicians, photographers. Like-minded people who were also looking for a place where they could share their work. That was the greatest thing of all, sharing what we were doing. It was no longer sand mandalas in the wilderness. It was a scene where you could get your work out there, and everyone was accepted.

Joey and Bradley were wearing matching tracksuits, standing with a group of people at the back of the gallery. They were talking about their paintings to a small group, and I noticed Joey was speaking up rather than letting Bradley do the talking for both of them. Steven was up front, playing the guitar and stomping on the new stage, kicking up some of the fresh, sweet-smelling sawdust. Pederson was in the alley behind the gallery grilling big slabs of meat and fresh vegetables. We spared no expense and had an endless supply of good whiskey, wine, beer.

A man named Charlie approached me and asked about the gallery. He was older, stark white hair and deep creased eyes. He was a photographer as well and had been doing it for thirty years. We talked about the gallery, and he asked about doing a show of his own. He pointed over to one of the photographs hanging on the wall.

"I love these photographs," he said. "Who did these?"

I walked over to where he was pointing. There was the photo Meredith took in front of the Chicago Art Institute of Pederson, the lion, the mutt. Next to it was one of her other photographs, a shot of downtown, overlooking High Street from above. I remembered that day. I was standing next to her when she took it. We were in the capitol building. I had taken her into the House Lounge to see the Benton murals. Afterward she wanted to go to the very top of the capitol dome. We found the door that led up and it was locked, so she used the canister opener in her field bag to pry the latch. It led to the inside of the building, the infrastructure of the dome between the inside and outside walls. We climbed the scaffolding to the top and opened the small hatch out onto the balcony, overlooking the whole town. We stood next to each other in comfortable silence, gazing out, a new perspective. It was one of those memorable days when it was just us.

"Meredith took those," I said finally.

"Where's she? I'd love to ask her about these."

"She's gone," I said.

"Gone where?" Charlie asked.

I wasn't sure how to explain, but I didn't have to, because right then she walked back into the gallery. Her hair was cut shorter, making her look slightly older and more distinguished.

"Meredith!" I called to her.

She saw me and came over. "I heard about this place," she said. Her skin was darker now, bronzed by the sun. We embraced awkwardly, unsure of holding on.

"We tried to call you. Where have you been? What have you been doing?" Questions kept piling up in my head, a compost of anger and elation.

"I've been traveling, working on a photo essay. I got some great shots, I'll show them to you later. And I have all kinds of stories to tell you guys. I've been on the road all day, but looks like I made it in time." There was a short silence. I didn't know what to say.

"Hi, I'm Meredith," she said to Charlie, breaking the silence.

"Oh yeah, this is Charlie."

"We were just talking about you," Charlie said. "I love you're work."

"Thank you," she said.

"Charlie's a photographer, too," I said to Meredith. "He wants to do a show here."

"I don't have any kind of portfolio with me," Charlie said. "But if you want, you can come to my studio and have a look."

"Meredith is the photography expert of the gallery," I said to Charlie. "She'd be the one to talk to."

"We'll both go," Meredith said.

"Great, come by tomorrow and I'll show you some of my work." He gave us his address and walked away.

Silence again. I didn't know what to say, where to begin.

"So where—"

"Hold on. I need a drink," Meredith cut in. "It's been a long drive."

"Sure. It's all in the back there."

"Cool, thanks." She turned and walked off, dissolving into the crowd before we had a chance to talk.

As the night went on, I wanted to talk to her, but she was always in conversations with other people. I could never catch her on her own.

The opening ran late as the crowd dissipated and the music came to an end. Eventually it was only the core people left. We locked the doors and sat around in the office while Meredith shared stories of her trip. Now everyone from the original gallery was back together again.

"I've always admired Dorothea Lange and what she did for the WPA, taking pictures during the Great Depression," Meredith said. I remembered the Lange print of the *Bean Picker* I saw on the shelf in her studio apartment.

"I wanted to do something of my own like that," she said, pulling out some prints of her photography, pictures of immigrants working in California vineyards, in Northwest cranberry bogs, in Florida orange groves. She told us stories of all the people she met as she showed us the photos. They were impressive, every single one. Her best work yet.

She never spoke directly to me, only occasionally glancing over with an apprehensive smile. I flipped through the photographs, listening, longing to have been there with her.

"It was incredible," she said. "I learned more about photography than I ever did in school. I have so much more tell you guys, but I'm starting to fade. It's been a long day, I need to get some sleep."

"Good to have you back," Steven said.

"Thanks. It's good to be back. I'm really glad you guys decided to give it another shot. I've been missing this." She finished her drink, stood up.

I stood up too, walking with her to the door.

"I didn't get a chance to talk to you," I said to her outside the gallery.

"Yeah, I'm sorry, I'm just fucking exhausted right now," she said. "I'll see you tomorrow, right?"

"Sure," I said. "See you tomorrow."

She walked off down the block, stepping confidently, her bag slung over her shoulder.

"Meredith," I called after her. She turned around. "It's really good to see you again."

She smiled, briefly, then turned and kept walking.

# Auto Contrast

I was sitting alone at the desk in the gallery office, behind the new computer, slipping into the alternate world of writing, thinking, thinking about writing, smoking cigarettes, and staring out the window. I heard the door open, footsteps walking the length of the gallery.

"Ready?" Meredith held the door with one hand, leaning into the office.

"Of course." We took her car and drove out of the town to visit Charlie and look at his work, talking along the way, more about her trip, about the ironwork Steven and I did. It felt like small talk, deliberately avoiding how things were left before she disappeared. I wasn't sure how to bring it up, what to say.

"Do you see the address?" She asked as we got close. "Help me watch for it."

We were in the middle of nowhere, some country road. We found the number on a board nailed to a fencepost, a dirt lane leading under a canopy of trees, shading the moon. We drove down it and found a mobile home, ringed with trash, one dull light shining in the window.

"This is his studio?" Meredith asked.

"Must be. It's the address he gave."

We both went to the door and knocked, not sure what to expect. An older woman answered, gray hair pulled tight behind her head, an ashtray in one hand and a filterless cigarette in the other.

She took one look at us and knew what we were there for. "Charlie's in the back. Go on in."

We stepped around the piles of old magazines scattered around the inside of the trailer and made our way to the back bedroom. Charlie was sitting at a desk in front of a computer, working through some of his images, applying automatic effects with Photoshop.

"Come on in, have a seat," he said.

We looked around. There was a bed. He had the only chair.

"Just sit on the edge of the bed, you can see from there. You two want anything? A sodie or some cigarettes? HEY DARLENE, BRING US IN A COUPLE SODIES AND SOME CIGARETTES."

His wife came back with two generic brand colas and one of the kitchen saucers with a few cigarettes she had pulled out of her own pack. She handed them to us and disappeared. A minute later she came back with an ashtray and set it between Meredith and I on the bed.

"Now, let me take you through some of this stuff."

He turned to his computer and pulled up his photographs on the screen. It started with a few tasteful nudes, heavily shadowed, photographed in different industrial settings. He was quickly skipping through them.

"Wait, slow down. These are really good," Meredith said.

"Hang on, these aren't the ones I wanna show you. This is the old stuff."

He skipped through and slowed down when he got to his recent photographs. He clicked through slowly for us. Sensual pictures of women in erotic poses, laying on their backs, eyes closed, slight arches of everything, degrading further until they were almost pornographic shots. And that's when the Photoshop images started. He clicked to treatments of flames surrounding the woman, some with animal print backgrounds, or a snake cropped into the image somewhere.

"Here you go, these are the ones I wanted to show you. This is my best stuff." Meredith and I look at each other in shock.

"Charlie, what about that earlier stuff?" Meredith asked.

"What do you mean? This is what you need to be paying attention to. Those old ones are fine, but *this* is cutting edge."

"Can we just see them?"

"Sure, here you go." He clicked back on his computer. There were images of Native American women, headdresses, bodies beautifully silhouetted.

"These are incredible," Meredith said.

"That girl was hit by a semi truck. She wasn't even supposed to be alive. She's covered in scars, but I framed her so you can't see any of them."

"Really? Why hide the scars?" Meredith asked.

"What I did was take these women that are deformed and frame it to make them beautiful again. I took all of that away. The lighting changes your whole perception."

"But why not show the scars? Those can be beautiful too. Even more beautiful. Now she looks like most other women. The scars would make it unique."

He turned in his chair and looked Meredith over. "You should let me photograph you sometime. You've got all this…healthy tissue." He devoured her every cell with his eyes. "You wouldn't need any lighting."

"No thanks."

"Fine, then be forgotten," he snarled, turning back to his computer. "Now let me show you some more of these other photographs." He redirected us back to his Photoshopped nudes. Meredith and I sat there for a while longer, uncomfortably looking at his digital productions, wanting to leave.

"Thanks, Charlie, I think we've got the idea," Meredith finally said. "We need to get going."

"Let me know when you want me to have an opening in this gallery of yours, I'll run some prints off and have them framed."

We got up and headed for the door. Charlie leaned back in his chair, puffing on his cigarette.

"And let me know if you change your mind," he said to Meredith, leering at her as she walked away.

We left the trailer, got back in the car, and pulled out of the drive. "What a fucking creep," Meredith said. "Let's go back to the gallery."

"Sorry about that," I said. "I had no idea."

On our drive into the town, she told me more about her road trip, all the photographs she had taken. We pulled up to the gallery. She grabbed her camera bag out of the back seat and brought it inside. Luckily, there was no one else there. I pulled a leftover bottle out of the drawer and poured us a couple of drinks. It still didn't feel comfortable with her, not like it was before.

She pulled out a camera. A different one than she was using before.

"New camera?" I asked.

"Yeah, picked this one up before the trip."

She handed it to me, a large, sleek DSLR, screen full of options. "I thought you were shooting with film?"

"Not anymore. Now I want to shoot digital."

"But what about what you said before, about film being better than digital?"

"I'm not saying it's better. It's just different. Photographers are all in love with old enlargers and film negatives, celebrating these things because they're rare now. But in reality it isn't happening in darkrooms anymore. It's digital, it's computers. I no longer want to try and go back to the past and recreate what the darkroom did. I read something in Weston's book that stuck with me. Something like 'Why do what I did with photography? Set your own standard.' The point is that if you go back and try to replicate something, then you're wasting your time. Those people already did it."

"But I thought you said film was more natural?"

"Yeah, but then I realized darkroom photography uses chemicals and processes to create different effects. It's artificially producing an image using whatever information it can gather. Digital does the same thing, only now we just click around on a computer. Besides, digital is closer to how the brain works. How the human eye, which is the only perfect lens, actually processes information. And there are things you can do with digital that film just can't do."

"You mean like what Charlie does?" I said, a little sarcastically.

"Don't get me wrong, Charlie's photographs were missing it. It didn't seem genuine to me. I want to see the scars, not hide them. And the new stuff was fake. Fake flames, fake animal prints. It just didn't seem honest. There's a downside to all this technology, too. It may be easier to arrive at, but it doesn't make you more creative."

As the conversation went on the tension loosened up. A warmth between us, talking the way we used to talk, staying up all night together in the last gallery. I poured us another drink and sat down next to her on the couch.

"I'm surprised, is all. Never thought you'd turn to digital. You seemed so adamant."

"I know, it seems naive now. But I'm glad I started out that way. I'll always love film, and I have a much better appreciation because of it. This is a great time to be an artist because we're still in the friction point of industry and technology. We get to have both worlds, because we're straddling between all these vintage processes on one end and this whole virtual thing on the other, before one is forgotten and the other takes over completely."

Neither of us spoke for a minute, finding that calm silence again, listening to the sounds of the Midwest night through the open window, the cicadas singing in harmony. She leaned back on the couch, settling in closer to me.

"Why did you leave?" I finally broached the subject. "I mean, why didn't you say anything? I thought—"

"I'm sorry. I had to. I wanted to talk to you, but I didn't know what to say. I freaked out after that night. I was afraid…because…I didn't want to get that close."

"Why not? What's so bad about that?"

She straightened back up, speaking in a nervous tone. "Because…I don't know…it's fucked up…I like you but…I don't want to like you…it just complicates things…I'm already committed to my work…and…maybe we could be happy, but…I'm not sure that's what I want right now—"

"What do you mean? I thought—"

"I'm sorry, that's why I had to leave…I don't know why I do that every time, why I run away…but I can't help it…I'm just afraid that—"

The back door kicked open and the rest of the crew came spilling in, carrying half-full glasses from Pat's Place, singing out the last of a Van Morrison song that had been piping through the bar. Meredith slid over on the couch, putting a little distance between us.

"Hey! What the fuck's going on!" Joey shouted, then started laughing.

We both looked at each other, and I knew it came off as awkward, the two of us sitting there, the way she didn't want to give anything away.

"How'd it go with the photographer?" Steven asked.

I looked over at Meredith. "Not so great," I finally said. "The earlier stuff was beautiful, but, I don't know, it's going nowhere."

# 6/8

Another Midwest winter thawed, blooming into dewy spring, then burning off with the swelter of another summer. The gallery had been open a few months, growing, synthesizing, more people netted with every new opening we did. It was no longer just the six of us. We were doing shows all the time, each one bigger, better than the last. Paintings, photography, screening films using a projector we picked up, showcasing live music on the pallet-wood stage, anything that came along.

Between these we closed the doors and used the space as a studio, where Bradley and Joey did all their painting. Steven, Meredith, and I used the office to work on our own projects.

At first I was starting to get somewhere with the novel I was working on, staying up late nights, the small clicking of the keyboard like tacking pin nails into the hard drive of the new computer.

But the closer I felt I was to finishing, the harder it seemed to find any time to work on it. Always more people coming and going in the gallery, so many distractions. After I while, I was barely writing anything. Sometimes I could catch a little here and there, putting on headphones to drown out the noise.

I sat behind the computer, listening to a waltzing melody, trying to remember something I had read about group size studies, when you get beyond a certain number and—

An enormous crash came from the gallery, followed by drunken laughter. I pulled my headphones back off, set them down on the desk, and went to see what it was, the cursor still blinking on a blank screen.

# Harvest Dinner

Steven and I carried two long folding tables out from the office and set them up in the middle of the gallery, between all the canvases hanging on the walls from the last opening. We had started the harvest dinner tradition, the one we only talked about doing in the last gallery. Every Wednesday night we gathered over a meal, indulging in the Great Conversation, passing around instruments, ironing out plans for the next show.

    We covered the folding tables in a long, paint-splattered drop-cloth. Chairs were pulled up. We had well over a dozen people. Everyone brought something to the table. Pederson had gotten a job at a winery outside of town, spending late nights walking the vine rows, plucking grapes, less tender under the moonlit nights. He was always good for a case of their least-sweet. He carried in twelve chartreuse bottles of Norton and set them in the middle of the drop-cloth with a grunt.

    Steven and I pulled the corks out of each bottle and spread them around, decanting on the altar of splattered paint. The meals became less opulent once he and I both blew through the money we had made from the ironwork. We paid last month's rent with what was left of it, but we weren't thinking about that. For now, the table was filled with adequate food, some of it stolen from the grocer, some from dumpster diving, whatever means available.

I sat near one end of the table. Next to me was Cardwell, short, squat, prematurely bald, a relatively new face. He did graphic and web design. He brought four whole rotisserie chickens from the supermarket deli. He ate these on a daily basis, part of some protein diet he was on.

Next to him was Sean, thick glasses over sharp, dark eyes. He brought a few loaves of day old bread from the dumpster behind the bakery. He worked behind a camera for the public access television station when he wasn't making documentary films. Always carrying a mini-DVD Sony Handycam, filming everything he could.

Across from him was Randal, a handsome Adonis, clean cut with a big, Roman nose, pin-striped pants, v-neck undershirt. He had recently finished law school but was putting off taking the bar exam. He made a mango chutney, a recipe he'd found in some fitness magazine.

Everyone was eating, drinking, talking over one another. A group of hungry artists, all of us poor but happy. Finding art in the taste we swallowed and ingested. Always hungry. Always voracious appetites, looking for the next experience. We were the chefs, the tastemakers of our own table. And this was how we lived, bringing our hands to our mouths. Wednesday night, the doors open to all.

Meredith sat at the other end of the table, as far away from me as possible. Everything was mountains and valleys with her. Over the last few months we occasionally had the gallery to ourselves, staying up late, drinking, talking the way we used to talk. But the more openings we had, the more there were always people around. Now it was impossible to find the gallery empty. It didn't matter anyway. Meredith had become completely absorbed in her work. It was all she cared about, all she ever did.

Next to her was Steven, sitting at the head of the table, talking to Gabe and Doss, a couple of installation artists.

"So we're all set for Meredith's opening this weekend," Steven spoke up, getting everyone's attention. "After that Gabe and Doss wanna do an installation."

"It's gonna be awesome," said Gabe, sitting next to him. He had dark hair, salt-streaks above the ears, bushy chops. "We're gonna go nuts and totally transform the space. Anyone who wants to pitch in is welcome."

"We could use it," said Doss. He was tall, lean, with wide, slumped shoulders. "We'll be moving a fuck-ton of material. The whole thing will probably take about three weeks."

"Everybody cool with that?" Steven asked.

"I'm in," I said. "We haven't had an installation yet."

"Me too," Meredith said. "Sounds like a lot of fun."

"Right. *Fun*," Bradley scoffed. "And where the fuck are we supposed to work while this is going on? This is our studio, you know."

"It's only temporary," Gabe said. "You'll have your studio back."

"Why not help out with the installation in the meantime?" Doss asked. "You can incorporate some of your paintings."

"No thanks, I have my own work to do. Joey and I will find somewhere else to paint." Bradley took a big lash of cheap whiskey from a bottle on the table and slammed it back. "Fuck it, let's get drunk. We're here to have *fun*, right?"

There was an uncomfortable pause, then everyone started talking and eating again and didn't pay any attention. I knew Bradley didn't mind the installation, it was all the new people being absorbed into the gallery he didn't care for.

After the meal everyone split off to smoke a cigarette or play music. I was still sitting at the table, overhearing the conversations around me.

"So you're a filmmaker?" someone asked Sean.

"Well, I make films, if that's what you mean. But I don't like to be categorized. If you're committing a *verb*, someone immediately wants to make you a *noun*…"

I reached across the table, grabbed a bottle of Norton, filled my glass. On my other side I heard Randal talking.

"I don't really do *art*, per se," Randal said. "I have done some modeling. Did you go to Art in the Park last year? Remember the human statue of David? Yeah, that was me…"

I lit another cigarette. I tried to remember the last time it was just the six of us from the original gallery. I couldn't.

When Cardwell approached and asked Steven and I to join him in the office, I was somewhat relieved to be stepping away.

"I wanted to talk to you guys," he said when we were in the office. He immediately took a seat behind the desk and fired up my computer, the only tangible thing I had left to show for those two months of hard labor. He scooted his chair into the desk, fleshy paunch wedged into the middle drawer, eyes like copper coins. He looked like one of Leonard Baskin's *Warriors*, a desperate collection of recessive genes.

He reached into his bag and pulled out a bottle of Makers. "You guys like whiskey?"

Steven and I both chuckled, drained the wine out of our etched Pat's Place glass and wiped them out with our shirts, set them on the desk. Pederson wandered through the door and walked over, setting his own glass down beside ours as Cardwell was filling them.

"So what's up?" Steven asked. Cardwell took his time, filling the glasses slowly. Pederson took his and stretched out below the open window. Steven and I pulled up a couple of chairs.

"Which one of you is managing this place?" asked Cardwell.

"Managing?" said Steven. "There's nothing to manage."

"Of course there is. Every project needs a manager. Even the anarchists have to organize, right?" He laughed lightly.

"What did you want to talk about?" Steven said, wanting to get to the point.

"I really like this place, what you're trying to do here. This town needs a gallery like this. An independent voice is a rare thing to find. Seems like everything else has some kind of ties to the Coalition, but you guys are doing it on your own."

"What are you driving at?" Steven asked.

"How are the sales going? I know I haven't been involved that long, but how are you keeping the lights on? It doesn't seem like anyone is buying anything. From what I've seen, no one even *tries* to sell anything."

"We've only been open for a few months," I said.

"A few months? I can't believe you don't have anything online yet. That's where I thought I might be able to help. I could make a website for the gallery. It's the only way to go now. We have to reach out beyond the city limits. Social media is exploding now, and we're not utilizing it. We need to broaden our audience, do a little online marketing. The people who come through here aren't the ones we're after, they're not the target market."

"What's wrong with the people who come through here?" Steven asked.

"Nothing, nothing. I'm just saying, the people here are all *creating* art, and that's great. But we need to find a market. Maybe we could work out some kind of agreement."

"We don't care about the market," Steven said. "What's your angle here?"

"Let me back up. All I want is for all of us to create something without having any limitations. I could put it where people will see it, lots of people. If you get it out there, and more people buy it, then you create more opportunity. That doesn't sound so bad, right? I could shoulder that burden for you guys, be like the gallery manager. And maybe just take a small percentage when something sells. Nothing big, just, you know, quid pro quo." He leaned back in his chair, looking off to the side, running quiet algorithms in his mind.

"Listen, we've been through this before, and I'm not doing it," Steven said. "We have something good here. It's organic, and everyone's free to do what they want. We don't need any kind of management."

"Okay, calm down. I'm just looking at possibilities. This is a revenue potential that isn't being exploited right now."

"Exploited? What fucking language are you speaking?" Steven stood up. "I've heard enough. Even good whiskey isn't a sufficient chaser for this bullshit. Find something else to exploit." He kicked back his chair, drained his glass, and shuffled off. A few seconds later he turned back. "Oh yeah, I just recognized a potential in this room." He grabbed the bottle of Makers off the desk, filled his glass back up to the brim, then walked out of the office.

"What's got him so uptight?" Cardwell asked me. "Art doesn't happen in a vacuum, you know. Everything is online now, so if you want the doors to stay open, you'll have to keep up."

"Don't mind that," I said. "None of us are any good at the business side of things, no one seems to even think about it."

"Yeah, I can tell," he said. "How are you paying rent?"

"I have no idea," I said. "We just ran out of money. We're gonna have to figure that out, soon."

"You said you used to work for the *Telegraph*, right?"

"Sure, a while ago. Back when it was still in print."

"Have you seen their new website?" he asked.

"No, I guess I haven't."

He pulled it up on the screen and twisted the monitor in my direction.

"It's been doing really well ever since it went online," he said.

I clicked through some of the headlines. All top ten lists, brief articles, blog posts, ads popping up or flashing in banners.

"I don't know, it seems a little hollow."

"It's not hollow, it's self-preservation. You have to blend in if you wanna survive."

"I see your point." I stood up and filled my glass. "But right now I don't want to think about it either."

"Keep it in mind. You seem to be the more reasonable one. Maybe you could talk to the others about it."

"Maybe." I turned and walked out of the office, leaving Cardwell sitting alone behind the desk, ready to sell whatever was in his hand, while Pederson lay under the window across the room, gazing and fishing lint from his sweat-puddled navel.

In the gallery, Randal was sitting at the table rolling up a joint. Joey was next to him drawing on the canvas drop cloth with a marker. Everyone else scattered around in little cliques. I sat at the table, my mind now stuck on the rent problem.

"I guess Bradley and I are gonna find our own studio," Joey said to me.

"You don't have to do that," I said. "You'll have the space back in no time. It's only three weeks."

"I know, but—" His voice was a little sheepish. "I'm not sure I can paint here anymore. There's all these people around all the time. It makes me feel like I'm performing or something. It's hard for me to get any work done."

I didn't know what to tell him. It was unfortunate, but understandable.

"Hit?" Randal broke the silence, handing me the joint.

"Sure," I said. I took a drag, coughed out a thanks, handing it back.

"Careful, it's high-gravity stuff. I use it to self-medicate."

I took another hit. "Medicate for what?" I asked without exhaling.

"ADHD. This works better than the Adderall."

"Did you say Adderall?" Joey perked up. "You got any extra, man?"

"Sure, I rarely ever take them, anyway. Too much chemistry for me." He took another drag off the joint and held it in. "My body is a temple." He exhaled toward the ceiling.

"What are you doing?" Bradley said, stepping into the conversation. "Don't give Joey speed. You don't know what he's been through." He stood over Randal, eyes now a little glassy and red, a bar mug full of warm Stag wobbling in one hand.

"Whoa, take it easy," Randal said. "Here, have some of this." He offered Bradley the joint.

"Fuck that. I can't stand pot," Bradley said. "I despise that odor."

"What do you mean, what's wrong with it?" Randal asked.

"It smells like failure."

"Yeah, well," Randal shrugged. "I guess I'm addicted to failure."

"What am I talking about? What the fuck do I care? It's not my gallery. You do whatever you want."

Sean came over with his camera, pointed it around the crowd. "Keep talking," he said. "Pretend I'm not even here. I'm just getting some footage for the doc."

Randal offered the joint around. "Joey?"

Joey was about to reach for it, but Bradley stepped in between. "What the fuck? Don't give Joey any of that either. He doesn't need induced paranoia."

"Really? Do you make all Joey's decisions for him?" The strings tightened between them.

"He's funny," Bradley said to me, laughing. "Who is this faggot prince, anyway? Where do you keep finding these people?" He reached down and tussled Randal's perfectly parted hair, and Randal immediately ducked the hand like a pugilist.

"Hey, careful! You don't want to mess up a work of art. You don't just walk into the Louvre and start penciling mustaches on the Mona Lisa, do you?"

"Oh, that's cute, hearing you talk about art. You think you know something now that you get to hang around here? What have you ever done?"

"Fuck you. I don't see you doing anything with *your* art. Seems to me like you're just hanging onto Joey and waiting to cash in. Way to go, you're excelling at mediocrity."

Bradley stopped laughing, pitched his glass down and splashed the beer right into Randal's face, spray hitting the lens of Sean's camera.

"Oops!" He started laughing again, harder, kept laughing. "Just having a bit of *fun*, right?"

Randal stood up from his chair, squared up to Bradley, chiseled jaw clenched, warm beer dripping from his chin. He was taller, stronger, but Bradley was full of fight and Randal had none. Bradley kept laughing, a low and wicked admission. They were like silverbacks from different jungles.

"This is rich," Sean muttered, adjusting the focus on his camera. "This is what drives a good story."

"What are you gonna do?" Bradley asked.

"Fuck you," Randal finally said, then turned and marched out the front door, wiping the beer from his face, the camera following him every step of the way.

# Exposure

Meredith came to the gallery to get ready for her opening. Pockets of people milled around, talking and drinking. She passed by them to the office, where Steven and I were working on our own projects.

"Hey," she said to both of us indifferently. "Who's that guy out there painting? Where's Bradley and Joey?"

"That's Ichi," I said. "Or at least, he goes by Ichi. That's his graffiti tag. We met him at the last opening, remember?"

"No, I guess I don't."

"Anyway, he's working on some paintings. I haven't seen Bradley or Joey lately."

"Okay, whatever. I gotta make some frames. You mind if I use your chop saw?"

"That's fine," I said. "It's over there in the corner with the other tools. You want some help?"

"No, I got it." She set everything up, bringing the chop out to the gallery and using it on the floor to build all her frames, working through the night. We were all preoccupied and didn't speak much.

Around two in the morning, she finished the frames and hung the last of her photographs.

I took a break and went out to the gallery. "Damn, these are staggering," I said, looking around at the powerful images she chose from her trip. "It'll be a good show tomorrow night."

"Thanks," she said. "Glad you like them."

I walked toward the office. "You want a drink? You've been at it for awhile."

"No, I need to go home." She scooped up her portfolio bag and headed toward the door.

"Sure. Guess I'll see you later then."

"Yep. Later."

She left, and I went back into the office, put the Elliott Smith album *Either/Or* into the computer, slipped on headphones to drown out the voices in the gallery, tried to write. I didn't understand her. One minute everything was fine, the next she was aloof, distant. I couldn't figure it out. I was glad she was back, but everything was mixed up.

2:45 A.M. I took off the headphones, shut down the computer for the night. Everyone had gone home, finally. I rolled a sleeping bag out onto the folding table in the office and went to sleep.

The next night was Meredith's opening. We filled the gallery with people again. She moved around the room, telling stories from her trip. Standing proudly, gin soaking into the foam of her cigarette, looking more beautiful than ever. She was in the spotlight, and everyone loved her photography. I was happy for her, the way she was glowing.

I met more people who wanted to be a part of the gallery, who wanted to do an opening of their own. People everywhere, filling the office, the sidewalk out front, the alley. Part of me was hoping for it to die down, for it to be just the six of us again.

A short, frail old gentleman in a suit came through the door. He walked around, studying the photographs, paying little attention to the crowd, all half his age, drinking and talking around him. After he carefully absorbed each image, he walked up to me, the only person who wasn't entangled in conversation.

"Excuse me, could you tell me who took these photographs?" he asked.

"Sure, she's right over there."

"I'd like to meet her," he said politely.

"Okay, I'll go get her." I went over to a circle of people, gently put my hand on Meredith's arm, interrupting what she was saying.

"What is it?" she asked.

"There's someone over here who wants to meet you," I said.

"Excuse me," she said to the rest of circle. "I'll be right back."

Meredith whispered to me as we crossed the gallery toward the suit. "Who's this guy, anyway?"

"No idea," I whispered back.

We walked up to him, and he shook Meredith's hand.

"You have a good eye," he said, the air of an academic appraisal. "I'm impressed with your work. Could be a very promising future with photographs like these."

"Thank you," Meredith said.

"I'd like to purchase something from you. I noticed there were no prices on the exhibit labels."

"Yeah, that was intentional. I didn't want people to look at a number, just the work."

"So how much are these? Do you have a price list I could look at?"

"There's no list. How much can you afford?"

"I'm sorry, I don't understand. Do you not have a price already fixed?"

"No. I thought I'd keep an open mind. I want them to be accessible for anyone who appreciates the work. I figured if anyone was interested I'd sell them on a sliding scale."

"Sounds very admirable. But you're a great photographer, and you should take it more seriously. If you want your work to be considered valuable, you have to apply a value to it."

"I do take my work *very* seriously. You liked the images, right? That's the value."

"Okay then," he pulled a leather checkbook from the breast pocket of his suit. "How much for all of them."

She looked at him coolly, nonplussed by his bearing, his checkbook. "Whatever you can afford."

"And what if I said I was poor, that I could only afford a few dollars."

"Then I'd sell them to you for a few dollars."

He slid the checkbook back into his coat pocket with a condescending sigh. "Then, I'm afraid I'll have to pass. This is not the way I do business." He turned to leave. "Best of luck to you."

"Sure," Meredith said. "Thanks for stopping in."

He walked out, got into the back seat of a car, and it pulled away.

Bradley came up, eyes wide. "Do you know who that was?"

"Nope," Meredith said.

"Samuel Cole."

Meredith didn't respond.

"You know, *Samuel Cole*, the owner of Central Bank."

"So what."

"So what? He wanted to buy your photographs. That's a big fucking deal. He's one of the biggest art collectors in the country."

"Good for him."

"So, that's the person you want buying your stuff."

"Why? So he can decorate another branch of his banks? I don't like how he came in and just thought he could buy up anything he wanted."

"You're a fool. If you want to make a name for yourself, you need to take people like him seriously."

Meredith shrugged it off, took a sip of her gin, lit another cigarette.

"Oh my god, if only I had a fucking shot like that..." Bradley said as he walked off, head shaking.

Meredith turned to me. "Maybe I was being kind of a bitch? What do you think? Did I make a mistake?"

"I don't know, I get what you're saying. But why not just name him some ridiculous price? Who knows, he probably would've paid it."

"But it's not the money. I don't give a shit about that."

"Maybe not for you, but think about the gallery. If we're gonna keep this place going, we need to sell something. We won't have too many chances like that one. Not all of us have the *luxury* of turning money down."

I shouldn't have said that. I knew right away I shouldn't have said that.

"Is that what this is about? You want me to sell out so we can make money? I don't know what you mean by having the "luxury," but if you think I'm being supported you're wrong. I have to *work* for my money."

"Sure. And you could afford to just travel all over the country for three months? Someone had to pay for it."

Again, the words came out before I thought about them. Not what I meant to say.

"Yeah, someone did pay for it. *Me*," she said, squaring up her stance. "What I never mentioned was that I worked in those fields, alongside the people I was photographing. And when I had enough gas money, I took off and did it all over again. *That's* how I could afford it."

"I'm sorry, that's not what I meant to say. Just that we need to figure out how to keep the gallery, that's all I'm worried about. It's a business, like it or not. If we wanna hang on to this, we're gonna have to compromise."

"Are we?" Meredith asked, eyes defiant.

When I didn't respond, she turned and walked away.

# Screening

The lights were out in the gallery. The projector was on, pointed toward the back wall, a film already playing when I walked in. People were scattered around, mostly on the floor.

I walked up to Sean, who was standing next to the projector in the back of the crowd.

"What's going on?" I asked him. "I didn't know we were doing anything tonight."

"I'm screening my new film," Sean whispered. "Steven said it was cool."

"Oh," I said. "Where is Steven, anyway? I need to talk to him about something."

"Don't know, I haven't seen him for awhile. He left before we got started."

I looked at the screen.

"What's wrong with the sound?" I asked.

"Shhh!" someone hissed.

"It's supposed to be like that," Sean whispered. "It's mumblecore."

"Hmm," I said.

"You know, low-budget indie stuff. I only had five grand to work with."

"*Only* five grand?"

"SHHHH!" someone else hissed.

"I know, right?" Sean whispered. "That's all my dad would give me. I was able to pull it off though. That's how it goes with independent filmmaking, you just have to figure it out."

I watched a few more minutes of the film, before retreating to the back office. I sat down at the desk, trying to figure out a solution for the rent problem. I found the cell phone in the middle drawer. I leaned into the chair, dialed up Travis.

"Hey, Travis—Yeah, it's me—I know, I know, things are crazy here. You should come down and see it sometime—No, you're right. You'd probably hate it—Anyway, can I get that number from you again?—The guy who hooked us up with the ironwork last Fall—I don't want to, believe me—I'm not even sure I'm going to, but I wanted to get the number, just in case—Yeah, who knows—Okay, got it. How have you been? I miss seeing you, especially on that nice drywall backdrop—Yeah, you go fuck yourself, too—Anyway, thanks, for everything—Bye."

I wrote the number down, hung up the phone. It might be tolerable to do it again, especially if Steven went along. But I knew there was no way he would. I sat there for a while, wondering if I could go by myself. Endure that cold, lonely existence for another couple of months.

I put the number in the desk drawer, slid it shut.

I looked around the room for things that could be pawned. I went to the corner where we had a few tools. Some of them were mine, some were Steven's. I wanted to talk to him, see what he would be willing to part with. I grabbed the chop saw, a few other power tools. Tools we used to build up the last gallery. In the other corner I noticed Steven's prized guitar. I thought about it, only for a second. I knew that was off limits.

I walked out of the office, carefully stepping around the people scattered on the floor, faces washed in blue light from the screen. Trying not to bump anyone with the chop saw as I wove my way through.

I opened the back door of the van and put the saw in, went back into the gallery for another load. Ichi got up off the floor, walked into the office behind me.

"You need a hand with that stuff?"

"Sure, grab those tools over there," I said.

We both took another load out to the van, then another. I looked over the pile that was now in the back of the van, the latent potential. It would probably be enough to pay the rent, already two weeks late, meaning in another two it would be due again.

Ichi lit a cigarette. He had a handsome, black-freckled face, half-Japanese looking with his dark, narrow eyes.

"Hey, I wanted to thank you guys for lettin me paint here," he said. "This is the first time I've done anything inside, you know, not in an alley or hangin off some building."

"No problem," I said. "Your paintings are really good. You should do an opening."

"Thanks. I've got a lot of new stuff finished. Pretty soon I'll be ready."

"You going back in?" I asked. "The movie's still playing."

"Nah, I gotta go. I wanna do some tags tonight. I got the perfect spot scouted out," Ichi said. "I'll see you later."

He walked off down the block. The movie ended shortly after that and people came out of the gallery, smoking cigarettes on the sidewalk.

"Hey, you seen Ichi?" asked one of the newer faces. "He didn't leave did he?"

"Yeah," I said. "He just took off."

"Ichi? Who's that?" asked another.

"What? You don't know Ichi?" the first person responded. "He's a rad artist. He's like *the* painter here. I think this place might even be like his studio."

I closed the door to the van, locked it, walked quietly back inside.

# Salvage

Gabe and Doss were walking through the gallery, taking measurements of the space, surveying the support structures. We were talking about the previous installations they'd done. They were pack rats, hoarders, builders, mechanics, weird scientists. Gabe was the driving force behind the aesthetic. Doss refined the ideas into something workable. Together they came up with these mythical, architectonic structures, transforming a space into something magical and interactive using mostly cast-off materials.

"This is the first time we've had an opening that wasn't photography or painting," I said. "It's refreshing, in some ways, not having to stress about the idea that something might actually sell."

"Yeah, I used to paint, but I could never make it work," Gabe said. "That's what drew me to installations in the first place. I'm a horrible business person, but with this, there's really no exchange."

"Good thing," I said. "Because since we've been open, we haven't sold a single work."

"It's fine, Doss and I do construction on the side. We can usually drum up a remodel gig between installations to keep us afloat. People may not be willing to pay a couple hundred for a painting on the wall, but they'll pay a couple grand for us to sand the floor under their feet."

"Plus it's a good source of materials. We reuse everything we tear out of someone's house to make something of our own," Doss added. "Besides, if you're sanding a floor, everyone expects it to look a certain way, there's not too much freedom in that. Here, we get to do whatever we want." He flicked the ember off his cigarette, put the butt in the pocket of his jeans. "Alright, let's get started."

"We're gonna make a field trip for materials," Gabe said to me. "You wanna come along?"

"Sure, I'll follow you in the van."

"Is anyone else coming?" Doss asked.

"I guess not," I said. "I haven't seen anyone today."

I found the keys to the van in the desk drawer and followed their pickup to a field outside of town with an old farmhouse falling in on itself. They had permission from the owner to take whatever they wanted. He was going to burn the rest when the snows came.

They pulled out a generator and some tools, and we started pulling the house down in sections, removing entire walls intact. Doss surprised me, lean but strong as an ox, could move mountains of material.

It took a couple of trips to move it all back to the gallery. We also raided the detritus from construction sites, dumpsters, stopped at flea markets. We got all of this together and were staring at huge stacks of salvaged lumber, fabric, glass, cable lines, shingles, chain link fence with vines still growing through it, old timbers, joists, materials with an age, a weathering, an immediate history.

We were taking stock, getting an idea of what was possible, when Steven and Meredith walked in through the back door.

"Murder and hell," said Steven. "Where did you find all this stuff?"

"We've been driving around town all day collecting it," I said.

"Damn, there's so much chaos in here," Meredith said.

"Great, isn't it?" asked Gabe. "Look at all this potential."

"So where do we start?" Meredith asked. "What are we going for?"

"That's what's so awesome about it, there's no set of rules," Doss said. "There's no right or wrong way it's supposed to look in the end."

"It's a collaboration, just pick a starting point and dive in," Gabe said. "It's pretty autonomous, but Doss and I will make sure there's a central nervous system that ties it all together. That's the most important thing. It's chaotic now, but in the end these things will all have a balance that makes it work."

We started the long process of assembling the installation. Working day after day to build it out. Everyone basically lived in the gallery, coming and going, making more runs for materials to complete an idea. Putting things together. Sometimes tearing them apart and rebuilding them into something different.

One day I walked over to the CD player and put on one of my favorite albums, went back to work.

"Yes! I fucking love this song!" Meredith shouted, going over to crank the volume up. It was *Pale Blue Eyes* by The Velvet Underground.

"Good call," Steven approved from the other end of the gallery.

We all agreed that it was one of the greatest songs ever made. Before it played through to the end, Meredith went back over to the CD player.

"I need to hear that again. Anyone mind?" she asked. Of course, no one did. She pressed the repeat button. When it was over, the song restarted from the beginning.

We would catch a nap when we could, making a pallet out of whatever was around, but slept little. Taking whore baths in the bathroom sink. Always a pot of coffee going, inevitably mixed with booze when the sun went down. Surviving on day-old bread pulled from the dumpsters while looking for more materials. The smell of toast cooking over halogen lamps like a bakery, a sawmill. *Pale Blue Eyes* still playing on repeat. What started as a joke, to see how long we could endure it, turned into a marathon of playing only one song.

Bradley and Joey walked in and saw the overrun gallery. They went straight to the back corner and gathered up their paint supplies.

"Look at all this shit," Bradley said to me. "Looks like you've installed the old gallery inside of this one."

I looked around. I hadn't thought about it, but he was right, it did look a lot like the last space. And for some reason, I found that comforting.

"I think it's cool, man," Joey said. "I can't wait to see what you do with all this."

"There's still a lot to do," I said. "Not too late to jump in and help out."

"I would stick around, but I don't think I'd be much help," Joey said.

"What's the point," Bradley said. "It'll get torn right back down."

"Sure, it's not a precious thing," Gabe responded. "It's totally different than painting, where you have to be burdened by the hope that it might last forever. But that's what makes it fun. You get to be a little more reckless."

"We know we're not carving marble or anything," Doss said. "Gabe and I have a whole ghost body of work in our past, none of it exists anymore. Just the memory of what it was, maybe a few photographs."

"I guess every kid thinks he invented masturbation," Bradley said to him. He turned to me. "Maybe you should charge admission, turn this place into an amusement park."

"Come on Bradley, stick around," I said. "It's not the same if you guys aren't part of it."

"No thanks. Joey and I found a garage across town we can use for a studio. You kids have fun." They went back to the office, packed up their supplies, and took off.

When the song came to an end, it backed up, started all over again.

We kept building night and day. If we hit a slow point, when nothing seemed to be working out, the momentum slowed, someone new inevitably showed up, reinvigorating the rest of us. Sean was there, sometimes helping, sometimes running the camera. Pederson showed up with another case of wine.

"What can I do?" Randal asked when he walked in. "Brief me on what's going on here."

"The basic idea is to make something interactive," said Gabe. "We're trying to create an immersive experience, and this is just the backdrop. It doesn't have to make sense, it just has to be enjoyed. It's something you're a part of more than something you look at."

"Sounds good." He reached into his pocket, pulled out a translucent orange pill bottle. "Here, thought you guys might want some of this." He dispensed a few of his little pink pills to all of us, creating a new surge on the installation as we all dove back in. The room was starting to take shape, form. You could start to see the big picture.

We kept working, working. The Velvet Underground song now playing for three straight days. Over and over, like a mobiüs strip, infinite loops all chained together. The volume was adjusted, but at this point no one would dare turn it off.

When the landlord walked in, Doss was on the ladder hammering cedar shakes all around the top of a pillar we'd installed in the center of the gallery. Gabe was taping a silhouette over the ladder's shadow cast onto the wall by the halogen lamp. Meredith and I were working side by side on the farmhouse.

"What is all this? Who said you could do this?" the landlord asked.

"It's an art installation," Gabe said.

"Art? What art? You're ruining my building!"

"It's only temporary," I said. "We'll put it all back the way it was."

"Don't placate me! You can't mitigate me! You still owe rent this month. You're late. Again!"

"Don't worry, we'll have it for you," Steven said. "We're only a little behind."

He looked fiercely at Steven, then at me, pointing. "I've been very considerate of you, letting you have this space. Now what have you done to considerate me?"

No one said anything. All you could hear was *Pale Blue Eyes*, still playing at low volume. Then someone, I don't know who it was, started laughing.

"You think this is funny? If I don't get the rent, I'm evicting all of you. See if you're still laughing *then*." He turned, started walking out. "And I want this gone next time I come in here," he added, then left.

"Damn, what's his problem?" Gabe asked. They all went back to what they were doing, as if it were nothing to worry about.

I put down my hammer and rushed outside. The landlord was getting into his car.

"I'm sorry about that," I said.

"No, I'm sorry. I knew this was a mistake from the beginning."

"We'll have the rent, I promise. Just give us a few days."

"You have until next week. That's it." He started the car, drove away.

I went back inside, back to work. Wondering if this opening would be our last. Meredith came over as I started putting together parts of the old farmhouse in the back of the gallery.

"Need a hand?" she asked.

"Sure," I said. "Thanks." She grabbed some tools, and we worked side by side. One of us would measure, the other cut. One hold up a board, the other nail it together. I thought of all the hours we spent in the darkroom or fixing up the last gallery.

"I like doing installations," I said. "It's very all-consuming, trying to solve the immediate problem of how to put all this together. It takes your mind off everything else."

"Yeah. I don't ever want this to go away," she said, hammering in a board as I held it in place. "We work pretty well together, you know that."

"I think so."

"You're working really hard for this," Meredith said.

"Sure, we all are."

"No, I mean the gallery. You've been working hard to keep this place going. You have a lot of drive. I admire that about you."

"Yeah, sometimes I feel like I'm all alone on this. I don't understand."

"I wanna figure out how to make this work, I really do. I know I've been a little distant lately."

"A little?"

"I know, I know. I don't want it to be like that anymore."

"Neither do I," I said, looking up at Meredith, hammer in her hand.

"We can make this work," she said.

I nodded, a little unsure if we were on the same page.

"Come on, help me hold this," she finally said, breaking the warm silence, hoisting up another joist.

# Installation

The installation was finally ready on the day of the opening. Or at least, we called it ready, since there was no real beginning or end anyway. Just a starting point, a lull, and a stopping point. A moment in time.

"This is perfectly okay," said Gabe, taking it all in. "Especially in context of this space."

"It's ironic and it's beautiful and it's stupid," said Doss.

"It is what it isn't," Gabe added. "Like this place. It's Artless."

The focal point was a pillar with an enormous purple martin house bulging out of the top like an inverted favela. In the back was a small-scale replica of the farmhouse, recreated to look as if it had rolled over onto it's rooftop and was upside down. A canoe made of broken crutches and seamed together plastic bags. A mural of masking tape. A birds nest of barbed wire. Kickarounds made of crates stacked on casters that were wrapped in fabric. A coffered ceiling over the pallet-wood stage with multiple levels, each one smaller and slightly turned, built to the golden mean, 1.618.

People filled the gallery that night, walking around the different installations, timidly at first. It was like watching a social experiment play out. Everyone observing from a distance, afraid to touch anything.

Gabe and Doss started pushing the kickarounds on their casters, skating them across the floor. Soon other people did the same, stacking them, rearranging them. Then everyone started getting more involved. People went inside of the rolled over house, climbing around on it. Pederson went to the outside wall, started drumming on it with his hands, pounding the rhythm out like some ancient Shamanistic heartbeat. Other people joined in, filling the gallery with a booming percussion. Gabe and Doss took the canoe and hoisted it over their heads, carrying it around the gallery upside down, parading it through the space to the resonance of the drumbeat. Other people took up the canoe with them. *Pale Blue Eyes* still playing in the background. It was part of the installation now, what it was built out of.

"Joey!" I said when he walked in. "You made it."

"Wow, man," he said. "This looks pretty wild. I didn't know what to expect."

"Where's Bradley?"

"He's not feeling good. I think it's all the polyurethane finally getting to him. He's been really sick."

"What? What do you mean?"

Joey said something, but it was difficult to hear with the drumbeat getting louder, louder.

Meredith came up to me, mad with excitement. "This is awesome!" she said. "I think this might be my favorite one yet!"

"Me too," I said. "Why don't you have your camera out? You haven't taken any pictures."

"Sometimes I think it's better not to take the picture. I just want to enjoy the scene right now, be a part of it," she said, then grabbed my hand. "Come on! Let's get in there!"

The canoe came marching around, trailing people like a Chinese dragon dancing through Eastern streets. Meredith and I jumped in under it toward the back. We crisscrossed through the gallery, around the installations. Meredith took my arm as we passed by the office and pulled me out from under the canoe. She said something, but it was so loud I couldn't hear her. She motioned toward the office door, eyes latent, emotional temperature rising. We ducked inside, and she immediately twisted the lock behind us.

She pulled me to her and quickly wrapped her arms around my neck, hormones clustering in the corner of my brain like a particle accelerator, firing electric. We collided in a surge, push/pull of bodies, like a forging of iron, tearing off our clothes down to the bare metal, all sound drowned out by the pounding beat in the gallery next to us, I pulled her closer, driving toward that arc light of release, the perfect weld that would break the metal before it ever failed.

# The Food Problem

We learned to live by carving a little fat from the thick, regenerative belly of America. After the installation was over, we all had a three-day hangover. Our immune systems finally crashed by sleep deprivation, pills, booze. I woke up in the gallery. A putrid smell like rancid butter all around me. Taste of stale ash like relighting a half-smoked cigarette.

I went to the bathroom and filled the sink with cold water. Splashed some on my face, head held down, hands gripping the basin to steady my weakened nerves, water dripping off me.

I dried off and went back out, where a few others were waking up from where they had fallen, bodies scattered around the office like a massacre. A harmonic, gregorian groan starting to fill the room as more people woke up.

"I'm starving," said Randal. We hadn't eaten anything substantial for days.

"I'm so hungry my belly is starting to chew on my backbone," said Doss.

A reversion to simple organisms, brains developed around the mouth, highly evolved alimentary canals.

"Let's go eat," I said, every word like a shovelful of gravel. "We need to recover."

Everyone pulled themselves together, and we loaded into the van to go in search of food. We drove across town to one of our usual hunting grounds. Pulled into the wholesale supermarket and parked the van. We walked inside the giant box, sensory overload crashing in on us, lights and sounds and colors, loud as American business, where everything was sold in bulk.

There were demos set up throughout the store. They were always giving out samples. We all fanned out in different aisles, grazing, pigeoning, hunting and gathering.

Pederson was a trained veteran when it came to these demos. There were processed turkey burgers on a little electric griddle. As they were being cooked, a crowd formed, their olfactories tickled by the sizzling, ground up foul. This is when Pederson began circling like a bird of prey. When the first round of samples was being neatly assembled and set out in little plastic ramekins, a shadow swept by and picked off the first one. He swooped again, bypassing an entire group of waiting customers. It didn't hurt that he had the look of a maniac, making people afraid to speak up. He was onto another booth before anyone knew what happened.

At first I waited in line like everyone else, but I soon learned that Pederson had the right idea. We weren't here to test the food, we were here to try and cobble together a meal.

I walked around the store and fed, a bite-size morsel a time. Chicken pot pies, shrimp scampi, teriyaki salad, fudge bars, cheesecake, concentrated orange juice, something called Dino Bites. All factory food, heavily processed, already chewed for you by the machines that made them. I turned over one of the display boxes and read the ingredient list. Aspartame, sodium benzoate, a list of compounds, as appetizing as the idea of balancing a chemical equation. I was starting to get tired of this food, living this way.

Steven was coursing the aisles, filling his pockets. Meredith picked up some food from the deli, threw away the packaging, and walked around eating it.

I walked by the literature section and found Randal looking through the diet and self-help books.

"Not hungry?" I asked.

"I haven't sunk that low yet. Is this how you guys eat all the time?"

"Pretty much. Some variation of it, anyway."

"You need to sell some art before you're all malnourished."

"Easier said than done. You got any great ideas?"

"Nah, that's not for me. If I were making money as a lawyer, I would do all I could to support the gallery, but I'm no good as an artist—" Randal immediately realized he had let his guard down, showing a rare humility. He anxiously picked up a magazine, the cover had a man pulling up his shirt, moguls cut down his shadowed stomach. Randal reached under his shirt, rubbing his own for comparison.

"Here's my art," he said, showing me his molded torso. "I wake up every day, look in the mirror, and make a promise to populate the world in my image."

Just then Steven turned the corner and was coming toward us. He raised his eyebrows, giving a worried glance over his shoulder. He was being trailed by an undercover employee.

"Shit, that's the loss prevention guy," I muttered to Randal. Steven turned the next corner as the guy was about to pass us. "We need to do something."

"Excuse me," Randal reacted quickly, stopping the guy. He grabbed up a 10-step self-improvement guide and held it in front of him. "Do you know if there are any books here for someone who has already achieved perfect health?"

"What? No, I don't know. I don't work here, sir."

"No? Okay, I guess I'll keep looking."

The guy sidestepped around Randal and hurried off around the corner, but Steven was already gone. I left and went to round everyone up, we needed to get out of there. Joey was the last one I found. He and I were walking out when we met Randal again at the door.

"You ready?" I asked Randal. "I think everyone else is outside."

As we walked through the door the alarm went off. We all looked at each other.

"Hold it there!" said the door greeter, waving his hand at us.

Joey looked at Randal and I nervously, shrugged his shoulders. Randal looked at me, I looked at Joey. Then Joey took a sidestep, slowly turned, kept walking out.

"Hold it!" The door greeter was coming over.

I was frozen, unsure what to do. Randal stepped in again. He walked right up to the door greeter, met him halfway. The greeter looked over Randal's shoulder, but Joey kept walking, without hurrying too much.

"They must not have demagnetized this," Randal said to the greeter, handing him a small brown bottle, the words *Opti-Nutrition Multivitamins* on the label.

The door greeter took the bottle reluctantly. "Uh...hold on—" He looked outside again, Joey was gone. He turned back to Randal. "I'll need to see a receipt for this," he said.

"Absolutely," said Randal. "It's right over there." He pointed over to one of the registers.

"Where?" asked the greeter.

"In the trash can where I threw it away, over by register six. Or it might have been seven, I'm not sure."

"You'll need to get the receipt to prove you purchased this," said the greeter, his nametag decorated with little colorful employee stickers, insignias of accomplishment.

"No I don't," said Randal, standing off with the old man. "You see, I've studied the law, and I happen to know the burden of proof lies on you."

"Well, I can't let you out of here until I see a receipt," the greeter maintained.

"And if you want to see that receipt, it's right over there. At register six, or if not there then it was five. I've reached a point in my life where I don't go digging through the trash. Go ahead, I'll wait here."

The greeter looked over at the registers, down at the bottle.

"Well?" Randal asked.

The greeter didn't know what to do.

"May I?" Randal asked, hand held out.

The greeter handed the bottle back to him. "Next time you need to hang on to your receipt. It's store policy."

"Understood," said Randal, taking the vitamins.

We got outside and started crossing the parking lot.

"Nice work," I said to Randal. "Thanks for covering for Joey."

"What are you talking about? I didn't pay for this," he said, grinning.

I was impressed at Randal, how cool he had been back there. But then I realized that when I first met him, he never would have done that. The gallery was corrupting him.

We found Steven at the wheel of the van, emptying his pockets. I climbed into the passenger seat, Randal in the back with Joey, Pederson, Gabe, Doss, and Meredith. Pederson sucking loudly in the back, teeth slicked by the lingering taste of artificial fat. We pulled out of the parking lot, our bellies full, rumbling from all the additives, preservatives, stabilizers. The rest of us emptied our pockets of food, letting it all spill onto the floor of the van below the console, enough food for the next day or two, at least.

"Anyone got ideas on how to pay the rent this month?" I asked. "The landlord gave us until tomorrow."

"We'll figure something out," said Steven.

"How?" I asked. "We're running out of options."

"I don't know," he said. "Maybe we can pawn something."

"There's not much left to pawn," I said. "I cleared pretty much everything out to pay last month. We need to figure something else out or we're fucked."

No one said anything.

"That is, unless you wanna sell your guitar," I suggested to Steven. "You said that's worth some money, right?"

"No. There's no way I'm selling that guitar," he said. "I would never be able to get that back again."

"Then what about Cardwell's idea?" I asked.

"What idea was that?" Meredith asked.

"He wants to manage the gallery. He's talked about making a website and marketing the gallery, creating an online presence."

"Cardwell as the manager? That sounds horrible," said Meredith.

"Yeah, but none of us are doing any better," I said.

"This is the same problem we had with Garner," Steven said.

"Well, maybe we should've given her a chance," I said. "Look what happened."

"Have you been by the old gallery recently?" Steven asked. "Have you seen what they did to it? You should, that'll change your mind."

"Whatever, that's fine. This isn't the same thing. Cardwell is just saying we can reach more people."

"We don't need to reach more people," Steven said. "The place is so packed full all the time you can't even work on something without being constantly distracted."

"But we don't sell anything!" I was getting irritated. "I don't understand, why are you all so against this? If we don't do something we're gonna fail! We'll lose the gallery!"

"Fine, then we fail!" Steven raised his voice to meet mine. "Who cares, we'll find another one."

"I agree with him." I turned back to Meredith, shocked that she would say something like that.

"What?" I asked. "You're with him on this?"

"I miss the old gallery, when it was just us. I don't want it to get any bigger."

I thought Meredith of all people would be on my side. I looked at Steven, at everyone. Then glared right at Meredith.

"I thought you wanted this to work," I said sharply.

No one spoke, the air thick and anxious. I stared out the window to hide my anger.

"Money, that's *our* hell, man," Joey finally mumbled to no one in particular. "It's not in our nature."

We rode the rest of the way in awkward silence, pulling up to the front of the gallery.

"Come on," Steven said. "Let's all go to Pat's Place. Randal, can you spring for a couple rounds? We'll pay you back."

"You keep forgetting that I'm not a lawyer yet. I only have 40 dollars left to my name," said Randal.

"That's okay, you'll die with more than 40 dollars in your bank account. Let's go spend it."

"You guys go ahead," I said. "I'm going to the gallery."

They all went next door, and I went inside the empty gallery. The remnants of the installation still waiting to be removed. I walked past it all and went back to the office. I felt desperate and alone, like an exile. But I didn't understand why they were so obstinate. It wasn't that big of a fucking deal. This was for the gallery. I didn't want to lose it again.

I walked over to the desk and sat down in front of the computer. I tried to write something, but I was still bothered. I could hear laughter from the bar coming in through the open window. I was stuck. I got up, paced around the office.

I looked over and saw Steven's guitar case in the corner. I became curious. A guitar that old. The way Steven talked about it. How much *was* it worth? I snapped open the case, pulled out the instrument. Inside the sound hole there was a faded label, serial number at the bottom. I went over to computer and did a quick search.

"Holy fuck," I muttered out loud. What I found completely blew me away. From what I could tell, it was worth somewhere between $15,000 and $20,000. I knew Steven didn't even realize it was worth that much.

I got up, carefully put the guitar back in the case. I couldn't believe it. So much money. We could pay rent for the next *year* with that. And *still* have enough left for Steven to buy another decent guitar to play.

I walked over, opened the case again. A skewed new perspective of the guitar, knowing it held that much potential. And it was just left out, sitting there, as all those people came and went. It could disappear so easily.

I could sell it. Give the money to the landlord, and we wouldn't have to worry anymore. Steven would be pissed, sure. But he'd get over it.

No. I couldn't. Steven was right, he would never be able to own that guitar again.

Or could I?

I needed a distraction. I walked out of the office into the gallery, looked around at the refuse from the last show. Beer cans and broken installation pieces.

I started to clean, sweeping the trash into piles, but quickly lost steam. I put the broom down, went back to the office, tried not to even look at the guitar as I walked over to the desk, opened the top drawer, reached into the back. Inside were more pills that Randal had given me. Chemical ambition was a useful surrogate. Filling in the void where passion would normally lead to motivation. Little pink orbs to help do the things you don't really want to do, but have to be done. I took 20 milligrams, chewing up the sugar and letting it dissolve in my mouth.

I went back out to the gallery, started cleaning again, the motivator kicking in as I picked up all the empties laying around, filling bag after bag with trash. Still hashing it out, trying to figure out if there was any other way.

I walked the last bag out to the dumpster in the alley and heaved it over, on top of a mound of empty bottles, cans, cigarette packs. There might have been a month's worth of rent in there, spent and thrown into the dumpster.

I went back inside. My mind was made up. I had to go to the pawn shop. I had to make sure this gallery didn't fail. This time it wasn't beyond our control.

# Ether

Time sped up, accelerated motion, everything passing by so quickly, before there was a chance to make sense of what was happening.

"...what's the point, anyway?" Randal was saying, as I drifted out of my head and back into the conversation. "There's all this time spent setting it up, but it really just comes down to these few scenes, so I just skip right to them." He was standing in the living room of his apartment, the remote control pointed at the television, tearing through his DVD collection. He would put one on, speed it up to eight times the normal frame rate. When he sensed something was about to happen, he would press play, slow it back to normal speed for one scene. When it was over, he sped it up again. He watched entire feature films this way.

He pulled out the disc, put in another one. Hit fast forward.

"You gotta see this," he said.

"I should probably go," I said.

"Hold on, here it is!" It was a live music documentary, *The Last Waltz*. The song was almost over by the time he hit play. "Just look at that! Listen to those harmonies!" He only wanted to hear that one part of the song. When it was over, he shut it off, pulled out the DVD, and went to grab another.

"Really, I need to go," I said. "I should get back to the gallery. We have the graffiti show coming up and there's still a ton of work I have to do."

"Don't you have help? Where's everyone else?"

"I don't know. I've barely seen the others since we did the installation last month. The gallery's becoming something big, just like we wanted, but for some reason they barely even come around anymore. I don't get it."

"Law of diminishing returns," Randal muttered, while sending a text on his phone and fast-forwarding another DVD.

"I can do it on my own," I said, standing up to leave. "You have any more of that Vitamin A, at least? That's the best help I can get, at this point."

"I don't know. You've been taking a lot of Adderall lately, you should probably ease up."

"I will," I said. "After this opening. I just need to get this shit done. It's fine. No different than using a hammer or a drill, really. It's just another tool."

"Okay, your call." He reluctantly went to his bathroom, brought out a pill bottle, shook out a few orbs onto the coffee table. These were a light orange, with a backwards G on one side.

"What's this?" I asked.

"I ran out of Adderall, no thanks to you. This is a drug I used to take, until it was black-boxed by the FDA, called 'Pemoline.' It's way more potent than Adderall."

"What do you mean, black-boxed?"

"Like, they don't know exactly what happens and they definitely don't know why it happens, but in rare cases, people have died taking this. Anyway, it was also given to B2 pilots flying 16-hour missions to bomb Iraq because it provided such heightened focus. Funny story, one time in law school the pharmacist looked at the script and said to me 'Whoa, we don't even use that in the penal system.' Also, I looked it up in the Physician's Desk Reference and learned it increases the incidence of cannibalism among rats—"

"Thanks Randal," I interrupted. "I gotta go now."
"Okay, sure. You want a ride?"
"No, thanks," I said. "I'll walk." The last time I was in Randal's car it was the same as his television. He kept the radio on scan permanently, listening to the first three seconds of each station before it spun on to the next. I slipped the pills into my front shirt pocket and left on foot.

I walked through the gallery door, pausing inside. I looked around, scanning the twenty or so unfamiliar faces, absorbed in conversation. No Steven. No Meredith. No Bradley or Joey. Not even Pederson.

I turned and walked back out, grabbed our makeshift sign with the arrow drawn on it, stuck it in the window so it pointed over to Pat's Place.

I sat at the bar by myself. Arvin walked over, and I reached into my pocket, pulled out some cash, stared at it for a minute, feeling the burden of where it came from. I counted it out, the little that was left after paying the landlord. I wanted to spend all of it right here.

"Well?" Arvin asked. "You want something or not?"

"Yeah," I said finally. "Give me a whiskey." He poured the drink, and I handed him some bills, leaving a generous tip, a small consolation for all the glasses we'd taken. "No change."

I lit a cigarette, took a sip of my drink. Arvin put the cash in the tip jar and came back over.

"I'm sorry, you can't smoke here anymore."

"What do you mean?" I asked. "Did they finally pass a smoking ban?" I knew California and New York had started the ban years ago, and other states followed suit. But things always take time to creep into the Midwest.

"No, actually I made that decision on my own," he said. "I never liked it. Now I'm doing something about it."

"Good for you," I said, and meant it. He handed me an empty shot glass and I put out the cigarette.

I spent the rest of the afternoon getting day-drunk, macerating my brain. I wasn't sure what to do, but I didn't feel like going to the gallery yet.

The door opened, bright sunlight pouring in from the street. Bradley walked over, took the stool next to me. He was pale, skinnier than before, eyes dark and sunken.

"Saw the arrow next door," Bradley said. "Thought I'd find you here."

"You look like hell," I said.

"You don't look so good either. When's the last time you showered?"

"I'm bathing my liver as we speak." I tipped up my glass, sucked off the ice cubes, then set it down. "Where have you been?"

"I got sick."

"Yeah, Joey mentioned something. That's too bad, hope you're feeling better."

"No, I mean really sick. Overexposure from working with these chemicals for too long, all the poly and silicone, breathing in all that toxic shit. It finally caught up with me. One day I threw up and immediately passed out. I was puking and coughing up my lungs for a few days after that. It scared the shit out of me. I thought my fucking heart was gonna seize up."

"Damn, that is serious, I'm sorry. You okay?"

"Yeah, I'm fine now. It's a good thing it happened, really. I was laid up for a couple of weeks unable to do anything. I was having the most fucked up dreams, like I was hallucinating. I saw myself going through these transformations, where every so often I become a completely different person. It made me realize it's time to move on. I need a paradigm shift, so I can soak up something new."

"Move on? What are you gonna do now?"

"I don't know yet. I think I'd really like to become a teacher. To help others who are in a rut. I could create a struggle in a controlled situation, give people the conflict they need to create good art. I wanna help others to do the best they can."

"The poly must have dulled your nerves. This doesn't sound like you at all."

"I know, sounds crazy. Whatever happens, I know I'm leaving. It's time for me to go. I came here to say goodbye."

"What about Joey? Who's gonna help him?"

"Joey doesn't need me anymore. He'll be fine. He never really needed help from me."

"Where is he? I haven't seen him for weeks."

"You know where he is. Same place Joey will always be, off somewhere painting, doing the only thing he really knows. Maybe someday he'll get discovered and people will recognize his work is great, maybe not. Either way, Joey will always be in a studio somewhere painting. That's who he is."

"You can't leave. What about the gallery?"

"What about it? I don't go there anymore, anyway. Maybe we never should have opened the doors in the first place."

"I thought this was the idea? To buck the old gallery trend by opening our own? You were a part of this, you know. You were there from the beginning."

"We're just a group of fuckups," Bradley said. "Throwing our ideas together and hanging them on the walls while the paint is still wet. It was fun, don't get me wrong. But it doesn't amount to much."

"You're wrong. It's much bigger now. You just don't like it because you're not at the center of it anymore."

"You're right, it is much bigger. So big I don't even recognize it. You've been pushing for this the whole time. Now you've got it." He threw back the rest of his drink, pushed the glass across the bar.

"Wait. Have you seen Steven? Or Meredith? Hell, even Pederson? They haven't been at the gallery for weeks."

He stood up and pushed his stool back. "Nope. You're on your own now. Good luck with that." He threw a five on the bar and walked out.

For a long time I sat there by myself, thinking about what Bradley had said. He was wrong, it wasn't what I wanted. Everything was getting turned around. But I couldn't let myself believe it was for nothing, that it didn't mean anything. Bradley was only sore because he didn't have his studio.

I got up and walked to the back where Bohinky was pulled up to a table in his wheelchair, chess board set up in front of him, waiting for someone to come along.

"Hey, Mark! You ready for a game?" he asked me.

"Sure," I said.

"We haven't played in a long time," he said, holding out two closed fists concealing a white and black pawn to see who started.

"I don't think I'll be able to give you much of a run today," I said, picking a hand. "Too much clouding my brain lately. I don't even know if I remember how to play this game."

"You're in the right place," he said. "I've been playing for forty years and I still don't know what I'm doing." He pushed his queen's pawn forward.

We fixed our eyes on the table, and the game began while Bohinky talked incessantly. Playing against him, you were always guaranteed two educations at once.

"Whatever you have on your mind, you can watch it play out right here," he said. "That's what draws me to the game. All of psychology, sociology, behavioral science, all of human civilization is played out right here."

I pushed my queen's pawn forward. "Everything is changing around me," I said. "I'm standing by watching as this whole big shift takes place."

He offered the queen's gambit. "Ah! A revolution! You know, every great revolution in history came out of a reaction against authority. Take the Great Reformation. This was all about the authority the church had over England, and out of that came Queen Elizabeth. Before, the queen had no power. She could only move one space at a time. Now she is the dominant piece on the board."

"That's not what I mean. Just that everything is happening so fast."

I take the gambit, gaining a pawn advantage.

"Of course it is. This is the Age of Information. Information always leads to the compaction of time. Look at the late 1400's. Back then you could only move the pawn one square forward off the front line, but with Columbus and the printing press, suddenly you have this spreading of human knowledge."

He threatens my pawn with a bishop, and I bring up another pawn to try and protect it.

"People were empowered to make their own judgments," he continued. "On top of that, we were crossing oceans. We were out conquering worlds. We needed to get to that endgame faster. That's how we get the *en passant* in chess."

He threatened my second pawn, and I moved another one out to try and protect it as well. I could barely speak and stay focused on the game, but I wanted to know more.

"What about now? Chess isn't changing anymore. The rules are fixed. Everything has been done."

He brings out his knight. I am running out of options to keep my one pawn advantage. I move the queen up one space.

"That's for you to figure out. I can only teach you about history and guide you to things in the past. You can be sure of one thing, though, it's never static. In fact, this might be the most exciting era of chess to ever come about."

Before I could ask what he meant, he began attacking on the chessboard, first taking the pawn, then quickly trading down piece after piece, making his move the instant I took my hand off of mine, only he was picking up more pieces than me.

"You're trying too hard to keep that one little pawn," he said. "You should have let it go and focused on developing something else." Before I knew it, my entire left side was completely exposed, and he had all the tempo. In just a few more moves, he had me.

"Checkmate!" He reached a kind hand across the table.

I shook his hand, examining the board, all the false moves, the other possibilities, places where I went wrong, all the while trying to make sense of what the hell Bohinky had been saying.

# Tag

I woke up on the floor of the gallery office. Startled, a feeling of vertigo, like walking up the stairs in the dark, getting to the top, and thinking there's one more step, but there wasn't.

"Hello?"

I heard the sound of the door shutting as someone came into the gallery. I looked around me. There were newspapers spread out over the floor, covered in paint splatters. Next to me was a cigarette butt, around it a burn ring where it had started to singe the paper, before going out. I must have fallen asleep with it in my hand.

"Anyone here?"

I sat up, cleared my throat. "Yeah."

He came through the office door as I tried to clear away some of the empty bottles around the room.

"Hey, sorry, is this a bad time?" he asked. He was maybe a couple years younger than me, carrying a laptop under his arm.

"No," I said. "It's no problem."

"I'm Marshall. I write a blog for the *Telegraph*. Just wanted to see if I could get a story about Artless."

"You write for the *Telegraph*?"

"Yeah, why you laughing?"

"Nothing, it's just that I used to work for that paper. How are Scott and Gary doing? And Jenny, does she still work there?"

"Gary left. He turned the whole thing over to Jenny. She's the editor now. Not sure who Scott is."

"Right, I guess he's long gone. So Jenny is running it now? How do you like it there?"

"It's okay. I don't mind it. When where you there?"

"It's been over a year now," I said, thinking back. "I have a lot of fond memories of that place. I guess I didn't really appreciate it until now." I went over to the desk, sat down. "So you wanna do a story?"

"Yeah, I have a blog that goes up weekly. I was hoping I could do a post about Artless. People are talking about it all over town."

"Are they?" I asked. "So what do you wanna know?"

"Well, maybe we could start from the beginning. How'd this get started?" He pulled a chair up to the desk, opened his laptop.

"It's kind of a long story," I said. "It didn't actually start here." I pulled out a bottle of wine and poured a cup for each of us.

"Drink?"

"Sure." He took the cup. I opened the desk drawer, pulled out a pack of cigarettes, but it was empty. I crushed the pack, tossed it in the corner, dug around in the drawer for another.

Marshall took out a cigarette and handed me one.

"Thanks," I said.

I lit the cigarette, and started telling him the whole story of the gallery. How it all started. The place on High Street. The six of us in the beginning. The first and only opening. The ironwork. Coming back and finding this place. All the shows we've done since then. Giving him all the details while he took it down, typing the notes on his laptop, making a light, rhythmic patter of keyboard clicks.

"That's about it," I said finally. "Now we're here."

"Cool," said Marshall. "So when's the next opening?"

"Tonight. In fact, I should probably get to work cleaning the place up and getting ready."

Marshall closed his laptop. "Alright, thanks for your time."

I shuffled to my feet, went out and looked at the gallery. The place was a mess. The byproduct of the constant party that went on there. Cleaning it, getting it ready for the next show, would be a long, arduous task for one person.

I went into the bathroom, locked the door. I reached in my front pocket, pulled out two of the pills. 40 milligrams. Enough to dial in the focus on the task at hand and fade out the rest. I crushed the pills up on the back of the toilet, scooted the powder into a line, snorted it up through the last dollar in my pocket.

When I came out, Marshall was still in the gallery. "Damn, you have a lot to do if you wanna have this place open tonight," he said, looking around at the mess. "You need some help? I don't mind."

"If you want, sure. Just need to get the place cleaned up. And I have to paint over this." I pointed to a section of wall. During some late-night bender, it somehow turned into a free-for-all, and there was ink and marker scribbled everywhere. Now it looked like the bathroom wall of Pat's Place, interspersed with the occasional dick drawing. "Ichi's gonna come in and do a big wall piece for the opening, so it just needs a coat of primer."

"Who's Ichi?"

"He does graffiti. You've probably seen his tag. They're all over town."

He and I started putting the gallery back in order. Picking up all the trash, moving chairs back into the office. He asked more questions as we worked. He wanted to know everything. I pulled out a bucket of primer and two rollers.

As we were painting the wall, Steven came in through the back door and went into the office. I dipped the roller in the paint, spread on more paint.

"Fuck!" I heard him yell. "No! Where the fuck!"

Marshall looked at me. "Hold on," I said. I put the roller down, went into the office.

"My guitar!" Steven said, freaking out. "It's gone! Wait, where's your computer? It's gone too! One of those little fuckers robbed us!"

I went over to the couch, scooted it off the wall, reached behind, and pulled out his guitar case.

"Relax," I said. "I hid it back here so no one would fuck with it."

"Thank god!" he said. "You had me worried."

"You probably shouldn't leave it laying out with so many people here," I said.

"Wait, what about your computer?"

"I sold it. I didn't get nearly what I paid for it, but it was enough to cover the back rent, at least."

"Damn, that sucks. I guess you still have the typewriter."

"Yeah, I guess so."

I went back out and started rolling out more paint. Steven came out with the guitar a minute later, went to the back door.

"Where you going?" I asked. "Ichi's opening is tonight."

"Tonight?" he asked. "Okay, I'll be right back. I need to work on something while it's still fresh." He walked out into the alley and was gone before I could say anything else.

Marshall and I finished priming the wall and set up some fans to dry it quickly. We kept working, cleaning up. With his help, the gallery was back in order by early afternoon.

Ichi came through the front door carrying a crate full of spray-paint cans. Cardwell came in behind him. He had a devious looking grin spread across his boiled chicken cheeks.

"What's up," Ichi greeted us. "Looking good in here. Who's this?"

"This is Marshall. He's helping set up for tonight."

"Right on," he said, shaking Marshall's hand. "Good to have you." He turned to me. "Everything ready for tonight? I haven't seen any fliers up around town. Don't we normally print some for the openings?"

"Sorry," I said. "I haven't seen Joey for a while. He's the one that usually prints them."

"Damn. How's anyone gonna know about it?"

"Cardwell's been promoting it online. He's got some of your stuff up on the Artless website."

"More than that," Cardwell cut in. "It's all over the web. We've got people signed up for the mailing list, tons of likes on Facebook, it's gone viral."

"Really? That's pretty fucking cool," said Ichi. "Let's pull it up, I wanna see it." He started toward the office.

"I can't," I said. "We don't have a computer anymore."

Ichi laughed. "Wait, you have a website and no computer? That's kinda dumb."

"I had to sell it. It's how we kept the gallery last month," I said. "It's how you get to do a show."

"I was just kidding, calm down."

"You can use my laptop," said Marshall. "I'd like to see some of your work." He flipped open the laptop and pulled up the website.

Cardwell pulled me aside. "Hey, I have something important to show you."

"Go ahead," I said.

"No, in the office," he said.

"You need anything?" I asked Ichi.

"Nah, I'm cool. I'm gonna start doin the big wall piece. Then I'll bring the rest of my stuff in and hang it up. It's gonna get pretty nasty in here. You might not wanna be around unless you have a mask."

I followed Cardwell into the office. He sat down behind the desk, grinning like a little Napoleon. A little Cardwellian.

"What is it?"

He took out a pleather checkbook and turned it over in his sweating palm. He slapped it down on the table.

"What's that?"

"Oh this? This is the beginning of a Business Plan."

"What are you talking about?"

"I went down to the bank and found out that by virtue of being a white, middle-class American, I am qualified for a loan. I couldn't believe how easy it was. Now we have some investment capital."

"Investment for what?"

"That depends. I figured since we're making some progress with the gallery, putting it online and all, it might have a promising future. I'd be willing to invest some money. That is, if I were *managing* this place."

"We already talked about this. I agreed to the website, but that's it."

"But I have a lot more ideas about how to make this place a success. We could make prints, mass produce them, and sell them online. Or merchandise, or—"

"Hold up, they just gave you a loan, no questions asked?"

"Well, I didn't exactly have the best credit in the world. In fact, the only way I could get the loan was to get my mother to cosign with me, which wasn't easy. I had to bring her the paperwork in bed. She's laid up with cancer, and some days she doesn't even want to look at me. She's still bitter about the fact that I abandoned her for all those years. But I caught her in a moment of weakness. Maybe it was all the drugs they have her on, but I put on quite a jag too. I broke down in tears right there at the foot of her bed. And don't get the wrong idea. It was all very real. I ran out on her too soon, and I never had anything to show her that would make her proud. But now I have the chance to do something. I'll pay her back the forty thousand and then some."

"Forty thousand? Are you serious?"

"Right here," he tapped the checkbook with his pudgy finger.

"Don't be a fool. You don't want to waste your money."

The landlord came into the gallery, started yelling immediately. "Now what the hell is this? Who said you could do that?"

We were always finding new ways to disappoint him.

When I came out of the office, Ichi was standing frozen, the handkerchief pulled down off his mouth.

"He's doing an opening of his graffiti art, so we're putting a tag on the wall," I said. "We'll repaint it afterward."

"You haven't paid this month's rent yet," he said. "I told you that was the last time I would be lenient. Now I want you guys out of here. Right now."

Ichi looked at me, full of confusion, disappointment. I shrugged. Nothing left to do.

"Wait, we have the rent," Cardwell said.

"What are you talking about?" I asked.

"Remember, we have some extra money, you know, in the *business* account." He went to the office and brought the checkbook out. "What do you think? Should I write him a check out of this?"

I hesitated, thought about what this meant. But there was no other option.

"Fine," I said. "Go ahead."

"Who is this?" asked the landlord.

"This is Cardwell," I said. "He's…the new…manager."

Cardwell tore the check out and handed it to him. "Here's this month's rent," he said. The landlord looked at the check, still unsettled. Cardwell immediately started writing out another. "And here's next six months after that."

The landlord took the checks. "Fine, but one more slip and I'm changing the locks. And I want this graffiti off the wall." He shook his head, then walked out, his big ring of keys clanging against his hip.

Ichi went back to work on his tag.

"Cardwell, don't think this means—"

"Listen, we can talk about it later. Right now we need to go out and celebrate."

I hesitated.

"Come on, we need to get booze for the opening, right? Let's go."

"Fine." I got into Cardwell's vehicle and went with him to the liquor store. He drove like a maniac, speeding around corners, burning through lights.

"Cardwell, slow down," I said.

"Loosen up, everything is fine."

"Slow this car down or I'm getting out!"

"Ha! How are you going to get out? We're going too fast!"

"Cardwell!"

He swerved quickly into a parking lot, threw on the emergency brake, screeching to a halt in front of the liquor store. He ran inside, where he proceeded to get one bottle of just about everything in the place. Every kind of liquor and mixer imaginable. He wanted to have a fully stocked bar at the gallery. To be able to make any kind of drink there was. This cost him a little over six hundred dollars. We sped back across town to the gallery, Cardwell still swerving and driving like mad, bottles rolling back and forth in the trunk, keeling like the hull of a sinking cargo ship.

When we got back, the gallery was noxious, spray-paint fumes sagging in the air. Ichi had a base layer covering the back wall and was filling it in. A guy was carrying in sound equipment, lights, a laptop.

"This is my friend DJ Y," Ichi said, introducing us. "He's gonna play tonight. That's cool, right?"

"Yeah, that's cool."

He rigged his equipment up on the stage while Ichi finished up his tag. While the fans pulled the fumes out the open back door, I helped Ichi bring in a few canvases and skateboard decks.

A guy ran in through the door excitedly, waving a copy of the daily newspaper in the air.

"Ichi! Have you seen this? You're in the fuckin newspaper!" He held it out, and there on the front page, above the fold, was a picture of a building on High Street, a billboard on the side just below the roof, with ICHI in giant letters across it. Below the tag was an ad with a glass of milk. Only I knew it wasn't milk, that when they photographed ads they used Elmer's glue instead, because it looked thicker, richer. I learned this from Meredith.

"Holy shit," I said. "Is this a good thing?"

"Hell yeah, I just tagged every issue of the daily!" Ichi said. "Of course it's a good thing."

"But aren't they gonna find out who you are?"

"I don't know, who cares. Don't you get how big this is?"

"Sure, that's great. But you're doing a show here. That tag is all over these walls. They're probably gonna send a bunch of cops down here once they find out."

"Stop worrying, man. They're not gonna put that together."

"I'll talk to Randal. He's a lawyer. Well, sort of. I'll see what he thinks we should do."

Steven came in, carrying his guitar. "Come on, let's have a drink," he said to me. "I got a new song I want you to hear."

"Hold on," I said. "We still need to hang these paintings."

Steven poured himself some whiskey and went into the office, settled in with the guitar.

We finished hanging the rest of Ichi's work to fill out the room. I stepped back, took it all in. The big tag covering the back wall. Canvases painted with softie letters, piece books spread out on a table. Painted skate decks mounted on one wall. Ichi really was talented.

I put away all the crates of spray paint into the office, finished up. Steven still behind the guitar, playing a low, whispery soundtrack.

I went back out as the DJ finished setting up and started playing. Soon, people started showing up, and the space quickly filled up. More people than we had ever had before.

Meredith walked in and fought her way through the crowd. She took my hand tenderly.

"Where have *you* been?" I asked.

"We need to talk. I'm sorry, I want to—"

"I don't have time right now," I said coldly. "I'm busy."

"Come on, let's go to the office and hang out. Let these guys handle it. I really need to talk to you."

"No."

She glared at me. "Fine. Is anyone else here?"

"Steven's in the office."

"Great, I'll let you get back to what you were doing." She turned sharply, disappearing through the crowd and into the back.

"Randal," I said when he came through the door. "We need your help." I explained how the tag had made the newspaper. "You could represent us, right? If something happens?"

"Whoa, whoa, I haven't even taken the bar yet. And even if I did, I can't break my cherry standing in court representing this place." He looked over the mobbing crowd, drinking booze, dancing.

"What the hell do you mean?" I said angrily. "Fuck it, never mind." My cell phone was ringing.

"Hello. Yes. Yes. 704 West Main." I hung up. The phone had been ringing like this all afternoon. Cardwell must have put the number on the website.

More people filed through the door. It was getting hotter, the air stifling. I worried it was getting too full. Wondered if there was some kind of fire code. The phone rang again. I silenced it. A young girl walked by me, drinking a beer.

"How old are you?" I asked.

"What? Are you a cop?"

"No, it's just we could get in trouble for…goddammit. Never mind."

I went back to the office and threw open the door. Meredith was sitting on top of the desk, Steven doubled over, both of them laughing wildly.

"Why aren't you guys out here," I said. "I could use your help."

The bottle of whiskey was going dry. They were still laughing at some earlier joke. Steven tried to speak, but it must have been too goddamn funny. I walked out and slammed the door shut behind me.

Somehow there were even more people than before. I could barely move. A thronging, dancing crowd, lights spinning over the stage, DJ on the ones and zeros, hand to one headphone, torso nodding to the beat, the whole thing reaching a fever pitch in my head.

I needed to step out, get some air, escape this atmosphere, the ether too thick. I walked past Ichi, a group of adulating people circled around him, doting on his work.

"Yo, there you are," Ichi stopped me. "This party is awesome! Can you believe it? I was just talkin to the DJ about doin this again tomorrow night. He said he's down for it. I was gonna see if you knew where Steven was so I could see if that's cool."

"What? You don't need to ask him. It's fine."

"You sure bout that? Shouldn't we check with Steven?"

"No, goddammit! I said it's fine! Let's do it another night!"

"Whoa, man. You alright?"

"Yeah, I just need some air." I turned and walked away. Everything was slipping, slipping, I was saying things before I could stop them. I bumped through the crowd and out to the front of the gallery.

There were people standing in groups, sitting all along the curb, smoking, texting on their phones, staring down at the screens. A binary crowd, numerators and denominators. Chain-smoking malcontents. I couldn't tell if I was losing my mind. They all seemed uniform. Wearing the same skinny, black jeans. The same tight-fitting hoodie. The same square-rimmed, plastic eyeglasses. All of them too cool, aloof, like toads lurking in the shallows.

I walked up to one of them, my temples throbbing. "Let me see your glasses!" I said.

"Why?" he asked without looking up from his phone screen.

"Because," my voice low, hoarse. "I want to know if they're *real*."

He looked up at me, and his eyes grew bigger. "Look, man. I don't know what you're—"

"Let me see them!" I snatched the strings of his hoodie, pulled and twisted them in my hand, eyes blinded by a color streak of self-destruction.

"Leave me alone! Who the fuck are you, anyway!"

He ducked over to the side as I tried to pull away his glasses.

"What the fuck is wrong with you!" A girl came up and threw her arms in between us. "Leave him alone you fucking creep."

He squirmed out of my grip and scurried down the sidewalk and around the corner.

"Who the fuck do you think you are?" said the girl. I looked around. Everyone was staring. No one knew me. I was a stranger.

A cop car rolled slowly past, window down, staring at the crowd of people. At the end of the block, the blinker came on, the car turned.

I needed to get back inside. I needed to find Steven and Meredith. I was a fool, I had gone too far. I just wanted to get away from all of this.

I went back in and pushed through the crowd to the office. I got to the door, and when I reached for the knob I saw the two of them through the translucent glass. She was still on the desk, but he was closer to her now. Because of the translucent glass I couldn't see what was happening, just two figures interlocked, embrace of intimacy. I couldn't look. But I couldn't look away.

Finally I turned and ran into the back alley, head full of madness, everything cracking up.

# Gentrification

I ran through the coin-gray night, kicking the lids off trash cans, smoking cigarettes, blood black as ink. A chemical void from the constant speed pills I'd been lighting through my neurons. Nothing left inside but a belly full of hot beer.

I found myself in the alleys downtown, the streets I used to walk alone. I stopped, lit another cigarette. Behind a Chinese restaurant I found the mutt next to the dumpster, chewing on a bone that had been tossed out. I looked around, no sign of Pederson. I walked up, hand held out, but before I could get close, it rose up, snapped its teeth at me, growling. As I backed up, the mutt laid down again to chew on the bone, keeping watch on me, gnawing, gnawing, until its gums started to bleed, then gnawing even more vigorously, as if the bone was rich with blood.

I kept on, passed the capitol, passed the glass Central Bank building, onto High Street. Up above on the side of a building was Ichi's tag, lit up in the billboard lights, covering the whole thing, advertising itself.

I kept walking. Think about what was happening right then in the office of the gallery. I couldn't believe Meredith was with Steven, of all people. I wanted to hate him for it, but how could he know? Meredith and I had never told anyone about what happened between us.

As I approached the old gallery, I noticed the vertical banners hanging on the lamp posts with "The District" emblazoned on each one in a carefully chosen font. That's what they called this neighborhood now. It had been revitalized. I went down to 124 High Street and looked into the clean, open window. The floors were refinished and pristine, shining in the streetlight. The stamped tin ceiling radiating. The brick wall exposed and clean. The whole thing had been revamped, and it looked beautiful. It was no longer the eyesore of the block. "The District" had closed around it like an oyster, pearling over the irritating grain of sand. It made me want to weep.

Paintings from the Coalition lined the walls, price tags dangling from the bottoms. I stepped back and looked at the sign. It was called "Cork" now. There was a menu taped to the inside of the window, listing expensive wines, charcuterie, cheese plates. It had become the worst thing possible, a place that people like us could never afford. It had become exclusive.

"Who cares. Fuck it!" I yelled out into the night, eyes glistening with saline. I flicked my cigarette at the storefront window, ember bouncing off in a scatter of orange spray.

I turned and walked off down the block. I needed to see Michael. I knew he could always be found in his private sanctum. When I got there, he was sitting sedentary on the front porch, staring at the hill across the street in the darkness. A conservation of overweight mass. His balding head like a piece of ripe fruit balanced on his shoulders.

"Michael, thank god you're here," I said.

"I am," Michael replied stoically, eyes still closed. "That I am."

"It's been a rough night," I said. "I don't know what happened." I sat down on the porch next to him and handed him a cigarette. "I need someone to talk to."

"Tell me about it, brother." He lit the cigarette and sat back and closed his eyes again. "I'm all ears."

I started pouring it all out, uncontrollable overflow of emotion. "Everything went to shit…I don't know…I wanted it to work, that's all…I got too caught up in it…I lost control…and no one else cared…they never considered the idea of actually running a gallery…of actually selling anything…but it's a business, right?…I don't know…the whole idea is ridiculous…putting art in a gallery so someone will buy it…art ruins walls…all I wanted to do is pay the bills…we have to, otherwise we're swinging a hammer…"

Michael was listening, smiling, a secret-knowing smile.

"Tell me everything is all love, Michael, because I'm full of hate right now, and I want to believe that. There is no hate, right? Tell me there is no hate."

"Nah, I've come to realize something, brother," he spoke around the cigarette in his mouth, fingers touching in some holy mudra. "It's true, there's no hate, but there's no love either."

"What's that supposed to mean?"

"Everything just *is*. It's all a dream, a virtual reality. We are all matter looking for the lowest energy state. Sit still. Breathe. Find your basal metabolic rate."

"So there's just nothing?"

"At the quantum level, no. Just energy, an idea, a thought. Nothing but stories. It's all just the story you tell yourself. The universe can't exist without them. That's the only thing holding all this together."

"Michael, you're not making any sense!"

"I'm not even here right now. I'm just trying to wake up from the dream."

"Tell me what I'm supposed to do!"

He didn't reply, his eyes still closed.

"Michael!"

His head began to shake, slowly at first, then more and more vigorously as he slipped away into some far off trance.

I lit another cigarette. Stories. Just stories. What the hell was he talking about? I thought about Michael and the way he lived his life, sitting around all day, stuffing his head with wisdom and virtue and vice until it inflated like a carnival balloon, burnt red from the sun, so buoyant that it floated above his own body. He was merely tethered to his corporeal existence, a balloon riding higher and higher, above the crowd, above the street scenes, above the towns and the cities of the world, and into the firmament. In some ways, I envied him. I imagined that someday he would reach escape velocity, and his bald pate would become another orb of the celestial world, revolving around the circus of the stars. And while we were all down here with our petty ambitions, he was seeing the world from above as simple heat and magnets, and he would burn with the rest of them, giving off a tremendous light.

Then, I had a moment of clarity. The story. I knew then what I had to do. I had to finish my own story, the novel I had started in the beginning. For once in my life, I needed to follow through with something.

"Thanks Michael!" I said. "You have no idea—"

Michael didn't answer. He was cold still in his chair. I couldn't tell, but he might have actually fallen asleep, dreaming away.

I jumped up and ran off the porch, left Michael's just before the sun was getting ready to come up, everything calm, beautiful, street lights fading into dawn, the beauty of a city when you haven't slept and everything is rising.

# Final Chapter

Taisir was getting ready to open Coffee Zone when I walked up to the window, peered inside. Brewing fresh coffee. Setting out cups. Baking sheet pans of cinnamon rolls. He unlocked the door for me. The smells wafted out, filled me, brought me to life, made me forget that I hadn't slept at all.

"Hala hala, my friend. You're up early. You need Rocket Fuel?"

"Thanks Taisir, give me the biggest cup you have."

I took my coffee and walked back to 704 W. Main. The afterbirth of a drunken debauch everywhere. Empty bottles, beer cans, stomped cigarette butts, trash, the DJ equipment still set up, lights and cords hanging like wilted plants.

I immediately went into the bathroom, dug the little pills out of my front pocket, used my ID and crushed two of them up on the back of the toilet, combing out a long, neat row. I slid the ID in the back pocket of my Carhartts, stood there, staring down at the fine line of light orange powder. Chemical ambition, the surrogate, filler of the void.

Then I realized, I didn't need that anymore.

I reached over, swept my hand across the tank, pulling all the powder off into the bowl. I had the motivation to finish the book on my own, because I had passion, a new kind of passion, even greater than before.

I dropped the rest of the pills into the toilet, loosed them in an unceremonious flush.

Through the office door I found Steven, alone, passed out on the couch, his boots hanging off the end, arm crossed over his eyes.

I went over to the bookshelf in the corner, reached underneath, and pulled out my old typewriter. I set it down on the desk and snapped open the case. Steven woke up, pulling his head out of the crevasse of the couch.

"What's going on?"

"Sorry to wake you," I said. "I have to write. I need to finish this thing."

"Sure, go ahead." He sat up, rubbed his eyes.

I lit two cigarettes, walked over to Steven, handed one to him.

"Thanks," he said. He sat back on the couch, blowing smoke into the ceiling.

I went back to the desk, pulled out a sheet of paper, rolled it into typewriter, squared up the page, stared at it. Fingers poised, motionless.

"You're pushing her away, you know." Steven said.

I looked up at him, caught off guard. "What?"

"Meredith. You're pushing her away."

"I fucked up," I said. "I know that. It's my own fault. I fucked up and now it's too late. She's a great woman. And you're my closest friend, and I'm happy for you, for both of you. Really."

"What? You think—? Wait, no. Nothing happened between us."

"I saw the two of you together last night, through the door," I said.

"What are you talking about? I would never do that. I know about the two of you. I've known for a long time. No, she was here all night talking about it. She's pretty torn up. She recognizes that she's been wrong too, her obsession with her work, being too distant. But she's been trying to reach out to you for a while, to make it right. But then you kept pushing her away. I've seen it, too. She really cares about you."

"She said that? And now she's gone?"

"Yeah, she did. She was going straight home to pack. She said she was leaving this morning. I'm sure she wanted to tell you, but it's probably easier for both of you this way."

"Fuck," I moaned, head in my hands.

"Everything okay?" Steven asked. "You've been acting different over the last few months."

"No," I said. "I've been fucking a lot of things up lately. I got carried away. You were right, from the very beginning. I should have listened to you. But I wanted everything. I kept pushing for more, more. And now it's all turned around, not what I had in mind."

"I'm sorry. I feel bad. Maybe I should have done more to help."

"It's too late. All I can do now is finish the book. It's the only thing left, the only thing to salvage out of all this."

"Sure, go ahead," Steven said. "I'll be right here. I'm gonna work on some music."

He snapped open the case and pulled the guitar onto his lap. He pulled out a new set of strings and popped one of the old ones off, then restrung a new, popped another old one off, then a new, changing them one string at a time so the tension wasn't lost. He slowly turned the pegs into tune, and started playing, humming a light, spidery melody.

I ran my forefingers around the black glass keys, tracing each letter slowly, deliberately, waiting, listening.

"I don't know how to end it," I said. "I don't know if it was a failure or what."

Steven didn't respond, sweeping his workman hands across the strings, *swick, swick.*

"I don't know if there's anything we could have done," I said.

He answered by humming louder, eyes closed, the way I first met him, heel of his boot tapping on the hardwood floor, keeping time, *boom, swick, swick...*

I finally started typing.

*Coming of age is getting old.*

I stared at the line for a second, sitting on the roller, horribly fake, contemptibly clever, a false start. I backed up, hammered a row of X's on top of it. Backed up again, hammered another row of XXXXXXXXXXXXXX over and over and over, slamming the keys, blacking out the pathetic dross. I finally ripped it off the roller and balled it up in my fist, tossed the wad of paper into the corner.

Steven paused. "That wasn't it," he said.

"I know," I said. "I didn't mean it."

"Try it again."

"I can't. I don't know what to say."

"Just be genuine. That's all that matters." He started playing again, humming.

I rolled in a fresh sheet of paper, started typing again, adding percussion to the room with each keystroke, the clear reverberating sound filling the office along with the guitar. This time I went at it simply, honestly, hammers swinging, worker of the world. This time it all started pouring out, *boom, swick, swick, boom, swick swick...*

Being genuine, that's what we tried to do. Whatever we did, at least we meant it. We wanted to make a living by being alive. But it wasn't enough. We didn't think about anything else. We tried to multiply our experiences rather than deepen them. We wanted something small and beautiful to last but it couldn't, and it doesn't need to. It didn't fail. It happened. We were a microcosm. One of the many, like iridescent soap bubbles inflating and popping everywhere. Not a movement, just a moment in time. We weren't beat, or lost. We were Artless. A sum of energy greater than all the parts. A nuclear energy, sometimes fusion, sometimes fission, generating enough power to light up a building, or enough power to move on—

I heard footfalls coming through the front door. I looked to Steven. He wasn't making a move. I got up from the desk and went out to see who it was. In the front of the gallery, I saw DJ Y and Ichi straightening out the equipment on the stage. A few other people came in behind them.

"Hey! Great time last night!" Ichi said when he saw me. "My first real opening, I think it went pretty well."

"We're gonna get things set up to do it again tonight," said DJ Y.

"Don't worry about the mess in here," Ichi said. "We'll take care of it."

"Go ahead," I said. "It's all yours, I'll be in the back." I turned and went to the office. Before I got there, I already knew Steven would be gone. I didn't hear him leave, but I knew he would. I didn't blame him. He had work to do.

I shut the office door, locked it, and went back to the desk. Back to work. Putting more pages through the typewriter, posting holes in the snow, pulling them out. Page after page.

More footsteps came into the gallery. I paid no attention. After a while I didn't even hear them, just the sound of the typewriter, everything else drowned out. Hours passed. Eventually the music started back up, the gallery filled with people again, but I didn't go out, just kept working, working, till the end of the line.

I had always imagined it would end differently, that we might burn it down, leaving by the light of the fire, together. But that wouldn't be true. You don't always get the ending you want. Sometimes, things just fade away.

Besides, it doesn't end just because the curtain closes over the people on stage. The story isn't separate from the audience, getting up out of your seats. We are not disconnected so cleanly. You go out into the daylight. Eat when you can. Sleep when you can. Fuck when you can. Work when you have to. Maybe you're affected by it. Maybe you remember your own moment in time, the people you connected with, the things that happened. Maybe you remember it when you spread a layer of mud across a sheet of drywall, or when you weld two I-beams together. It's not what you do, it's who are. It doesn't matter, as long as you're being genuine. As long as you mean it.

# Coda

I pull the last sheet off the roller, gather up all the pages on the desk, the floor, and shuffle them together in an uncollated stack. I fold it over lengthways, pull a rubber band out of the middle desk drawer, slip it over the roll of pages. I close the case over the typewriter and snap the metal latch shut, slide it back under the bookshelf in the corner.

I pick up the manuscript, feel the weight of it, the sense of relief, satisfaction. It's finally finished. Bind it up. Give it away. Deduct the tare. Break the spine until the pages lay open. Tear out the ones you don't like. Write over it. Make it yours.

When I walk back out into the gallery it's in full swing again, right back where it left off last night, thronging with people again, dancing and partying. The only lights are the ones over the DJ on stage, swirling and fanning out over the crowd, silhouetting the sea of people. I bump my way through, manuscript tucked under my arm. No one notices me. No one says anything. I go to the front of the gallery and turn to look at the crowd. Most of the faces I don't even recognize. And that's okay.

I turn to leave.

"Where you going?"

I look over. Marshall is sitting against the wall in the corner, laptop on his knees.

"Hey Marshall," I say.

"Hey, what's up? You're not leaving, are you?"

"What are you working on." I look at the laptop. "That for the blog?"

He snaps the laptop shut. "This? No, it's nothing, really."

"So you're a writer," I say.

"No…I don't know…I wouldn't call myself that."

"Sure you are." I reach in my pocket. "Here, take this." I hand him a key.

"What's this?" he asks.

I nod over to the front door. "You can use the office if you want," I say. "It's a pretty good place for writing."

"Really?" He turns the key over, eyes lighting up. "You're giving me a key? Just like that?"

"Of course," I say, smiling. "How else?"

He puts the key in his pocket. I am about to leave. Then, off in the very back corner, where I just came from, I see Pederson. Big, silent sculpture, the hem down his blue jeans like a parting-strip. It feels good, one familiar face in the sea of strangers. I want to talk to him, more than ever. I bump my way back through the crowd toward him. People sweating, rubbing heat against me. I pull the manuscript in closer so I don't drop it.

I look up and see Pederson again as he turns, walks out the back door, into the alley. I keep slogging my way through the crowd toward him.

I finally push through and open the back door, step out. The door pulls itself shut behind me, half muting the music on the other side. I look down the alley. He's already gone. But there, standing at the corner, smoking a cigarette and leaning against the brick, is Meredith. She smiles when she sees me, flicking her cigarette across the alley. I walk up to her.

"Meredith. Listen, I'm really sorry," I say. "I haven't been myself—"

"No," she interrupts. "It's my fault. I wish I would have been more open, from the beginning. I wish—"

"I know," I say. "I know."

"I wish we could start over," she says.

"Yeah," I say. "Me too."

"So what do we do now?" she asks.

"I don't know," I say. "Are you leaving?"

"Would my answer to that affect your decision to get involved?" she asks.

"Would you change your answer if it did?" I ask.

"No," she says.

"Then, no." I say.

# Epilogue

www.artlessgallery.com

## Acknowledgements

Steven Carrel, Joey Wagner, Bradley Wieberg, Mark Pederson, Leslie Webster, Travis Steck, Michael Seabaugh, Taisir Yanis, the Parents, Gabe Meyer, Brian Doss, Jennifer Neff, Carla Steck, Michael Finklestien, Andy Opperman, Alan Tatman, Joe Cardwell, Andrew Lyskowski, Sean Brite, Carly Peña, Chase Thompson, Heather Hoffman, Mitchell Brandt, Sarah Lacy, Aaron Little, Matt Steck, Sarah Zurhellen and Lisa Knight.

Thank you.

Made in the USA
Lexington, KY
12 June 2014